MAGDA

A DARKLY DISTURBING OCCULT HORROR TRILOGY – BOOK 3

S. E. ENGLAND

ISBN: 9780993518386

1st Edition: EchoWords 2016
www.echowords.org
www.sarahenglandauthor.co.uk

About the author

Sarah England is a UK author. Originally she trained as a nurse before a career in the pharmaceutical industry, specialising in mental health – a theme which creeps into much of her work. She then spent many years writing short stories and serials for magazines before her first novel was published in 2013.

At the fore of Sarah's body of work is the bestselling trilogy of occult horror novels – *Father of Lies, Tanners Dell* and *Magda*; followed by *The Owlmen*.

You might also enjoy, *The Soprano*, a haunting thriller set on the North Staffordshire Moors, or *Hidden Company* – a gothic horror set in a Victorian asylum in the heart of Wales. *Monkspike* is her latest novel.

If you would like to be informed about future releases, there is a newsletter sign-up on Sarah's website. Please feel free to keep in touch via any of the social media channels, too. It's good to hear from you!

www.sarahenglandauthor.co.uk
www.facebook.com/sarahenglandauthor
www.twitter.com/sarahengland16

***

Four and Twenty Blackbirds

'Sing a song of sixpence,
A pocket full of rye.
Four and twenty blackbirds,
Baked in a pie.

When the pie was opened,
The birds began to sing;
Wasn't that a dainty dish,
To set before the king?

The king was in his counting house,
Counting out his money;
The queen was in the parlour,
Eating bread and honey.

The maid was in the garden,
Hanging out the clothes,
When down came a blackbird
And pecked off her nose.'

Prologue

Ruby Dean
Drummersgate Forensic Unit
August 2016

The tube is hurtling through the subway at breakneck speed. Blurry faces flash past on blackened tunnel walls and alarm is beginning to spread. Something is badly wrong. One or two people lurch forwards, struggling to hold onto ceiling straps; others grab the seat in front. Still it accelerates – racing perilously along the track with carriages rocking dangerously from side to side - at times lifting off the rails.

This tunnel is going on for way too long…What's happening? What is this?

A woman holding onto a pole by the exit turns to fix me with a stare, crimson painted lips catching in the flickering half-light. Silently she mouths a disembodied question that resonates around the black bowl of my head. "Don't you *know*, Ruby?"

Know? Know what?

But there's no time to think. We're going to crash. Any second now. A loud bang sounds from somewhere further back and a window blows out. Still we pick up speed. Faster and faster, faster and faster, faster and faster…A woman falls to the floor and panicky shouts break out.

"Hey, what the hell's going on? Pull the cord! Someone pull the damn cord."

A man lunges for the emergency brake, but is thrown aside in the chaos.

Faster and faster, faster and faster, faster and faster.

Then suddenly the brakes screech to a halt. Bags and bodies catapult from seats.

And the carriage doors hiss open.

For several moments there is only the shocked mayhem of passengers and their belongings strewn across the carriage in a haze of burning electrics. Some people are crying and others are bleeding - beginning to reach out to helping hands - when a computerised voice echoes around the station.

"Step off the train, Ruby Dean. You have reached your destination."

Everyone turns to look in my direction.

How do they know I'm Ruby?

This isn't even a proper tube station – it has no name, no lights. It's as black as a coalface.

But the hatred inside the carriage is now a living thing, growing with every accusing glare – a palpable, intensifying understanding that this hellish journey is somehow the fault of the girl by the window; that I am the one who has brought them here.

"You have to get off the train, Miss Dean. Get *off* the train."

Their voices chime in. "Get rid of her. Get her out."

Angry and peevish, they shove me in the back, down the aisle and off the steps to a crumpled landing on the platform below. Pain shoots up my ankle, but by the time I've turned round the doors have snapped shut and the tail lights shoot into the tunnel, leaving me stunned and alone in a hot, black, airless pit that stinks of rotting garbage and human waste.

For a full ten seconds there is nothing but silence.

And heat. An equatorial heat that's dirty, oily and wet – impossible to withstand. Sweat bursts from every pore and panic blasts through my veins. This is the kind of blackness that renders you blind; without a pinprick of light. I can't even see the track, visible only a moment ago. And the air is almost globular, forcing me to gulp down the rotting-corpse taste of it slithering down my throat, clogging my nostrils. This must be what it's like to be buried alive, to swallow filth. I'm going to die. I am. I'm going to die.

Stop... stop...listen...shh...

A whisper... laughter...someone is here with me..."Oh no it's far worse than that, Ruby... far worse."

I whirl round. "Who's there? Is someone there?"

Children: the sound of children snickering and giggling.

"Who is it? Who's there?"

Like a sleepwalker with my hands stretched out in front, I stumble towards the voices – and straight into something netted and sticky. It spans my face, tangling in my fingers, and suddenly I realise what it is...A huge cobweb...lacing over the whole of my upper body, threading into my hair. Frantically I back out of it, slapping at my arms, chest, and face...my heart rate off the scale. Please, please, please, not giant spiders...I'm going to be sick.

The giggling escalates. *She...she hates spiders...she...shh...*

Breathing hard now, crouching down low, panting, and trying to think. If only I could see some difference in shade or shape within this solidity of blackness – anywhere, in any direction. But there is nothing. Absolutely nothing. No stairwell. No lift. No sheen of a wall. Not the faintest glimmer of light or movement. Even the tunnel has disappeared. I cannot see a thing.

"Do you give up yet? Do you give up hope, Ruby?"

"Who are you? Who's whispering?"

Something brushes the top of my arm – something light and fast and I swipe at it, a fresh wave of sweat breaking out, tears stinging my eyes. Spiders must be crawling everywhere, hanging in hammock cobwebs all ready for me to walk into. What if they're in my hair right now? Or stuck to my back? I have to get out of here. Come on, find the exit...come on, Ruby you can do this. Which way to start walking, though? Which way?

An announcement comes over the Tannoy, "Ruby Dean, you have arrived at your destination. There is no exit. I repeat. You. Have. Arrived."

The voice stops me dead.

Of course...I know where this is, don't I?

"You are a traitor, Ruby Dean. There is no way out."

Only now do the other occupants begin to show themselves.

They rise as spectres from the gutters and the drains – diseased corpses with fetid whispers, and empty eyes glazed with madness. Their gnarled fingers claw at my hair and face. Too close, too many…More and more of them materialise - stroking my arms, tugging at my clothes, excitement breeding excitement. But something else is fast approaching. Something that frightens them. The creatures pause, chests rattling with wet, rasping breaths. Whatever it is drenches them in terror. I hear it too…bestial howls now echoing through the subway, iron shackles clunking against the stones. The mad and the sick slither away in a hissing recoil; as shuffling forwards in their hundreds, no thousands, are those with no souls at all; the ones oozing with depravity and sadistic malice – those entirely drained of humanity. And it is with this group that he arrives.

"Ruby Dean to Platform One," the intercom voice announces. "Your grandfather is here to collect you. Ruby Dean to Platform One."

And in the next instant he is there before me – the rancid stench of him reawakening every single diabolical, abusive hate-filled violation he ever inflicted: Old Spice aftershave, stale urine, whisky…the snap of a nappy pin as I'm lifted from my cot…

His ice-hard eyes laser through the darkness as raw terror rips from my lungs.

"No, no, no. Help me please, help me someone, help me… Oh God. God help me!"

A woman's laugh pours scorn all over my fear. She is the red glow of a cigarette butt, a coil of acrid smoke. "No one's coming, Ruby. You are a bride of Satan, don't you remember? Baptised and sworn in – just like us. Exactly the same."

"God, please help me. God! Dear Lord, please, I beg you…"

4

Lucas Dean steps towards me.

"No. No. God in heaven, please–"

"Wake up, Ruby."

She is a presence, a feeling – a tinny voice from the surface of a deep ocean. My spirit cries out to her with every atom of energy I have left. "Celeste?"

"Ruby...come on, Ruby. You must wake up."

The power of her light wraps around me and I cloak myself in it, fighting my way up and up and up....to the tiny specks of glitter far away.

And when I open my eyes again the stars are back in the window, sparkling over open moorland; and I'm lying in bed on soaking sheets.

"You really must learn to protect yourself better," says Celeste, already fading. "That was almost impossible – I nearly lost you."

Swinging my legs over the side I put my head in my hands. I am Ruby Dean. I am Ruby. I thought I knew all the fragmented parts of myself – thought everyone in the system had been identified and we were safe. Clearly not. It appears there is a watcher – a Judas inside my own mind. And now I daren't go to sleep.

***

Chapter One

Jasmine Cottage, Chesterfield
August Bank Holiday Weekend, 2016

Becky stopped chopping vegetables and stared out of the kitchen window. What a God-given evening – glorious, purple heather coating the moors for mile upon mile under a deep indigo sky still tinged with gold. The thick, stone walls of the cottage had baked in the Saharan heat; and their white cat, Louie, lay motionless across the windowsill amongst the flowerpots, snoozing; waiting for a cool breeze and the scent of dusk.

The piercing beauty was almost too much to bear. She took her fill of it. What a long way she'd come in the last eight months. Gone the dark days of winter when it seemed her world would disintegrate in a descent of lonely madness. She and Callum had married last month and unbelievably, at the age of forty-four she was going to have a child. She'd never thought it would happen and hadn't even bothered to take precautions, thinking it never would, but it had. The baby in waiting was a girl and would be called Molly. They liked the name and so Molly it was. Her ex, Mark, had bought her share of the house in Doncaster and along with the divorce the transaction had gone through quickly. So now she had a new husband, a child on the way, and two teenaged step-children all in a very short space of time. Hmm…not that Callum's kids were exactly thrilled about their dad having a new wife, but that would come. These things took time to settle.

"Well, Molly," she said, talking to her as if she was in the room. "By the time you arrive in November we've to get this house ship-shape and I've an agency nurse to train up. Standing here staring at the scenery won't get things done, will it? And your dad's going to want something to eat before he goes to work tonight, as well."

There was always a downer – Callum's hours did leave her alone a lot but at least he'd recovered sufficiently to return to work and that was the main thing. As it turned out he'd been off for six months, having to learn how to walk properly again, the extent of his spinal injuries pretty severe. But he was on the mend now, almost as good as new, he insisted, with a war wound on the side of his head to show for it. She smiled as he passed through her thoughts. In her eyes the scar only made him more handsome.

"We 'aving tea anytime soon, or what?" he said, ducking under the lintel.

He seemed enormous in this poky kitchen, it always struck her. People in days gone by must have been tiny. The cottage was an end of terrace in a row of three, incongruously built in the middle of a field on the windswept Chesterfield moors. Driving past a couple of months ago they noticed the 'For Sale' board and Callum had pulled over. "Now why would anyone put those there?" he asked. "Just the three of them like that?"

Becky shook her head. "I don't know but I kind of like it."

They bought the end one. All three had long rectangles of garden with sheds at the bottom; and not too long ago they'd all had outdoor toilets tacked onto the back. These were lean-tos with roofs made of corrugated iron, now used for storage since the days of a weekly tin bath in front of the fire were long gone. It might be romantic to think of people mending and sewing by candlelight, she'd said to Callum, but in reality those freezing mornings with no heating and only a cold wash under the kitchen tap must have been tough.

The kitchen was crammed into a small, gloomy corner, which badly needed knocking through to the dining room and opening up. Locked in a 1970s time warp, it sported yellow Formica cupboard doors, peeling wallpaper and a free standing cooker; but the aspect was stunning and that's what had clinched the deal. To wake up, throw back the curtains and breathe in an

7

eternity of open sky with nothing but the sound of a kestrel hovering on the current of a breeze, was euphoric and all they could wish for after the darkness of the previous year.

On hearing Callum come in, she quickly tipped the board of mushrooms and peppers into a frying pan and pretended to dodge out of his way. "Get off you great brute, do you want to eat tonight or not?"

"Depends what else is on offer, wench."

"Nothing else is on offer. Can you get the plates out – this'll only be two ticks."

"What we 'aving?"

"Chicken stir-fry."

"Rice or chips?"

"Oh, very classy. Chips? With a stir-fry? It's noodles – rice noodles."

"They give you chips in the Chinese with stir-fry. If that isn't class, I don't know what is."

"No, well you wouldn't. You want educating," she said from inside a cloud of steam. "Can you get some glasses as well?"

"I don't know about a Chinese restaurant, it's more like a Chinese laundry in here."

Becky laughed, flushed from the heat as she served up. "Here you are. Now no complaints mind, or it'll be lettuce for the rest of the week – that soggy dark green, home-grown stuff we used to be force fed as kids, with radishes."

He bolted his food like a starving orphan, staring hungrily at her plate the second he'd finished. "Don't you want that?"

"God, it's dangerous to even put your fork down in this house. I just wanted a sip of water… Oh, go on then." She pushed her plate over. "Have it."

Nurses ate fast but blimey, policemen were worse.

"I had a very deprived childhood," he said. "Our Carol would 'ave it off me if I didn't eat quickly enough. And she pinched me."

"I'd have pinched you, as well."

"By the way, do you feel like inviting Toby and his new girlfriend over for a meal at the weekend – bottle of wine, that kind of thing? It'd be good to 'ave a catch-up – I've 'ardly seen 'im since I've been back."

"Girlfriend, eh? He never said anything to me about a girlfriend when I spoke to him on the phone. Is she new? What's her name?"

"Amy, he said. I think it was Amy. Yeah, he just met 'er apparently. Said she had hypnotic eyes."

They laughed.

"Ah, love's young dream."

"I'm glad for 'im though – he's really been through it, the poor, little sod. I'll be honest, I never thought he'd go under like that, though, did you?"

"No, but then these things can come back to bite you on the arse when you least expect them."

"I'd like to bite you on the arse."

"I'd like to see you try."

The two of them bantered and bickered as if they'd been married for years, both of them, she thought as he sauntered down the drive to his car, ecstatically happy.

"That's right," she called after him. "Leave me with all the washing up!"

He looked over the car roof and waved. "Get it done, wench, and stop mithering."

She laughed again, and after he'd driven away began clearing the table, startled for the zillionth time to feel a tiny kick inside her. "Oh hello, Molly, you okay in there?"

Concentrating on the washing-up while her thoughts flitted all over the place, not settling on anything in particular, it was therefore with some surprise that when she looked up the windowsill was empty. "Oh! Where's Louie? Typical – I was just about to cook him some fish. Did you see him go, Molly? No, of course you didn't." She laughed. "Oh well, no doubt he's off mousing – it's a nice, clear night and the owls are out. Good hunting, I expect."

Another twinge caught her mid-breath and she plonked down on a kitchen chair for a moment, tea towel in hand, until Molly settled.

Late August and the light had dipped to a sultry haze, dust motes fizzed in the dying rays, the air a heady mix of honeysuckle and scented roses. She sat totally still. How wonderful. There wasn't a sound.

The moment came and went, but it was almost like blinking and not being quite the same again afterwards. As quickly as that. Had it been déjà-vu she wondered? No, that was when you thought you'd experienced the same thing before, wasn't it? She frowned. This had been more like being in her own body but seeing through someone else's eyes altogether. She swayed, slightly dizzy. *Ooh, what a weird feeling...*

The clock on the wall ticked solidly onto the hour. Initially she just glanced at it, then did a double take. Good grief, an hour had passed. When she'd sat down the sun had been a crimson ball sinking over the horizon...yet the kitchen was now quite gloomy; shadows crept along the floor, and the vivid colours of a summer day were rapidly seeping into dusk.

Despite the lingering heat she shivered as she stood to lean over the sink and pull the window shut. Perhaps she'd fallen asleep? No denying the dragging fatigue of an insomniac, that was for sure. It probably came with the territory – pregnancy, new house, stress...all of those things... Yes, it must be that.

She eyed the narrow, wooden staircase leading up from the hallway.

Well there was no putting it off – it was that time again.

She sighed. If only Callum wasn't away. If only there hadn't been that message from Ruby, 'Tell Becky to look up Lilith...'

And if only she hadn't.

***

Chapter Two

Lilith, Lilith… The name that had frightened Celeste so badly just before she died. She'd been scrying, using her gift as a medium to try and uncover what was happening in Woodsend; but whatever she'd come into contact with that day had possessed the power to destroy her within hours. Coincidence?

Oh, why did this message have to come through for her personally? And why now when she'd finally got settled and happy? Still, there was no one to blame but herself for going ahead and researching it, opening up doors that should have been firmly shut. And locked. Maybe it was better not to have the knowledge? It was almost as if once you recognised these dark spirits they recognised you. The thing was, Ruby was rarely wrong. And there was the rub. If you didn't believe there were other dimensions to those we only perceived with our five senses, you sure as hell did after you'd met Ruby.

Becky wandered from room to room methodically checking all the doors and windows. The middle terrace next door was empty, having been allowed to fall into disrepair after the last tenants vacated, and the one at the far end was inhabited by an elderly couple who, although they gave her friendly waves, clearly had their work cut out with her on crutches and him almost bent double with arthritis. It wasn't the isolation though, that gnawed at the edges of her mind, but a much deeper, far more insidious fear – something that had latched onto her, prickling the back of her neck, causing her to suddenly glance over her shoulder, or start at an imagined sound. And that something, she realised, would have to be dealt with whether they lived in the middle of a city or on a beach in Bali.

Taking a deep breath and giving herself a stern talking to, Becky switched off the downstairs light and headed upstairs, as usual avoiding looking up at the landing as she climbed. If she did she would see her - a young woman with long, wet hair standing under the light; the same conviction, the same image, creeping into her mind every evening.

The bare bulb flickered slightly when she got to the last step, and she hurried into the bathroom and shut the door. Why on earth had she got such jitters? Everything was fine during the day, it was just at night. Shivering, as if invisible moths were fluttering up and down her arms, her back, and in her hair, she hunched over the sink to brush her teeth. And now there was something else to add to her overactive, fertile imagination. She'd just had to go and read about Lilith possessing women through mirrors, hadn't she?

Fleetingly she glanced at her reflection purely to remove her eye make-up, then washed, rubbed in moisturiser and grabbed her dressing gown. The electric light seemed too bright, surreal somehow, as if she was a character on a stage, observed from a dark and silent auditorium.

She flung open the door to the landing. No one was there. *Of course not...of course there bloody wasn't...*

Forcing herself to breathe properly, to systematically unwind the muscles knotting in her stomach, she pushed the bedroom window wide, leaving the curtains open to catch any hint of a breeze. It was stifling up here; one of those nights where people lay sleepless and exhausted on top of the sheets, waiting for the early hours to cool them down. She lay back on the bed and closed her eyes, leaden with exhaustion, and although still partly alert for creaking floorboards, fell quickly into the oblivion of sleep.

Seconds later she woke with a shock. Someone had shouted, 'Good evening!' loudly and directly into her left ear. She sat up. Was that a dream or was it real?

She waited for her heart to stop banging so hard it hurt - squeezing from arteries and slamming through pulse points. It was a dream that was all...had to be... Anxiety did weird things to you – keeping you on night watch instead of letting you drift off trustingly. What time was it? She reached for the alarm clock.

Bang on three am. Weird, just weird…it seemed like she'd only been asleep a matter of seconds...yet it had been hours.

Moonlight bathed the room through the long sash windows; night's shadows falling across the bed in boughs of heavy leaves. All was perfectly still and silent. Reassured, she eased back against the pillows again, her breathing steadier now, when a glint of light in the dressing table mirror caught her attention and she found she could not look away. It was a strange effect and the thought occurred that perhaps it would be a good idea to reposition one or the other, because reflected in the glass was a never-ending corridor in the cheval mirror opposite; a corridor, in fact, of corridors.

Lilith…Said to possess souls through mirrors.

Oh for God's sake, Becky!

She sat up again. This was no good, no good at all. If only she hadn't read all that twaddle. Coming on the back of all she'd already suffered it had rooted in her mind and now just would not go away. *Wired and fully awake in the witching hour. Great.* She lay a hand on Molly. This was fear for the sake of it – fear breeding more fear and so it went on. In Celeste's language, fear itself was a spirit – one which could paralyse you, part of your brain displaying graphic images of oppressive dark shapes and skittering shadows where there were none. And it would feel oh-so-real. If that was the case, then surely, she rationalised, it should be possible to re-train your own thoughts and replace the fear images with benign ones – those of love and faith and sanity, for example? So maybe if she pictured decorating Molly's room? Or planting out the garden? Enjoying a glass of wine outside on the patio with Callum on a gorgeous summer evening?

The nice images came and the nice images went, lasting a second or two at most before her mind flicked straight back to where it was. There were so many theories, from scientific to ancient pagan beliefs, regarding human fear, but in the end the only thing anyone could do was whatever brought them comfort when they were alone and scared in the dark. Nothing was watching her. Nothing was going to pull her hair or shake the bed or snatch the covers. And there was no one on the landing. It was all in the mind. She had a will of her own and she was not having this. Not anymore. Enough was enough. 'Go away' she told the fear within. 'Go away and don't you dare come back.'

For goodness' sake, what had all that business with Ruby done to her? Would she ever properly recover and feel normal again? Callum seemed to remember nothing of his experiences except being chased through the woods by flesh and blood thugs with torches. All the supernatural, sanity-challenging aspects had passed him by, thank God. Still, that kind of left her isolated, didn't it? Celeste was dead; poor, damaged Ruby had problems even coping with daily life; and Kristy Silver – the specialist who had tried to help both her clients and her colleague, Jack McGowan – had decided to emigrate with her ex-husband and live in Australia. She wanted daylight, she said, as much sun, sea and surf as possible – and who could blame her? She was even retiring from psychiatry to re-train as a GP. A sad loss to the profession, but after what she had suffered it was highly understandable – a miracle she could practice medicine at all really; unlike Jack who had lost all that he was, and by all accounts still continued to struggle with his sanity.

Kristy might well go on to live a happy life, and Becky hoped that would be the case. There was little doubt though, that the experience would always haunt her, that she would fear dropping off to sleep or being left alone in the dark, wondering if the television set would switch itself on or things would move around in her room, and if the nightmare would start all over again.

With renewed determination, Becky forced herself to shut down the remembered images of Kristy as she had last seen her. If she gave in and thought about it she'd never sleep again.

No, the only person she could safely talk to about this was her staff nurse and best friend, Noel. Maybe Toby? No, no – not Toby. Toby needed the light, having suffered a breakdown. He'd been way too young and impressionable, despite being in the CID, and not nearly well enough protected spiritually. Hopefully though, he'd be okay in the long run. Callum, his boss, was watching out for him and so was she. It had been a wise move for him to return to his parents for a while: no one needed to be alone in a house at night after facing what he had.

He occupied her thoughts for a while. On a high after the arrests, Toby had been part of the team putting together the case for prosecution, and it had been that which had sent him toppling over the edge. It seemed odd he'd cracked once the imminent threat was over, and that it was later, much later, when the team was working under Tanners Dell, that he'd finally collapsed. Like Kristy, he was another who preferred not to rake it over, though. Perhaps it was enough that he'd recovered and they should be thankful for that? And now it seemed he was well enough to think about girls again too, so that was alright.

Would this Amy be kind, she wondered? Would she take care of him? It wasn't a quality young men looked for exactly, but Toby needed someone with a good heart whether he knew it or not. Oh really, she smiled at herself. She wasn't his mother...but she had come to feel very protective towards him nevertheless. Guilt, no doubt. Yeah that was the guilt talking.

A faint waft of night air perfumed with sweet honeysuckle cooled the perspiration on her face, and once more her leaden eyelids began to close. Drowsily, her thoughts churned over the message from Celeste. How uneasy it had left her, researching Lilith that afternoon. There didn't seem much to fear when you analysed it, but nevertheless it had left what she could only describe as an awareness – an awakening of knowledge that had seemed to open some kind of channel.

Lilith had many legends attached to her depending on which civilisation, religion or century you identified with most. According to one story she was an Old Testament character who claimed to have been created whole and was therefore equal to Adam. Sexually confident, it seemed she had emasculated Adam and as a result he had subsequently taken Eve, a more subservient woman to be his wife, the latter having been crafted from one of his ribs. Banished into the wilderness, Lilith was now full of vengeance. Revered by modern feminists for insisting on sexual equality yet reviled through the ages for being a frustrated sexual predator who hated children and killed pregnant women, she was reputed to be a harbinger of disease who flew through the night to wreak her revenge. Hardly the stuff, Becky thought, to terrify a right-thinking person, and probably a myth fabricated to serve the purpose of various religious leaders throughout the ages.

However, it wasn't that which had chilled her, rather it was the far more credible, modern day worship of Lilith. Summon her and the unholy alliance with Samael would spark the black flame; after which Lucifer himself could be raised. Oh, how richly rewarded these people would be by Satan for inflicting pain and degradation on others, for defiling everything sacred; without mercy, without compassion, sullying the soul given to them by God. Was it an excuse for being a disgusting, self-serving human being with no conscience? Or did whatever they invoke really manifest as a malevolent presence none of us could either understand or control?

Surely they realised, because they must believe in it, that the demonic was too dangerous to summon? That they would no longer be in in the driving seat? That it didn't give a damn about rewarding them with more sex and more money once it got here? These idiots were mere conduits... Or perhaps they didn't quite believe in the dark side after all – thinking it was just a bit of a thrill until it was all too late? The genuine, sickening testimony from the broken few who had been victims of ritual satanic abuse and escaped, often only to find themselves disbelieved, was so horrific it could not have been fabricated. The same acts carried out by ancient druids in the sixteenth century were still being carried out today; and it was so far underground, so tight, the rest of the world simply didn't know, see or care about the victims spat out afterwards. But why did they do it if there was nothing in it...if it didn't work? That was the thing...

Well, knowing what she now knew, especially with it being so personal, hadn't helped one bit. She couldn't sleep – not when every time a pipe banged or a board creaked her eyes snapped open again and her heart lurched. She stared into the gloom. A branch rustled silkily outside the window, its silhouette fluttering on the far wall. Silence hissed in her ears. So who or what had shouted into her ear? Was something here now staring at her...they could see her but she couldn't see them? God, if ever she woke to find a pair of eyes fixed on her in the dark she'd die of a heart attack.

It could happen...

Right, that was it! She threw back the top sheet and padded over to the light switch, passing the cheval mirror mid-way. Then stopped. And turned. A tiny movement had caught her attention and she stared at her reflection. For several minutes she stood there, voluminously pregnant in the ethereal greyness of pre-dawn, gazing hypnotically into the glass, unable to pull herself away....chilled now...swaying...

And when it happened it was so fast her mind almost didn't register it.

With a gasp of horror, hands shaking violently, she lunged for the light switch, back flattened to the wall.

What the fuck was that?

Electricity floodlit the room. She scanned everything in it, turning around and around, half expecting there to be someone behind her. Everything was normal. Absolutely normal. She swished the curtains shut. Shot back into bed. Pulled the covers up to her chin, shivering uncontrollably. The urge to tear downstairs, get out of the house and run into the drive was overpowering – there was a feeling of menace in here, like a presence.

No, no, no – she would not give in to this. Instead she plumped up the pillows and reached for her Kindle. It was all in the mind. Every bit of it. Sending her half mad. Anyway, there was no way she would sleep until the sun came up so the best thing to do would be to read for a while.

What was it, though?

She stared at the unopened Kindle.

A dream, a hallucination, her own demons, memories from a movie or online images? That was fine…yes…she could cope with it, rationalise it…Or was it Lilith…possession through mirrors…

She flicked on the Kindle. Her imagination had run into overdrive. It was stupid and had to stop. But it wouldn't stop. It kept on and on.

She scrolled down to the book about third trimesters, determined not to recall what she'd just seen, or thought she'd seen. But it shot straight back into her head.

As she'd stared into the cheval mirror, a fleeting image of a woman's face had appeared in the mirror opposite, multiplying infinitely down an eternal corridor.

Her hair was long, black and dripping wet; her eyes totally white.

***

Chapter Three

Woodsend Village

Toby wandered along the riverside path from Bridesmoor to Woodsend. This case was going to take years to wrap up: there were still so many unanswered questions – not least where Ida Dean had got to. It was, in short, a total mystery. If she had been in Tanners Dell on the night of the raid she could only have fled further into the network of underground tunnels, and there were only so many exits, none easy to scale – especially when the surrounding area was heaving with officers. However, if she hadn't been present at the satanic ceremony then she would surely have been at home in Woodsend when the police came knocking? From what he understood though, Ida would have been an essential presence at the Black Mass. Well, one thing was certain – no way could she still be around here; the whole place had been pretty much taken apart. He pictured her shooting skywards on a broomstick and half-smiled. Bloody, horrible old witch.

Right now though, right here in this moment, with sunshine catching on the water in sparkling sprays, it was hard to believe so much evil had been committed amid all this natural beauty. What was wrong with people? All this having power over others or acting out debauched perversions seemed totally alien to him. That the whole thing had lasted decades and locked down an entire community, depriving the villagers of their right to live freely, was frankly astonishing. Christ, but they'd had it all sewn up though, hadn't they?

Even now, eight months after the arrests, local people still wouldn't linger down here by the river or walk their dogs in the woods. The dogs, it was said, wouldn't go in - crouching on their haunches, growling at a sinister presence humans couldn't see. And although every person residing in Bridesmoor had been visited by the police over the last few months, all without exception had refused to talk – said they'd seen nothing and heard nothing. Fear, it seemed, was their legacy. Maybe it always would be – at least for the next generation and all who could remember Lucas Dean and his sons. But it was now over, it really was: they were free if they chose to be. It was odd how an atmosphere lingered, even when the threat had long gone.

He shoved his hands deep into his pockets. Anyway, it was good to be back at work; good to feel part of the human race again; and especially good to be out here on an afternoon like this, with the warmth of the sun on his back and the smell of fresh, wild garlic in the air. It was mind over matter that was all – people here needed a positive attitude now, to reclaim this stunning countryside as their own. It wasn't the Deans' and they should take it back.

Hang on, that's weird…

Stopping short, he frowned. Surely with the sunlight behind him, his shadow should stretch out ahead? But it didn't. It spread sideways instead, almost as if there were three of him. He checked over his shoulder for a possible cause, but there was no one else there, nothing in fact, which could explain it. Now if he'd had a huge bear on his back it would have made sense. Maybe a cloud? He looked up. The sky was clear. Come to think of it, this wasn't the first time he'd had a feeling of being shadowed or followed, even in full sun. He'd put it down to depression and the disturbing images he had when asleep. They called it the black dog, didn't they, depression?

Yeah, that must be it – it was in his own mind…and it would lift…

Ahead lay the forest leading up to Woodsend – a village no longer inhabited. With the Deans imprisoned and the row of decrepit council houses on Ravenshill awaiting demolition, there was no one here anymore; and therefore nothing to be afraid of. Even so…he glanced over to the cool shade of the forest, at the trees which lined the path like grim sentinels – and shivered. It was a spooky place.

Oh come on! Could he really say that trees and fresh water and luscious green grass scared him? At worst it was only ghosts of the past, and those he could deal with. In fact, it had been scientifically proven that imprints of energy could remain in our own time dimension, particularly when something traumatic had happened. Anyway, all he had to do this afternoon was take a good look round – see if there was anything they'd missed or he could add before beginning, at long last, to write up the concluding report on Tanners Dell before the trials began this autumn.

Forensics had completed their examinations, the entire area scrutinised for every last vestige of evidence. The caravans at Fairy Hill had been removed and the Deans' place taken apart floorboard by floorboard. A grim job that had been. Ida Dean's laundry room had been full of frayed, greying sheets, cotton nappies, and children's clothing ingrained with the kind of stains no amount of washing could ever remove. And on the shelves were racks of glass bottles containing a variety of herbal mixtures, including lethal concoctions of belladonna, hemlock and wolfsbane. Paul Dean's computer contained thousands of images of child pornography and hard porn; and in the loft they found a large collection of torture, horror porn and snuff movies. That the place was a stinking cesspit surprised no one, that there were human remains underneath the floors, did. It had taken weeks to sort through and catalogue; every member of the team now undergoing professional counselling.

From underneath the abbey over two hundred skeletons – animals, small children and babies mostly, plus several unidentified adults – had been disinterred. Not all were recent either – many dated back centuries, which was odd because the tiny, ringed cemetery was full of the many orphans the sisters at the abbey had tried to help, their gravestones clearly engraved with names and dates. So why there were skeletons dating back to the sixteenth century underneath the building as well, no one had yet worked out. Who had put them there? And where had the sisters themselves been buried? God, that really was odd now he came to think of it. It would be interesting to get to the root of this because the village seemed to have had quite a dark history long before Lucas Dean had even been born. What on earth went on here? Well anyway, he was a detective not a history scholar – his job was just to try and get the police evidence wrapped up so the likes of Ernest Scutts and Paul Dean would be banged up for a very, very long time.

On nearing the entrance to the woods, a tomb-like chill wafted against his face. Toby hesitated, looking back at the sun-baked river bank and sparkling water instead. Surely a few minutes relaxing first wouldn't hurt, would it? Turning round he sank onto the grass and kicked off his shoes, raising his face to the sun. It was so wonderful to be in the light again that was all, and the water tumbling over the shiny rocks was dazzling, mesmeric...He leaned back to soak up the warm, golden haze. First day back: he'd been off a long time after working in the vault underneath Tanners Dell and it wasn't something he was going to forget easily – if ever – those nightly visits from dark shapes crawling into his mind, paralysing him in sleep, forcing him to endure the torment. Night after night he'd woken screaming, sopping with sweat, heart hammering into his ribs.

But it was alright now. It was... He lay down on the toasted earth. It was all going to be just fine...

He was startled awake by a cacophony of rooks bursting into the sky. Sitting up, he looked at his watch. *Oh no, flaming hell – two hours had slipped by.* A light breeze lowed in the trees, the sun having dipped behind them. Best get a shimmy on or Sid Hall would be ringing. Sid, his sergeant, should have retired this summer but he'd hung on after Scutts had been arrested. Gut instinct, he called it. Yeah, more like he wanted both Callum and Toby on their feet properly first. He jumped up. Sid had been like a father to him and no way would he let him down.

The temperature in the forest was noticeably chillier as he climbed over the style and jumped down; and despite it being a public right of way, the main track up from the river was

22

overgrown, making it difficult to see where it was. Still, he thought, with the reputation of the place it was no wonder really – who would want to wander through here out of choice? At least it was dry and if you pushed the ferns aside not too difficult to pick through. After a while the sound of the gurgling river behind became muted and he stopped to catch his breath, listening. Curious: there were no sounds of life in here at all. No birds. No rustling in the undergrowth. The air was close too – trapped and stale – and although only four o'clock and still daylight, in here it was dismal and grey, the canopy of leaves shadowing the ground almost to dusk. He marched on, eventually passing a cottage on the right so overrun with foliage it could easily have been missed. Woodpecker Cottage presumably – where that poor boy had been brought up, the one Kristy had taken care of? He looked on ahead. The path seemed to be getting much darker as the forest deepened. There was a sense of being very alone.

His own breath came loudly in his ears as the climb steepened. Maybe this had been a bad idea? Surely the Deans' old place should be in front of him by now? Trekking on, he began to break a sweat, until gradually the ground levelled off and there in front, appearing through the tree trunks, was a chimney stack. He stopped to get his breath, leaning against the trunk of an old oak. God, he was so unfit. He used to run and work out every day – he really must get back into it as soon as possible…In fact…

Wow!

Abruptly his mind chatter ceased. To the west a prism of sunrays beamed through the woodland, giving the illusion of a brilliantly lit corridor surrounded by a spectrum of pink. Almost, he thought, like a moon rainbow. And at the end lay a ring of shining white stones.

Without thought or hesitation he immediately started walking towards it, veering off the main path, tripping over roots, branches snapping in his face, in order to take a better look. The team had examined this, of course, but no evidence of any kind had been found at the site, its existence marked down as little more than an aside.

*What a magical sort of place, though…*He crouched down to examine it close-up. The stones had eroded into smooth boulders with age - thirteen in all, the largest positioned at the western point. And in contrast to the outlying area the grass inside the circle was lushly verdant. He looked up. The treetops were far enough apart to let in dappled light. But more than that, the oak trees, old and gnarled as they were…also appeared to form a circle, towering overhead like guardians.

Walking into the middle he twirled around and around, still looking up: yes of course, ancient pagans would have relied on the position of the sun, moon and stars for their rituals – working closely with the laws of nature – and from here would have had a perfect view. Wow, there was a real sense of history here – an atmosphere – like reaching back in time…

What happened next, however, was something he could never explain.

A blinding pressure suddenly rushed to his head – a pulsating, sickly throbbing – and he staggered as if drunk. *Whoa…* At once the sky became a multi-coloured kaleidoscope, the tree canopy a spinning vortex. Grasping at thin air he tried not to fall as the white stones whizzed round in a crazy carousel, picking up speed until they blurred to a whole.

Outside of the circle the forest instantly blackened to night and a hypnotic, low hum emanated from within. He clasped the sides of his head to block it out, reeling as the ground began to buck and rise beneath him. Groups of hooded figures were gathering in every direction, gliding sedately at first, then rapidly rushing forwards with torches of fire. He tried to reach for one of the stones, but the earth rose up, slamming hard into the side of his face, and as he lay stunned, a ring of torches formed around him.

What the fuck was this? What was going on? This was madness… He was mad… madder than he thought…

Grasping at blades of grass, clawing into the soil, intuition screamed at him to get out of the ring. The nearest boulder gleamed brilliant white but oh-so-far-away. Repeatedly he lunged for it, slithering on his belly as if climbing uphill, until finally his fingers made contact with the satisfying solidity of the stone. Clinging on by the nails, he levered his bodyweight up inch by inch, until finally he had a better purchase and could hurl himself out; rolling over and over onto the hard, dry earth into the cool silence of the forest.

For a long while he lay on his back panting hard, swallowing down the vomit in his throat. Thumping pain cramped the nerves in his head like the worst of migraines but… he glanced around several times in every direction…it seemed he was alone again… all was gloomy and still, just as before.

He flopped back.

What the fuck? Seriously – what the fuck was that?

The only experience he'd ever had remotely like it was after a stupid experiment with magic mushrooms and a bottle of 8% cider as a teen.

He tried to sit up but fell back again, cracking his head and blacking out.

When he next opened his eyes it was night. He blinked, puzzled. Stars glittered in between the treetops; it was bitterly cold with a light frost on the crunchy leaves beneath him; and the branches were stark - a smell of smoke and bonfires in the air.

This didn't make any sense at all. Slowly his eyes adjusted to the darkness and he shook his head at the sight of a shadow before him. *What the hell….?* An explosion of shock thumped him square in the chest. The blackened, dead-eyed body of a woman hanging by the neck was swaying in front of him.

***

<u>Chapter Four</u>

Bridesmoor
May, 1583

Fifteen year old Magda turned breathlessly to her younger sister, Cicely, and pulled her up the hill. "Come on, we're almost at the top now."

The evening was unseasonably humid, the steep path slippery, rainwater still dripping from overhead leaves. Cicely took Magda's proffered hand and together they climbed the remaining few feet to Five Sisters Abbey, panting, a light sheen of sweat on their faces.

"You first," said Cicely, indicating the high stone wall.

Magda nodded. It was the least she could do. "Give me a lift up, then."

Cicely made a stirrup shape with her hand and Magda stepped into it, levering herself onto the top. She reached down for Cicely. "Put your foot into that hollow bit there – the crack between the stones – and hold onto me."

Cicely, being only thirteen and small for her age, was light - still a child - and Magda swung her up with ease.

"It's so beautiful," Cicely said.

Beneath them, the Tudor garden shimmered in the blue haze of an early summer evening. Scented with damp earth and fresh, new roses, it had been intricately laid out in parterres enclosed by clipped box hedges. Gravel walkways enabled easy maintenance, with stone archways separating one part of the garden from another; and partly hidden by evening shadows small flights of steps led to further secret gardens; stone statues and fountains punctuated the lawns, and an ash arbour sat in the shade of the wall. Enchanted, they stared, eyes shining. Each small square of roses had been carefully planted with various colour combinations, from white to pastel pink to the deepest ruby red. The girls nodded to each other. Perfect.

"Look over there too," Magda said, pointing towards an outbuilding that would be useful for a hasty retreat. They could vanish into the forest as if they had never been here. Besides, they agreed, the nuns would surely not notice a few missing blooms. Everyone knew they lived in luxury while the villagers starved. Ambrose said it was because of all the good work they did for the orphans: these were women of God and it would be blasphemy to question it.

Magda worked quickly, losing herself in the swish of leaves and rasp of the knife as she dropped roses into her basket, determined not to notice the tears wetting her sister's cheeks. No doubt Cicely was thinking about what was to come. Well, what had to be done, had to be done. Tomorrow her sister would be the village May Queen, paraded through the streets in a cart adorned with flowers. After which she would be married.

The marriage ceremony itself would begin at dusk in the stone circle they had just passed; ending at midnight with a supreme sacrifice. It had to be made for the gods of fertility to be appeased or there would be nothing but death and destruction. Ambrose had proclaimed this as fact and no one doubted him. Already the plague had claimed a third of the local town's population, and the famine of last winter had left people in the surrounding villages starving: the old, the weak, the bairns – all had perished before February was out.

Her sister would have a beautiful crown of roses – she would make sure of that. The wedding dress of white wool lay across her bed in their small family cottage all ready for the big day: how pretty she would look wearing that, waving to onlookers as it led her and simple-minded Ezra to their grand finale. Not as pretty as she herself would have looked, but the attention would have to be on Cicely tomorrow. She and Ezra were the only maidens over thirteen, the only ones who could save the village from pestilence and famine. It would be an honour – a day of glory – and it would be their last.

An owl hooted nearby, cutting into her thoughts. Startled, she caught her thumb on a thorn. "Ouch!"

"Magda?" Cicely rushed over, dabbing at the swelling bilberry of blood with her only handkerchief. Her face was shiny and wet from crying, and Magda put her arms around her, burying her face in her sister's tumble of strawberry-blonde curls, so starkly different from the straight, raven black of her own.

"We've got enough now. Let's go home."

Cicely suddenly stepped back, searching her sister's face. "Did you hear that?"

"No. What?"

They stood as statues. "There," said Cicely. "Listen."

Both turned in the direction of the darkening forest, as a low, steady whistle shivered through the branches.

"It's just the wind," said Magda. "Come on, let's get back."

The light had dipped to midnight blue, a soft mist hovering over the ground as the girls hurried down the track, Cicely in front, occasionally glancing over her shoulder to check on Magda.

One more night sleeping with her sister. One more season before the village would know if the crops came good. One more day, week, month before they'd know if the plague was coming for them… It was only to be hoped Cicely's sacrifice would not be in vain.

The Old Coach Road from Doncaster had been closed for weeks now, with the epidemic having taken over eight hundred people in less than six months. It had, the townspeople claimed, arrived with a tradesman on his way from London to Edinburgh. He'd been taken sick, fallen from his horse and cart, and lay on the roadside in a fever. A kindly woman had taken him in and now the death toll was rising fast. Within days of contracting the pestilence people collapsed with a high fever and vomiting, before exhibiting the terrifying death knell of excruciatingly painful swellings in their groins or armpits, otherwise known as buboes. They died in agony, often within hours. Crosses were nailed to doors and bodies quickly buried. The sudden, widespread deaths cut a swathe through a population ignorant of either cause or cure.

Ambrose said it would come for them too. Whole villages had been wiped out, and if they didn't die of the plague they would likely die of famine if the crops failed again this year. Either way, their deaths, compared to the swift, clean end Cicely and Ezra would face, would be prolonged and torturous. Conviction amongst the villagers grew: Ambrose, their parson, was the most influential man for miles around, and the only one who could save them.

As the older sister, it was supposed to have been her, of course. She who should have been tied to hapless, fourteen year old Ezra, have her throat cut and her blood drunk from cups...

But Ambrose had been watching her for a while.

One evening as she walked back through the woods, damp from bathing in the river, her thin cotton dress still moulded to her curves, he caught up with her. They walked abreast for a while. Few words were exchanged. Rather, it had been an understanding that occurred, a live and glitteringly dangerous thing, which grew and took shape.

"Are you ready for the ceremony, Magda?" he asked.

Aware of a heightened energy, of his darting glances towards her breasts and the way the late sun silhouetted the shape of her thighs, she smiled. There was only herself and her sister. It would have to be one of them.

The woodland thickened as they neared Tanners Dell, and she let him pull her down into the long, dewy grass. And turning aside as his stale breath blew into her face, and his fingers feverishly pulled at her underclothes; she allowed him to pummel her soft flesh and push himself inside her.

It was over quickly.

Afterwards he rolled onto his back, slavering and wizened.

He was just an old man, she thought. With no power at all really.

***

29

Chapter Five

Jasmine Cottage
Present Day

Becky began to top up the others' glasses with more wine. Perhaps a bit more alcohol would loosen Amy's tongue? There was so much she wanted to know but the girl was withdrawn to the point of rudeness, deftly avoiding eye contact and sidestepping questions. How disappointing.

"There's plenty more where that came from," she said.

"Not for me thanks," said Amy.

Oh, well that was that then.

"Stop trying to get her drunk," Callum said. "I know you – you want to fish for information." Looking at Amy, he added. "It's because she's a psychiatric nurse – she has to analyse people – see if they're bonkers or not."

Becky laughed. "Says the detective." She glanced at Toby. "You're quiet as well. You alright, love? Here, have some cheesecake – you need a bit of padding if you ask me."

Toby patted his washboard stomach and shook his head. "That's a five mile run, is that! No thanks, I've got to get fit again – been off too long."

"Well, I think that's really cruel. Now every time I look in the fridge tomorrow it'll be sitting there, begging me to eat it."

"Tomorrow? I'd put money on it not getting through the night," said Callum.

She punched his arm and he pretended it hurt, then filled up the wine glasses again.

Amy snatched hers away. "Not for me."

"You can if you want, you know? We're getting a taxi back."

"No. Really, Toby." She smiled and nuzzled against his arm.

She looks ever so distracted, Becky thought, like she wants out of here as soon as possible. Well maybe she was too young for a dinner party like this, although she and Cal weren't exactly stuffy. "Shall I put some music on? John Legend, okay?"

Amy smirked.

"Oh no, torture," said Toby. "Have you got any Rudimental or Massive Attack?"

"Yeah, lots," said Becky, popping on the John Legend CD. "Now listen to this and be grateful it isn't Bananarama."

"Who?"

Sitting down she re-filled Toby's empty glass yet again. Blimey, he was knocking it back.

"Rude boy. So, come on, tell us – how did you enjoy your first week back at work then? I suppose you've got to write up the report now? The trials start in a couple of months, don't they?"

"Actually, I only went back yesterday, Becky." He downed his fifth full glass of Rioja, immediately holding it out for another. "Ta. Yeah–" He gave a dry kind of laugh. "I had to go out to Woodsend – just for a wander, to tie up loose ends, that kind of thing."

"It must be eerily quiet out there now with no one living there anymore? At least you were safe to take your time and have a good look round without the risk of running into any Dean brothers. You're braver than me, though. It must have a really creepy feel to it after all that's happened?"

"Hang on, no one living there? So what about Woodpecker Cottage then? The one that's all overgrown?"

"No," Callum chipped in. "It's been empty for a long while, has that. Thought you knew?"

"Well, yeah...It's just a bit odd, that's all because there was a lamp on downstairs when I walked past. It didn't really register at the time. It only hit me later when I was driving back."

"I'm surprised it's got electricity." said Becky. "But maybe it was an oil lamp or something – a tramp or a squatter? My God, I wouldn't want to stay the night there, would you? They must have nerves of steel."

"Why?" said Amy.

They all turned to look at her, eyebrows raised.

"Well, because of what went on," said Becky. "Toby's told you about the devil worshipping, I assume?"

Amy nodded somewhat vacantly and Becky tried not to stare too much. There was something so disconnected about the girl; like some of her wiring had come loose.

"It's a place with a very dark history, Amy. Children were abused there."

"Not now, though? It's just woods and trees and stuff – just a place?"

"Yes, I expect you're right."

"Of course she's right," Callum said. "What 'appened were bloody awful but there's no one there anymore – not in Woodsend anyway. It's just a place, and a gorgeous one, too."

"Apart from it being the scene of hundreds of unmarked graves, you mean? Come on, there's got to be some sort of negative imprint there – remember they used those woods for rituals involving human sacrifice. The cemetery became a satanic church. You yourself found evidence of black witchcraft in the caravans at the back. We're talking about decades of devil worship…Well all I'm saying is that something like that has to leave its mark."

"How, though?" said Callum, reddening in the face as he became increasingly animated. "I'm not arguing with the facts – yes all of that is correct and we finally got hold of a band of nasty, sadistic murdering paedophiles; but what you'd have us believe, my sweet, is that the area itself – woods and flowers and stones – are haunted and can scare you? Honestly, Becky, you don't half come out with some crap."

"No, actually, light of my life, what I said was there might be an imprint of all that bad energy in the atmosphere. We are all made up of energy you know? Even inanimate objects. And it's been proven scientifically that in places where a particularly traumatic event happened – terror or a sudden death for example – that the negativity can linger and 'haunt' a place. Unless you're a totally insensitive buffoon with the skin of a rhino's arse, that is."

"Becky's right," Toby said. "There's something in that."

He flushed as the focus of attention switched to him.

"Now this I've got to hear," said Callum.

"Right, well, I um…had a bit of a funny experience yesterday–"

"I knew there was something," said Becky. "I knew you weren't quite right. Go on."

He hesitated. Then drained his glass. Twiddled the stem. Finally the words came out in a rush. "Okay. Well, there's a ring of stones in the middle of those woods – you know, like an ancient druids' circle – they're all over the country, aren't they? Everybody knows about rings of stones–"

"Go on," said Becky.

"Right, well it's the only part of the forest floor that's got thick, green grass growing, not bracken and dirt – and by that I mean it gets the light – so I looked up and that's when I noticed the trees around it. A huge ring of gigantic oaks have deliberately been planted around those stones, like in a concentric circle."

"Oak trees take hundreds of years to get to that size," said Callum. "That's all ancient woodland, that is."

"Yes. I wouldn't like to say how old they are but the trunks are colossal, the branches all twisted and gnarled – some of them arcing down to the ground, and the roots are like these giant claws you could almost climb under. Anyway, I don't think anyone in the team picked this up because the report said there was nothing of note at the site; but it occurred to me the whole set-up had been purposefully designed long before the Deans showed up, and I started to think about the history of the place – with skeletons being found under the abbey that were hundreds of years old as well–"

"My God, I never would have linked those," Becky said. "I thought the skeletons they found might have been plague victims, but now you mention the ring and the oaks, it does make you wonder. I suppose you've got the anthropologists in?"

He nodded. "Oh yes, that part of it was handed over months ago; but it has piqued my interest as well. It isn't connected to the crimes of recent decades, obviously, but–"

"But maybe that's why it was chosen! Like evil was drawn to it or something?"

"Oh for Pete's sake, Becky," said Callum.

"Anyway, Toby – sorry about him – you were saying about the history of the place?"

"Yeah, well that's why I was in the middle of this ring, thinking about the history of it all, when it was like suddenly I'd had fifteen pints and a couple of joints. I'm not kidding I couldn't stand up. The ring was spinning round like hell, and next thing I was on the floor having this horrible nightmare, one of the worst, except I was wide-awake. I managed to crawl out and the minute I did it all stopped." He clicked his fingers. "Over. Just like that. And I was lying there with a killer headache and sweat pouring off me wondering what the fuck happened. Only I couldn't get up. Every time I tried I fell back again, and I suppose I must have hit my head on the ground because when I woke up it was dark and… Christ, are you ready for this because it gets worse and even more unbelievable?"

"Oh my God, Toby," said Becky. "Are you okay now? I mean, do you think you should have gone back to work?"

"Yeah well this is just it – you're all going to think I'm going daft again and this is the problem, that's why I don't want to say."

"No, we won't," said Becky. "I promise you, absolutely not. Go on."

He glanced at his girlfriend, whose face was blank. "Amy, are you alright with this? I've had to deal with some bad stuff but I'm not loopy, I promise."

She smiled and nodded, her eyes more alight than they had been all evening.

"Okay, well I must have conked out like I said, but when I opened my eyes again it was dark and cold and smelled of wood smoke; the leaves had fallen and all the branches were bare... and there in front of me was a woman hanging by the neck from one of the trees. The wood was creaking and her long black dress was flapping in the breeze. I just sat there staring, and then slowly I realised there were loads of them – all these women hanging, their necks broken, everywhere I looked–"

No one spoke.

"I ran like a bleeding bullet – onto the main road and down to the car. It was only then I remembered about the light being on in Woodpecker Cottage when I passed it on the way up. I never thought at the time – stupid – but I didn't."

For a moment the four of them sat in silence, listening to John Legend singing, 'All of me...'

"Seriously, do you think you've come back to work too early mate?" Callum said.

"No, don't assume the obvious, Cal. It's a very strange place is Woodsend with a weird history. And anyway, if it makes you feel a bit better, Tobes, I've had something odd happen to me too, recently," said Becky. "And I don't know, maybe it could tie in somehow, I'm not sure."

"Oh, I love all this," Amy said, as if she'd only just switched on her personality. "All these spooky stories."

Becky hesitated briefly, but seeing Toby's stricken face decided to continue. "Okay, well let's agree on the principle that traumatic events can linger in an atmosphere, yes? Apart from him." She inclined her head towards Callum and rolled her eyes. "Obviously. Well the thing is, I know Celeste – remember, the medium I told you about - had a bad feeling about Woodsend and that woman was never, ever wrong. It was when she first went to live there, but I assumed it was because she'd tapped into what the Deans were up to. Now though, I'm thinking it may well go back much further because she said some very peculiar things the afternoon before she died...about Ida Dean in particular...that just didn't make any sense at all at the time. We all assumed Ida was just Paul Dean's wife, a bit player, someone who helped channel evil spirits with her witchcraft. But here's the thing, Ruby told me–" She stopped and looked at Amy. "I have a clairvoyant friend."

Amy nodded, smiling.

"I never used to believe in it either but it's shocking really – she's just spot on about everything – stuff she couldn't possibly know. Anyway, I had a message from Celeste through her about the real Ida Dean. I'm thinking on my feet here but this may link in, so bear with."

"You mean like a spiritual message?" said Toby. "From beyond the grave?"

"Oh, you're not going to repeat all that twaddle, are you?" said Callum. "You know, a satanic sect I can get my head round, but all this demonic stuff and messages from dead people–"

"Well, how did Ruby know the name for Ida that Celeste came up with then? Celeste died within hours of telling me and Noel. She had no access to Ruby during that time and neither of us would have repeated it to a girl so unstable – why would we – to anyone at all even? So eight months later Ruby tells me to look up this name. To find out who Lilith is!"

"Who's Lilith?" Toby asked.

"A bloody demon," said Becky, who permitted herself a smile. "Okay, I admit it does sound bonkers."

"You're not wrong."

"Oh shut up, Cal."

"Anyway, I looked her up, didn't I? And to be honest I really wish I hadn't. Apparently, she's a harbinger of death and disease, particularly to pregnant women and the new-born, and reputedly she possesses women through mirrors."

The others sniggered. Even Toby had his colour back.

"Don't tell me," said Amy. "So you looked in the mirror and this scary demon was looking back at you."

36

Becky stopped smiling. "Actually," she said. "You're not far off."

"Get away," said Callum.

"She had no eyes," said Becky, suddenly serious. "They were all white with no irises. I couldn't stop gazing in, almost obsessively, just couldn't drag myself away until...well, until it seemed like she was gliding out of it towards me, and then I broke away."

"How do you know that she was Lilith?" Amy asked. "The one Celeste said was really Ida Dean? I thought Ida Dean was a real person."

"She is, love," Callum said. "Flesh and blood and on the run." He shook his head. "Demon..."

"What they were doing in Tanners Dell was raising demonic spirits, Amy. And Lilith is a female demon who brings harm particularly to women. There is something about hatred for women in that place, although I can't prove it, of course, and I'm just guessing. Oh, and she's the only one with white eyes. I still can't really piece it together, except that I am now pregnant and I helped bring down that satanic sect. So if she was raised–"

"Holy crap!" Toby stared at her open mouthed. "You've broken the memory. That's what it was in the vault just before I got ill. One minute I was fine and the next thing I was in a hospital bed and couldn't move, couldn't even wash myself. And no matter how many times I tried to remember what happened I just couldn't. But now I know – it was right after I looked at this stone carving. It went right through me."

Becky frowned. "What did?"

Toby was wide eyed, excitable. "Yesterday I just wanted to see if anything would make it all fit together so I could file the full report, wrap it up, but...fuck! Sorry...sorry...it's just that it's come back to me now you've said about the eyes–"

The music had finished but no one noticed. Everyone had turned to stare at Amy, who was laughing so hard her face was distorted, tears streaming down her cheeks.

"It's just all so ridiculous," she said, dabbing at the mascara smudges and trying to sober up. "Sorry, I thought it was a joke."

**

Chapter Six

Drummersgate Forensic Unit
Next day

"Ruby wants to see Alice."

Becky unlocked her office door. "She's said that? Just now? How funny."

Noel followed her in. "Why?"

"Because it was only half an hour ago I finally had a report from the adolescent unit – I've just come off the phone to them. Take a pew, I'll put the kettle on."

Noel slumped onto the armchair by the window and put his feet up on the desk. "God, I'm knackered."

Becky spooned instant coffee into a couple of mugs. "Rough night?"

"Mmm..."

She turned and wrinkled her nose. "You stink of booze."

"Do I? Sorry, I didn't realise. It helps me sleep, that's all."

"Slippery slope, Noel."

"Yeah…, yeah, I know…Becks, you remember Harry? The priest I told you about who did the exorcism on Kristy?"

She sloshed a drop of milk into each mug, handed one to him and sat down, holding onto Molly with her free hand. "Yes, of course."

"Ah, are you suffering?"

She smiled. "No, not at all. I just feel very protective… Yeah, okay, I'm no spring chicken and I feel like a sweaty carthorse, my back aches and my legs have started to swell up…bet you're glad you asked. I could go on with the list if you want? "

"No, you're alright. You going to be okay to work?"

She took a sip of coffee. "Yes, I think so. So far so good. Anyway, why do you ask about Harry? He and I never met, but of course I remember you telling me about him. Kristy's going to Australia soon by the way, have you heard? Can't say I blame her – fresh start and all that."

He nodded. "I don't blame her either. I cannot begin to imagine what she's suffered. Anyway, it's just I might go and see him, that's all."

"Are you still having nightmares?"

"God, yes. Aren't you?"

"How bad is it?"

He shrugged miserably.

"Ah, Noel. I suppose I didn't see what you saw – I didn't witness an exorcism or frankly I'd be in here – locked in Solitary. It was bad enough seeing her like that so it must be a hell of a lot worse for you. Is it like reliving it every time you go to sleep or–?"

"Yes and no, more a feeling of being constantly watched. I've got this thing about keeping the light on because I could swear that while I'm sleeping there's someone suspended over me in the dark, staring at me from the ceiling. It's human but shaped like a crab with its head on back to front…I dream it's really there, but when I wake it's gone. Then the minute I shut my eyes again it's back, sort of like a continuous nightmare that reverts exactly to where it was before, determined to send me mad… Oh I don't know. Maybe time will help."

"Well, drinking won't that's for sure. In fact it'll make it a whole lot worse, but you know that." His eyes were bloodshot. An already lean man, he'd lost a considerable amount of weight too. "I've never seen you like this before. You don't even drink much normally. It's serious, isn't it?"

He nodded.

"I wonder why it's getting worse?"

He shook his head. "It's wearing me down, Becky."

"What do you expect from Harry? Have you thought about counselling?"

His eyes locked with hers. "Becky, you and I both know this is something a counsellor can't fix. You know what this is."

She nodded. "Yes, yes I do and I'm sorry. It's just I wanted to give you normal sound advice and not jump straight down that route again. I get enough stick at home about it."

"You're not still affected as well, are you?"

She nodded. "Not like before. But it kind of stays with you...never really goes away, I'm afraid. Anyway, I'm sure Harry's the best person to go and see – good idea. And I'm always here for you, you know that."

"Thanks, I know, but you've got other worries now and besides, surely you want to try and forget?"

She took another sip of coffee. "I seriously wish I could, but to be honest I've got the exact same feeling as you about being watched. I'll tell you something now. Do you remember the day Celeste died, her telling us that Ida was really Lilith? Well a week ago Ruby came out with the same name – said Celeste, who's her spirit guide now by the way, was telling me to find out about Lilith because I was with child. I don't suppose you ever gave Ruby that name?"

"No, of course I didn't."

"No, sorry. Sorry. Well it's bloody spooky that's all. Lilith is supposed to be a demon that hates pregnant women and kills the new-born. All nonsense you might think, except she's got white eyes – exactly as Celeste described – and oh, Noel, I couldn't tell anyone else this for obvious reasons, but when I'm alone at night I see her in my bedroom mirror."

"A year ago I'd have said that's your imagination and hardly surprising, but–"

"Yes and I'd convinced myself it was precisely that - I'd seen those images time and time again researching Lilith, and we know how the subconscious mind can play tricks on us when we're tired or scared to death?"

He laughed. "You're not kidding. But how is this demon woman supposed to actually hurt you? I mean in the real world?"

"Well, she can't, can she?"

They sat without speaking for a few minutes. In the corridor a tea trolley clattered, and in an upstairs room a phone rang and rang.

"So why is Ruby suddenly asking for Alice, do you think?" said Becky. "She hasn't mentioned her daughter to me at all. Not once."

"It came out of the blue this morning," said Noel. "I went in with her meds and we got chatting, then all of a sudden she said, 'I need to see Alice.'"

"She didn't say why?"

"Nope. That was it. After that she turned to stare out of the window humming that infernal nursery rhyme, her eyes all glazed over."

"She's gone very internal again, hasn't she? Talking to her other parts, of course. It's an amazing landscape she's got in there. Have you seen what she's drawn for Claire?"

"The rooms and tunnels in her mind? I know, it's incredible. It's such a shame Amanda resigned because Claire hasn't got the time to do it really. I'm convinced if she got the right person Ruby could, if not recover, at least function in the real world again, aren't you?"

"Hmm, well we might have word on that soon." She smiled. "I've got to train up Sandi next to cover my maternity leave, but I do know Isaac's released more funding, so with Claire promoted to consultant hopefully when I come back we'll have a full complement of staff again."

"Thank Christ for that. Sometimes I feel like I might as well bring a sleeping bag and move in."

"Ditto."

"Just going back to Alice for a minute, though, what did the report say? Is there something we can pass on to at least reassure Ruby? She seems very agitated all of a sudden."

Becky gulped the rest of her coffee and checked her watch. "Oh, sorry, yes. Finally they replied – good of them, eh? And it's not much either – just a two-line memo stating she's responding well to speech therapy and is now back on the unit."

"Back?" Noel shook his head in confusion.

"Quite. That's why I rang straight away, and this time I got through to a therapist, who said she was new – Judy Harper. It seemed she was fostered out, can you believe? She lasted three days before screaming the place down and attacking the other children. Oh, and worst of all, she then went missing. They found her wandering around Tanners Dell for God's sake."

Noel frowned. "I don't understand. So the child is rescued from a satanic cult, had her tongue cut out, and they put her with foster parents after just a few months? I don't get this."

"I don't either. And as you know I've asked repeatedly for news of her progress and repeatedly been fobbed off. I've been so busy and preoccupied I had to assume she was being well taken care of. Now I'm not so sure. Not so sure at all."

"What about a visit from one of us then? They need to work with us if we're going to reunite mother and daughter at some point."

"Absolutely. And she'll have DID like Ruby: they need to be treating her for multiple personalities, and sooner rather than later. I mean, what if she runs away again? Ruby ended up a drug addicted prostitute at fourteen – we can't let history repeat itself." Becky stared at Noel as the thought occurred. "And *she* kept heading back to Tanners Dell too, didn't she? Hmmm….running away to return to a place of terror – now why would they do that? It doesn't make any sense."

"Well this is why we need to talk to Alice's psychologist. I don't know either. Ruby's the only case of DID I've ever looked after."

"I've had a few, but no one with poly-fragmented DID and I've never had to look after a victim of RSA. There are things we don't know… but I do know these children need to feel safe. They need to *be* safe before any kind of treatment can start. They'll get nowhere with Alice until she feels that trust, and if they foster her out again she's hugely at risk. For God's sake it's supposed to be a secure unit she's on."

"But no one will be at Tanners Dell even if she does manage to get there, have you thought about that? The place is sealed off with police tape. Deserted. And the police knew where to look and brought her straight back, so why do you think she's at risk? Surely these people will be long gone?"

"Because Callum says they're positive from what Ernest Scutts and Crispin Morrow are bragging about inside, that they didn't get all of them – not by a long shot."

"What exactly have they got to brag about?"

"That they raised Lucifer and they did a good job; and that we have no idea just how good a job yet. They've got them both in isolation now. One of the blokes unfortunate enough to be sharing a cell with Scutts was found howling and screaming the walls down at three in the morning. It took four wardens to hold him down."

"Alice has suffered enough. We need to make sure she's safe."

"Yes," said Becky, standing up. "And I've got a strong suspicion she isn't."

***

Chapter Seven

Bridesmoor.
1583, September

The rain set in around mid-August and drizzled on, turning berries to mush and the crops black. They would starve again this winter. And the plague had spread. Several cottages now had crosses nailed to the door in an attempt to stem the contagion, which had finally reached Bridesmoor, though no one knew how: the main routes to town had been blocked and no one had ventured either in or out.

Speculation on their misfortune was rife, spilling onto the church path after Sunday service. Perhaps, it was vengeance from the gods, or more likely witchcraft: the pestilence had been brought on the wings of a raven or the breath of a wild fox. Both of these red-eyed familiars had been seen skirting through the woods recently; ravens cawing from the forest, their blackened wings flapping into the autumnal evenings like the ragged cloaks of old churchmen. Harbingers of evil, said the elders who knew about these things and had seen it before. They no longer dared venture into Five Sisters woods after the witch had been hanged, hauled from her cottage by the mob many years ago. Her restless spirit haunted those woods, they said, and now she was back to wreak her revenge…in the guise of another…

Every lone woman, especially those who offered their services as a midwife, used herbs as medicine or kept animals, locked themselves indoors and barred the windows. In town, the gaols were full of women accused of witchcraft. Stripped and shamed, birthmarks became proof of the devil's mark; the testimony of women whose young had died after being wet-nursed was used against them; even the word of children as young as five or six claiming an elderly lady had looked at them strangely, was justification enough to hang them.

At just after ten o'clock when the rest of the family were fast asleep, and the sound of her father's snores reverberated through the walls, Magda slipped out of the cottage. The night was black; the sky a rumbling, ominous brew of bruised clouds that blew swiftly across the moon. Pulling her cloak around her she dropped the cowl hood low over her face and sprinted across the fields into Carrions Wood unseen. No way was she going to be blamed for this second year of bad luck. The guilt would not gnaw through to her bones, or burst through her skin in bubonic pustules; she was a survivor and there was power in that. Power in what she could do. Power over men. Men who would protect her.

Ambrose had kept his word, allowing her to slip away during the sacrificial ceremony so she would not have to watch her sister's fresh, virginal blood soaking into the lush grass. Once the young couple had been slaughtered, the frenzied celebrations had begun - with spiked wine and dancing until the precise moment the full moon shifted into the centre of the ring, at which point the crowd fell quiet, the young couple were buried where they lay, and the party trooped gravely home.

Now the villagers would be saved. Now they could rejoice in the knowledge that abundance would swell on the hedges and weigh down the trees, fatten the animals, plump the grain and produce healthy new-borns. Good times were coming.

As payment for her life, Magda permitted Ambrose to maul her body; his pathetic groping laudable, the musty old-man stench of him repugnant. But he kept in place a protective veil between her and those who eyed her suspiciously – her own mother for one. So for now…for now…the most influential man in the area would serve his purpose. The power though, oh, the power – what a taste it had given her.

William was waiting where he said he would be – by the twisted old oak to the east side of the mill. If he hadn't a wife she would be safe, would she not? Warm, comfortable, fed, and free from the pact with Ambrose…*If he hadn't a wife…*

The heat of him pulsed in the blackness of the woods as she drew level on this wild night. Grabbing her waist, he immediately swung her round to the hard slam of his lips, the grip of his fingers digging into her flesh. They fell to the ground as one; he hitching up her skirts, pulling at her undergarments, she arching her spine to take him in fully. Together they clawed and gasped like animals, tearing at each other's clothes, locked in the moment they had been desperately craving. Ever since one July evening after another loathsome pawing from Ambrose, when she'd wandered along the river just that little bit too far.

With dappling sun dancing on her bare skin she had waded into the water wearing nothing more than the white, cotton dress, which had captured Ambrose, letting it ride to her thighs, the cool freshness of it washing away the foul memory of tissue-dry hands that had poked, prodded and pried.

A handsome man in his mid-forties, William had been on his way home, as she knew he would be, when he stopped to watch her bathe. Deliciously conscious of his intense stare, she leaned back to rinse her hair, reclining in the flow, letting the soaked cotton of her dress cleave to her flesh as it rose further up…and up…

Now, silvery leaves crowded overhead in a ring of spectators, peering down from a black sky as repeatedly he rammed into her, pounding her spine into the dirt of the forest floor. He had her by the hair, levering his hips so he could plunge harder and harder and harder. "You dirty bitch, filthy harlot, village whore…"

This man, she wanted him. The black hair, the glinting hazel watchfulness of his eyes, the only man around here with money, respect and property; how his muscles strained against the white of his shirt and filled his breeches as he strode around in black leather boots and coat tails. A head taller than most, William the miller exuded dominance. They said that pale, weak wife of his could not bear children, miscarrying repeatedly… They said he beat her…well, that's because he didn't love her. How could he? This was a man who should possess a strong, beautiful girl who would bear him healthy children, roll around with him in his bed and satisfy him in every way, which she most definitely would. A man who needed to meet his match.

Her strong thighs wrapped around his back as the ferocious intensity of his lovemaking grew with each powerful thrust, dizzying her senses, sanding the skin off her back, crushing her arms with his weight as he shoved her shoulders into the ground, baring his teeth until at last, "You fucking, dirty little tart, damn you filthy, fucking disgusting bitch…" With a roar he finally released his weakness and his pleasure and his pain.

And inside the blackness of her mind she smiled. She had him.

He rolled onto his back, wreathed in sweat, panting, and she inhaled the raw, masculine scent of him, reaching over to stroke the black curls away from his elegant face. Oh, his wife had to go. Somehow Lisbet had to go. Did ever a woman want a man as badly as this? She could give him everything he wanted and more. The sons he should have…

"I'm pregnant," she whispered.

Not a sound broke the empty silence of his answer.

***

Chapter Eight

Mental Health - The Child and Adolescent Unit
Present Day

Becky was shown into the art room by the receptionist, who pointed to a pale, solemn-looking girl by the window. The psychologist supervising her was one of those women of indeterminable age – short, grey hair cut around her ears, no make-up, pleated skirt and flat, comfortable shoes, although with a virtually unlined complexion. Late forties or early fifties? Becky smiled, already liking her as she stood and held out her hand. Behind the glasses, her eyes were a deep, cornflower blue.

"You must be Becky? We're just playing a little game, aren't we Alice?"

Alice did not respond, concentrating instead on carefully packing a doll into a small cardboard box.

"Hi," Becky said, taking the proffered seat. "Thanks ever so much for agreeing to see me, Judy. I really wanted to talk to you."

Judy kept her voice low. "Likewise." Nodding towards Alice, who was humming distractedly, she added, "I don't think she's with us at the moment but best to keep our voices down all the same."

"Yes, of course," Becky murmured back. "I'm just so relieved to be able to talk to someone about this. The thing is, like I said on the phone earlier, we've had Alice's mother, Ruby, with us for nearly three years now, and she's making good progress; but as I'm sure you can imagine she'd like to see Alice. Anyway, I've tried making contact with the staff here for months but had no response. This is the first chance I've had.

Frowning, Judy lowered her voice to little more than a whisper. "I'm glad you came, Becky. I'm not particularly happy about the situation either. I only had the referral four weeks ago and that was by default. And I was surprised – very – that Alice hadn't been assigned a psychologist before that, and even more shocked to realise she'd been sent to foster carers, particularly when I found out they were based in the same area she came from."

"Sorry? You've lost me – come again?"

"Bridesmoor. She was sent to a family in Bridesmoor."

For several seconds Becky stared open-mouthed while she computed the information. "Wait a minute, you're kidding – they sent her to Bridesmoor? And you've only just been assigned? But…I don't understand. So she didn't see a psychologist for seven months? At all?"

"Nope. Looking at her notes she had intensive speech therapy, and after being assessed by the psychiatrist he was of the opinion that what she needed the most was a family environment."

"Good grief. I wish I'd known sooner, but I never had a single reply to any of my queries – I must have sent a dozen emails and rung Dr Mullins' secretary as many times again. You're the first person I've managed to speak to either on the phone or in person."

"I don't think I'd be here either if it wasn't for the fact that a senior registrar was on locum duty the night Alice was re-admitted. I'd worked with him before and he remembered me; so I agreed to come and do the assessment, then basically fought to stay on because I was so concerned. This is clear-cut RSA and Alice needs specialist help: I was most vociferous and threatened to make a big fuss. Fortunately the ward sister, Isobel, backed me and so here I am. I work privately as well as for the NHS and I'm on contract for this one – we sometimes get grants from various charities. Anyway, the consultant really doesn't want me here so the appointment is very tenuous."

"Sounds like he's got a control freak problem."

"You've got that right. Pretty rich when he's a psychiatrist, wouldn't you say?"

"Oh, the stories I could tell," Becky said. "If only they could diagnose themselves."

"Me too...we should have a drink one day and swap horrors. Mind you, there are some weird nurses around as well."

Becky laughed.

They watched Alice select plastic spiders and snakes to put in the box with her victim, before taping it up – with some difficulty because she had odd, crooked fingers that seemed too long for her delicate hands. Rocking to and fro as she worked, the growling noise emanating from her throat was both threatening and aggressive.

She was a lot smaller than most thirteen year old girls, with almost no signs of puberty. The resemblance to Ruby was startling: fine hair the colour of weak tea hanging around her face, alabaster skin so transparent the blue veins were visible around her temples and jaw line; and she had those same ice-blue eyes all the Deans had. Also like Ruby, Alice was trying to make herself as small and unnoticeable as possible - physically retreating into her shell, hunching into her body and avoiding eye contact - as she blocked out the world, rocking and growling.

"She upsets the others with that," Judy said, "That growling. They said she skitters around on all fours sometimes like she's a dog, particularly at night."

Becky frowned, watching the girl dig a hole in the sandpit Judy had provided, before proceeding to bury the little coffin.

"Hello Alice?"

Alice ignored her.

"Alice? My name's Becky. I wanted to say hello to you, to check you're okay. Can you say my name?"

"She's been given a prosthesis but she won't use it," Judy said. "I don't think she wants to talk to us today, do you Alice?"

On the table an array of toys had been set out – but hardly normal toys. Judy had supplied items which allowed Alice to express what had happened to her without having to answer questions directly. That her tongue had been removed had certainly stopped her from exposing secrets, but it seemed this girl was every bit as mentally damaged as her mother.

Becky's eyes filled with tears. She looked away. Dear God, what had these awful people done? This child should be out rollerblading or shopping in town like all the other girls her age – talking about the latest clothes and pop music downloads. And to think she'd come into hospital under the protection of officers only to be left with such little help. What bloody incompetence! And from people who were well trained and paid from the public purse. God, it made her so mad. Her glance fell to the hideous toys – plastic insects, imitation syringes, lengths of string, and a small plastic camera.

She nodded towards a toy knife. "I take it she's acting out what they did to her?"

"I'm afraid so. Actually, it's taken me weeks to get this far. She's not supposed to 'tell' anyone, you see? Especially a therapist. We're the most dangerous of the lot."

"How so?"

Judy glanced at the clock on the wall and said to Alice, "Have you had enough for today, Alice? Shall we let the girl out of the box now? She hasn't done anything wrong, has she?"

Alice shook her head, rocking so hard on the chair it was going to topple over.

"Is this what they did to you?"

No response.

"You know it's wrong what they did?"

The rocking stopped dead. As did the growling.

"You're not there anymore, Alice. You are safe now." Judy reached out to lightly smooth away a strand of Alice's hair but the girl flinched violently.

"It's okay. I won't touch your hair if you don't like that."

Alice turned to stare out of the window again, humming again but more softly, her gaze distant and glassy.

"You are not there anymore, Alice. You are here now and you are safe in hospital. Alice – look at me, Alice."

Slowly, the child turned around, peeping through her hair.

"You don't have to trust me – that's for you to decide – but if you want a hug I'm here." She opened her arms. "Would you like to hug?"

To Becky, the miserable nod was all too familiar. This child had never been loved. Never. It seemed Judy had gained a glimmer of trust though, because Alice suddenly clung to her. Minutes ticked by and still she held on, refusing to unfasten her grip from Judy's neck.

"Okay, okay. I'm here."

A gravelly noise erupted from Alice's throat, which sounded like, "Promise…"

"Yes. I promise. Now come on, let's get you to your room for a lie down."

Becky tagged behind, as Alice held onto Judy all the way down the corridor. Clearly she was behaving just like Ruby, having regressed into a toddler personality with powerful attachment needs. Once in bed she rolled onto her side and stuck her thumb in her mouth, tears drying on her cheeks.

"She'll be like that for a few hours now," Judy said. "Come on, let's go and have a proper chat."

***

"Honestly, it's so emotional, so draining – this job can really take it out of you," Judy said as they walked into the staff kitchen. She shut the door behind them. "Unfortunately, one of the methods these people use to keep children from talking is to instil a fear of therapists, nurses, teachers, policemen – anyone in authority, basically," she said, switching on the kettle and rooting around for cups. "The message is simple, 'Tell anyone and you'll be tortured or forced to torture another child.' What they do is encourage the victim to confess to one of the sect, who will be dressed in uniform or pretend to be a kindly therapist. The treachery is then exposed and the torture begins. It's designed to be so bad, so painful and so terrifying that the child will never tell a living soul ever again: we're talking about near drowning; taping their eyes open and spinning them round for hours…forced ingestion of human excreta… Oh, it's easy to destroy trust and that's how they do it."

"Have you worked on many cases of ritual abuse?"

"I've studied and worked in this field for over twenty years now; spent time in Australia and the United States, too. We have to remember the survivors are the clever ones, and in the minority. I can't afford to get angry, though, I just have to try and help the kids who made it through all that, to function and find some kind of peace."

"Oh God, poor Alice. It's evil beyond all belief, isn't it?"

"Sure is."

"So what happened at the foster home, do you know?"

"It went badly wrong as you can imagine. From what Dr Mullins told me – and he was quite dismissive, make no mistake this was not up for discussion – Alice had done well in speech therapy and after several assessments was deemed by him to be making good progress. Her notes say she was uncommunicative, vague and superficial in character, but beginning to improve in terms of washing herself, eating properly and taking her medication…"

"Which was?"

"A mild sedative."

"That's all?"

"Yes. But remember Alice will have learned a long time ago to comply with anyone in authority. Compliance equals survival, so of course she would have seemed acquiescent when she was both on a sedative and trying to protect herself. That didn't mean she didn't need help. Anyway, she was fostered out."

"And the whole team was in agreement?"

"Apparently." Judy handed Becky a mug of coffee.

"Lovely, thanks."

"Does Ruby have DID too?"

"Yes. Very poly-fragmented, but I don't think she was subjected to mind-programming. There aren't any indications of it, anyway."

"Are her fingers normal?"

"Yes."

"Did you notice Alice's? They used mousetraps on them as a form of punishment. And she screams the place down when the telephone rings – runs and hides under the table shaking and rocking. They will have convinced her that they know when she's telling tales and the ringing phone is to let her know they know. Her drawings show eyes inside her own head: they've told her they can read her thoughts and know everything she thinks, says and does. It takes a very long time, if ever, before a person abused in this way will ever tell another living soul because they truly believe they will be tortured or killed if they do. You have to give them time to gradually realise they're safe and the bad people were lying. So you see, since I came along she's actually become more demonstrative – in other words it looks as though her behaviour is going downhill, when in fact it's the direct opposite and we are only now beginning to make progress."

"Do you think Ruby might have gone through this kind of programming too, at least to some extent?"

Judy narrowed her eyes. "Well, she grew up with the same family involved with the same satanic cult, but from what you said on the phone I'm not sure. This is quite sophisticated, you see, so it could be more recent. Someone knew precisely how to manipulate Alice's alter personalities – how to get them to betray, kick and abuse her. She's terrified of letting them out."

"How do they kick and abuse her?"

"Sudden migraine attacks. Sudden pain in her stomach or chest. She'll draw a picture of a hob nailed boot and an angry face; oh, and eyes – so many liquid, black eyes – and knives that twist and turn inside her. Alice has some ferocious alters that she keeps locked up. When she feels more secure we can start dealing with them. But when she wasn't safe, or didn't feel safe, the monster alters took over, which is why she was fighting the foster carers, cutting herself and daubing blood all over the walls. The final straw was her writing in lipstick on the bathroom mirror, 'Gonna kill you, bitch!'"

"And of course they'd have had no idea how to handle it or how to protect the other children?"

"God, no. She was brought in by the police and sectioned immediately. That's when the registrar I mentioned earlier called me in to help. There aren't that many of us who know how to treat this. In fact, I suspect Dr Mullins is way out of his depth, but won't admit it. To be honest, I've had very few cases anywhere near as bad as this myself, and they could speak. Alice is by far the worst. The most damaged for the longest period of time. Apparently she's given birth at least half a dozen times too, all aborted. "

"Oh my God, I feel sick."

"She drew a tiny perfectly formed baby with a zipped pouch or purse around it, then a flower and a note saying, 'RIP'."

Becky stared blankly at the wall. There were no words.

"Is there any hope for her?"

"Yes, oh yes. That's the good news. But there's no quick fix, no easy tried and tested formula – in the end it comes down to the human bond, and to trust. We'll get there if Mullins will just back off and let me do my job."

"Judy, is there any danger you'll be taken off the case?"

"I'm fighting tooth and nail to stay, and I've applied to hospital management for the full-time post they've had vacant for over a year."

"A year? Ah, I see – so can they not find anyone or–?"

"Everyone who's applied has been turned down, apparently – according to Isobel."

"By Dr Mullins?"

Judy shrugged. "Well, he'd have the final say, but there has to be a symbiotic working relationship so I can't be sure. I must say I don't care for the man one bit but I'm here for Alice not him, so stuff him."

"What about your husband – does he mind you getting all this stress? I know mine does."

She laughed. "He's used to it. No, Mike's a very busy orthopaedic surgeon so we're... well you know we've been together a long time. We have stuff to do."

Becky smiled. There was such an air of security and permanence with this woman. "Can I just ask you a couple more things before I go?"

"Of course."

"Well, first – why did Alice go back to Tanners Dell when she escaped? Ruby used to keep going back there too, and I don't understand why someone who escaped from such a terrifying place would want to return?"

"Did she? Ah...interesting...maybe someone did know what they were doing with her then? Hmmm, well, the first thing to realise is the biggest fear for an abuser is the victim will tell - they are terrified of their victims, which is why they spend time programming them. But another trick is to use one of the alters to betray the host, which of course provides an inbuilt security system. So by the use of a trigger – say a phone ringing three times before going dead for example, the alter will go 'home.' Alice's alter was going back to snitch on her, or so the alter thought. You and I know it's just a way of getting Alice back to her abusers. And after what you've just told me about Ruby it seems one of hers may have done the same thing."

"I've got a big worry about that – my husband's in CID and I happen to know some of this sect are still out there, you see?"

"Didn't one of the women escape without trace?"

Becky nodded. "Exactly, yes – Ida Dean totally vanished."

"Well, I can promise you Alice won't be fostered out again anytime soon. I'll make sure of it and so will Isobel. But I don't think it's a great idea she's brought over to see Ruby just yet, do you? We've a long way to go."

"Definitely not, no. But at least I can tell Ruby I've seen her now, and she'll be happy with that."

"Is she able to understand what happened to her yet?"

"Yes, but there are complexities, like her clairvoyance and poly-fragmentation, and we had a particularly nasty episode after she was hypnotised and …well, we lost two consultants to mental breakdowns because of it."

"I did hear something to that effect, well I heard about Jack McGowan anyway. I knew him a few years ago – a good man, excellent doctor."

"Yes, yes he was. He was the one who did the hypnosis on Ruby. I was in the room too – but after that he was never the same; and frankly neither was I."

"You mean one of her alters was demonic in presentation?" Becky gasped.

Judy nodded. "You wouldn't believe what I've witnessed over the years."

Becky exhaled slowly. "Thank God. I cannot tell you how happy and relieved I am to find someone who understands. Honestly, I could cry."

"It affected you badly, didn't it?"

Becky nodded. "I'm so glad you're here and you're who you are. Can we meet up again soon, please? I really feel there's some hope now."

"Of course, I'd love you to. It's actually very useful for me, as well." She glanced at the clock and stood up. "Oh no, I really must dash – I have a meeting across town. You know it's funny but talking about Ida Dean something's just come to mind I think I should mention. There was a woman lurking outside in the yard a few weeks ago who made me feel a bit uneasy. She was watching Alice very intently, but because I was new I thought she must have been staff. Anyway, when I looked up again she'd gone. Later I thought, 'I wonder if she was Ida Dean and I should have said something?' But to be honest I'd nothing to go on – just a fleeting glance - and I've not seen her since."

Becky was shrugging on her jacket. "Outside here, do you mean? What did she look like?"

Judy screwed up her eyes. "No, no it doesn't make sense. And no one can get into the yard who isn't a member of staff. Anyway, this woman was young – very young – younger than Ruby."

"Ida Dean would be in her late fifties at a guess."

"Yes, yes of course. I was new, as I said, and hadn't really looked into how Ida was related to Alice; where she fitted in."

"She's not. Alice is the progeny of Ruby and sadly, Ruby's father – Paul Dean. Ida never formally adopted anybody."

"But she was married to Paul Dean?"

"That's what we've been led to believe but I can't say I've seen the marriage certificate. It wouldn't surprise me if they had some kind of demonic ceremony if they did anything at all."

"And Ida escaped…hmmm… You see that's what made me automatically think she might have come back for the girl; but like I say – this was a young woman so it couldn't have been her."

***

<u>Chapter Nine</u>

It bugged her, gnawing away at the edges of her mind on the bus home. Ida Dean was on the loose. And who knew how many others there were too? Those people were bound to the sect by the gruesome acts they had committed, and were no doubt regrouping.

But why did Alice still pose a threat to them? Maybe she'd been groomed for a higher purpose, or more to the point could expose things they would definitely not want known? Either way she was in huge danger, something which really hadn't occurred to her before today; all this time she thought the child was safe. No wonder Ruby was agitated - Ruby who intuitively knew about these things.

The blurry image of a young woman hovered in her mind, a focused stare through the glass, willing Alice to look up. That's all it would take – just one glance and the child would vanish into the underworld again without a trace.

How would she have got access, though? You either had to be a member of staff with a security key card, or have a visitor's appointment, which required registration at the main desk. These children were considered to be high risk and as such were closely protected; often from their own families.

No, it didn't make sense.

When I looked up again she'd gone…

Deep in thought, the mobile phone ringing nearly catapulted her off the seat. Becky fumbled in her bag, catching the call just before it went to voicemail.

"Hi, Toby."

"Hi! Becky, where are you?"

"On my way home. Be there in about an hour. Why?"

"Nothing much. I fancied a chat, that's all. I know it's a bit of an imposition when you're off duty but–"

"Ah no, don't be daft. Come on over and I'll put the kettle on. Cal won't be back until late anyway – he's in Goole."

"Yeah, I know. He left me writing up the report on Woodsend. God, there's a mountain of stuff to get through."

The line was quiet for a moment as if he wanted to say more.

"Was it something in particular? I'm guessing it's to do with what we were talking about the other night?"

"Yes and no…um–"

"Okay, tell me later. Look, while I've got you, and this may be something or nothing, but I've just seen Alice's psychologist and she mentioned she'd noticed a woman watching Alice from the yard at the back of the unit. Now the thing is, that yard is locked and this woman was not a member of staff, so I'm just a bit uneasy: she doesn't fit Ida's description but what if Ida has an accomplice and Alice is at risk of being snatched? It's just a feeling I can't shake."

"Why would they do that, though? I mean, Alice can't talk and she's mentally ill – she's not going to give evidence in court, is she? Why would anyone want to snatch her?"

"That's what I was trying to work out. Anyway, I'm just passing it on – call me paranoid."

"Back atcha with that one! See you later, then?"

Becky ended the call. He was putting a chirpy face on, but that lad was still very disturbed; his six month nightmare was far from over by the sound of it.

***

Just over an hour later they were walking up the front path to Jasmine Cottage, Becky holding her aching back and trying not to waddle – conscious of, as Callum had put it so sweetly, looking like she had a pumpkin between her legs.

Toby, though…Toby was visibly wired. If she didn't know better she'd say he was on something: his eyes were darting round in the sockets as if he expected someone to spring him any second, and he'd developed a disconcerting habit of constantly checking over his shoulder.

"Are you alright? You seem a bit nervous."

"Yeah, Becky – honestly, fine, really, yeah…much better."

Either side of the path, sprays of lavender scented the air and the cottage garden hummed with the drone of dozy bees. Becky glanced over at the stone terrace hoping to see Louie stretching out on the warm stones. It was strange he'd vanished. Nine years old and neutered, Louie had clearly been happy here after months in the RSPCA. What a shame…really…what a disappointment.

She put the key in the lock and they stepped into the cool, musty hallway. "Come in, Toby. Just fling your jacket anywhere. Have a seat."

"Thanks."

She threw open the windows and flicked the kettle on.

"Ooh, that's better – bit of fresh air. Tea or coffee?"

"Tea please, Becks."

"Right you are." She rummaged around for mugs and tea bags. "It's a pity your girlfriend turned the other night into an embarrassment to be honest, because I really wanted to hear what you had to say. Still, Cal wasn't much better, was he?"

"No, he's even worse – like he's in denial or something – he just won't have it. Anything to do with spirits or religion and he shuts down like a trap door. Anyway, there's no way on God's earth I could talk to anyone other than you about what I need to say. I hope you're ready for it?"

She filled the kettle. "Let me get the tea made then we can talk properly. So you seeing her again then, this Amy? She was very pretty."

He shrugged. "Think so. If I haven't freaked her out too much."

"Well perhaps it's best not to tell her anything more, she's a bit young. Mind you, so are you…but she must be what…twenty?"

"Twenty-three."

"Do you want milk and sugar, I can't remember? I'm all over the place at the moment."

"Just a drop of milk, ta. Didn't you have a cat? Where is he?"

"Yes, Louie. He seems to have vanished, though, the ungrateful swine."

"Typical, that. Maybe it's down to the ghost in the mirror you were talking about – they know about that kind of thing, do cats."

She brought the mugs over and sat opposite him. "Gee, thanks - that makes me feel really great stuck out here on my own."

"Sorry, I was only kidding. Trying to lighten the mood. You don't really think this place is haunted, do you?"

"No, but I think I am. Anyway, let's talk about you. Where were we before the laughing policeman and giggling Gertie interrupted us so rudely?"

Toby took a sip of tea. "Well, I couldn't have said anymore anyway with them there; don't know why I started in the first place."

"Drink. You'd had about six huge glasses of red and counting."

"That could be it."

"So let me get the facts straight – you were down under Tanners Dell with forensics when you collapsed? Everyone thought you'd slipped on the wet stones and banged your head, which is why you couldn't remember anything, yes? But you and I know it's more than that and now you've remembered the cause? I have to tell you I'm bursting to know because I only recently had that message about Lilith, so if it's to do with her I am seriously interested. I want to get to the bottom of this."

He nodded. "Yes, oh yes it's to do with her alright. To be fair, it's extremely personal and I find it embarrassing as hell, so I really do need you to keep it to yourself. If Cal hears about this I'll be a bloody laughing stock. I don't even know if it'll help either of us but from what you were saying it just might."

"Are you still having night terrors?"

"Becky, I haven't told the GP a fraction of this - as far as he's concerned I'm fine and dandy. I don't want him giving me anymore sedatives and I don't want putting in hospital again either. Having mental health issues is never a good career move, is it? And besides, things are a hell of a lot worse if I'm unconscious."

"How do you mean?"

"They're not like nightmares you can wake up from, Becky – these night terrors are completely different. I read up about them. There are studies showing they don't belong to dream sequences – that they're caused by external factors – it's been proven they can physically paralyse you. So something other than fear or imagination is causing this, something real. Becky, I swear something's watching me – just waiting for me to lose consciousness."

She looked at his young face, ringed with sleepless shadows, and the wider than wide eyes, the way his hands gripped the mug and his legs jittered constantly.

"Well, first things first - I've never heard of that. You can read all sorts of unsubstantiated stuff online if you're not careful, Tobes. Look, let's start at the beginning and we'll talk through it properly, okay? Remember I've been through some pretty horrible stuff myself that no one to this day has been able to explain, and so have the entire team, so don't hold back – tell me everything and we'll take it one step at a time. It does help to know we're not alone, you know? And you're not – both Noel and I are experiencing the same thing."

He nodded.

"Good. Right, so let's start from where you went into the vault."

He immediately turned his head away.

She waited. The buzzing of the bees seemed to intensify and the air stilled while he gazed out of the window. After a while there was nothing but the sound of the clock in the hall ticking the time away.

When he finally faced her again his eyes were unfocused and glazed, fixed on a far point only he could see, almost as if he'd slipped into a trance.

"Toby?"

There was no response.

A tiny flicker of alarm caught in her chest. "Toby, are you alright? Can you hear me?"

After a long moment he blinked repeatedly, almost as if he'd only just realised where he was. "Sorry, what?"

"Didn't you hear what I last said?"

"Yeah, to go into the vault?"

She nodded. "You went a bit fuzzy on me. Look, only do this if you want to, if it helps. If it's too traumatic we can stop anytime."

"Becky, will you promise to keep this to yourself? I'm deadly serious. Even from Cal? I just–"

She nodded. "Yes, of course. Absolutely."

"Right. Right…okay…" He took a deep breath and then the words flew out. "Well, it was absolutely freezing down there back in February – the floor was slimy and slippy, walls dripping and everything black dark like down a pit. My fingers were numb and I couldn't stop my teeth chattering – every day it was like you just couldn't get warm when you got home either – horrible – and it'd been going on for weeks. I suppose looking back it must have got to me, and loads of the others went off sick. Anyway, that particular day I'd gone on ahead, further down the corridor beyond the main room where most of the team were working. It was bad enough in there: I don't know what we expected – maybe not something so sophisticated - you'd think an underground cave for Satanists would be just that, but it turned out to be old and grand like a masonic hall. In the middle of the floor there's this really intricate mosaic-tiled circle engraved with animal heads and hieroglyphs, and symbols carved into the stonework – the all-seeing eye, scales and pillars–"

"That does sound masonic."

"I agree except it isn't a freemasons' lodge and never has been. But that's what I was struggling to understand, you see, because a lot of it was ancient. We brought in some academics but the guy leading the team got spooked and wouldn't work down there. They had to dig it up piece by piece, which is why it's taken so long - I've still got his reports to go through. Anyway, what I do know is that much of it was imported and may date as far back as the 12th century; they're still working on where from. The more recent stuff though, was set up like a satanic church – crudity overlaying the finery if you like – with crosses hung upside down and vile pictures of bestiality and orgies. It was a freaky enough place but kind of staged with red curtains and candelabras: just a front for what really went on as it turned out."

"How do you mean? What's worse than conjuring up the devil and sacrificing human victims?"

"Like I said – are you ready for this?"

"I doubt you could shock me."

He laughed bleakly. "Want a bet?"

"Go on then - I'm ready."

He drained his tea and put down the mug, still staring at her.

"Toby, you're freaking me out. This must be really bad?"

"Okay, here goes, don't say I didn't warn you. Right, well, leading out of that room is a rabbit warren of tunnels. You have to feel your way along inch by inch because it's coalface black, and you can't see the way back either because somehow it shuts behind you – I can't explain it except you're turning corners so behind you is solid wall again. And it stinks like a sewer - really hard to breathe. I must've been holding my breath because I felt dizzy from the off. Anyway, I put my night vision glasses on and at that point I could still hear the others in the main room. I was just thinking, you know, I wonder what's through here and through here…and so on….

And then I came to the first room and it totally threw me. I just wasn't expecting what I saw. There were heavy duty chains hammered into the stone floor, leg irons and clamps; and a chair with cuffs and manacles facing the far end so whoever was in it could only see the wall in front of them...It was like some kind of medieval torture chamber. I tried to backtrack at that point but I couldn't, and accidentally stumbled through to another one...down a step...and this is where it morphed into some kind of suite of chambers. I could hear dripping water and the floor was like ice. Literally, it was one baby step at a time with my arms outstretched. And this one was longer, more like a tunnel...I just had to keep walking through, hoping I'd come out the other side...but it wasn't a walkway at all, it was another torture chamber. You ever heard of a strappado?"

Becky shook her head.

"It's where they stretch someone's arms back using a pulley until they wrench them out of the sockets. They used to use it to torture women during the witch hunts. And hanging from the ceiling were iron hooks – you know, like meat hooks? And in the corner was a tin bath and some buckets. Graffiti was smeared on the walls – God knows with what, it looked like blood – and then I trod on something and picked it up. I'll never, ever get over it... never."

"Do you want to say?"

"No, but I'll tell you. It was a mousetrap, Becky, only with someone's finger bones still in it...I dropped it and all I could hear was my own blood pumping in my ears in this endless dripping, freezing silence with more and more archways to more and more torture chambers to come and...and... Oh God, imagine being down there with masked figures over you, knowing what's coming...hearing screams...not being able to see or to get out–"

Becky reached over for his hands and squeezed them tightly. "Go on – just get this out, don't lock it inside."

"You can smell it, you know? The blood and the fear and the filth. And you're just thinking it can't get worse but then it does and after that you can't un-see it.

It's some sort of maze down there: we've mapped it now but I didn't know at the time – all I knew was I no longer had any bearings or clue how to get out again. Panic was rising up but all I could do was keep on going, hoping I'd hit on a main route back, when suddenly it was the end of the tunnel and I'd reached the very last room.

By that time I had no idea where I was and I couldn't hear another living soul. And there in front of me was a nightmare - lit up in the bluey green haze of my night vision glasses. And this is where it all gets so much worse. Becky, I was staring at an operating table with racks and racks of medical implements – syringes, scalpels, scissors and receptacles – and around it a ring of chairs like it's a fucking viewing gallery...what... I mean can you imagine, what the fuck they were doing? And on the shelves were glass jars with...oh God–" He looked away and blurted it out in one breath. "There were human eyes, tongues, foetuses...stuff like that...all preserved in formaldehyde; and coffins full of dead snakes and spiders with decomposed bodies inside–"

Neither of them spoke for several minutes.

Becky walked over to the cupboard and poured them both a brandy.

He knocked his back in one. "I wish I could rid myself of the images, I really do. It started then really, with the nightmares and this overpowering blackness weighing me down, like life was never going to be the same ever again for me. The others saw it too – it's all documented and photographed; it's real, but they weren't on their own and they knew what was coming. I'm not saying it didn't affect them because I know it did, but God, yeah... well, it was the shock of it and the atmosphere: really oppressive and menacing – I still carry it with me, never shook it off."

"It must have been terrible."

"I would have got over it though, I'm sure. Really, I'd have been alright even after that. And everyone else saw it so I knew I wasn't going mad. But no one else went in to her, you see?"

Becky shook her head in confusion.

"What I've told you in confidence is documented and will be presented in court. Obviously I wouldn't want to repeat any of that to anyone else outside the police service, but it isn't that...I just had to lead you up to this bit, so you know how it happened and how I felt."

"But that was the last room, right?"

He nodded. "Yes, the last room."

"So?"

"Becky, swear on your life you won't repeat this....I mean it - even Cal? He's seen the photographs but he doesn't know what happened to me personally. No one does. Even I didn't because my memory blocked it, until the other night when it all rushed back. The only reason I'm telling you now is because it may, just may, help one of us or both of us."

"I promise."

He leaned forwards then, lowering his voice as if he didn't even trust the shadows. "That last room- it had a door. I thought it was maybe a cupboard for where they kept documents or some evil artefacts or something and just thought I'd take a quick look. It was a tiny space and I had to crawl in on my knees. There was nothing in that room, though, Becky. Nothing. I was relieved – truly had my guard down, actually exhaling and getting ready to backtrack and start shouting to the team – when I noticed the ceiling. I lay on my back to shuffle out and get a better look at the same time."

He closed his eyes tightly, concentrating, determined to relate what happened as accurately as possible. "You know those Greek goddesses carved in glossy marble – you see them in stately homes and gardens? Well, it was like that only it was on the ceiling looking down at me – totally out of place and completely incongruous – and through night vison glasses the white stone shone light green and it was a bit eerie, but not really scary, not compared to what I'd already seen. To be honest what was going through my head was that this was their icon or

69

something, an expensive bit of marble, and now I wanted to go back.

"The problem was that although I was desperate to tear myself away I actually couldn't. I just could not stop staring. The face had bulging eyeballs as large as peeled eggs, and long hair coiling down a naked body with a snake wrapped round it. There was quite a dreamy feeling really, like being lulled...and then suddenly the little door slammed shut and I nearly had a bloody heart attack. I tried to get up but I couldn't, and in less than a second I swear the atmosphere got so intense and oppressive it made my head pound and I felt physically sick. And I still couldn't move – at all. I can't tell you the panic...my body was going to explode. I kept trying to get up but my legs were paralysed and my chest was weighed down with lead, and the walls were folding in. I couldn't breathe, I couldn't shout and I couldn't move. And all the time I'm fixed on this sculpture in the ceiling, and it's growing bigger and bigger – floating down on top of me – and still I couldn't take me eyes off it–

And then suddenly it was real.

It was like, how can I explain this – like a waking dream? There was fresh air on my face and I could hear birds singing. I was me, a real person, but in a totally different time and place, seeing things through different eyes. And there's a woman walking towards me. If I said a massive 3D cinema screen with surround sound that would relate it dead on: this young girl coming out of a rushing river on a summer's day... She's got long, dark wet hair and all her clothes are see-through, and I felt excited even though I didn't want to be and full of lust like you would not believe, like I've never felt before – violent – and then just as the dream faded and the hard, cold stone was in my back again I heard a whisper, a kind of nasty snickering in my ear... and I might have imagined it but I don't think so. Someone, a woman's voice, said, "Ah, so that's his weakness."

Anyway, the next thing I remember I was outside and there were flashing blue lights everywhere."

_***

<u>Chapter Ten</u>

Bridesmoor
October, 1583

Magda's mother dragged her inside by the hair and threw her against the kitchen table.

"Did you think I wouldn't find out? That I wouldn't hear what they're all saying about you? You're the village harlot, Magda! Everyone's talking about it – why Cicely and not you? To think I kept asking myself over and over again – why? Well, by God we know now, don't we?"

The slap whooshed through the air, cut into the side of her face and knocked her sideways.

Magda buckled onto a chair. "What do you mean?"

Her mother leaned in close, gripping Magda's shoulders with her rough, calloused hands and shook her. "You and 'im, you evil little bitch. How could you? What kind of low life, nasty piece of work does that make you, Magda?"

Magda thought fast. Who was she talking about – William or Ambrose? Had someone seen them? How had this happened?

Her mother took a step back, her normally kind face contorted into a sneer, shouting until her face turned puce. "I always knew I shouldn't have taken you on. You were a bad 'un right from the start. I should've bloody known. Me and my soft heart – and this is where it got me."

"What? I don't understand."

But even as she flinched from the harsh words, she knew. Deep down, had always known. She didn't fit in and never had.

Outside the bruised sky dipped rapidly into the inkiness of night and a sharp gust of wind rattled the window pane, whistling under the door. "You're with child I expect? You'd 'ave to be."

Magda searched her mother's eyes – the light blue of a summer morning, deeply set in ruddy cheeks. So like Cicely. So like her brothers. "T…t…took me on?" She stuttered. "Who am I then?"

"And that's your main concern, is it?" She shook her head. "Well, all I can say is I'm glad you're not my flesh and blood. You can get out, you murdering little witch. I don't want you under my roof another minute. It makes me sick to look at you."

"I need to know who I am."

"Pack your bags and get out of my house. Get as far away as you can an' all because if I find you I'll thrash you to the bone, so help me God."

A sheet of rain lashed against the window. "But where will I go?"

"Try the father of your child. Oh, now let me think – which one could that be?"

Magda stood up, shivering as she edged out of the kitchen. Who had started this gossip about her? Ambrose could not expose her without there being a rebound on himself so why would he have done that? And why would William?

"Probably any one of the men in this village for all I know," her mother raged on. "You're no daughter of mine, Magda. I brought you up to be respectable, fed and clothed you, and this is how you've repaid me. When I think of my poor, beautiful Cicely…with her throat cut so you could go whoring round the village. Oh just get out." She picked up the nearest object to hand, a washing mangle, and threw it hard in Magda's direction, screaming until her throat was hoarse. "Get out! Get out! Get out!"

With no time to grab anything except the cloak she'd left on the table barely moments before, Magda stumbled into the muddy yard just as thunder rumbled in the distance and rain spat needles into the dirt. Where would she go? How had her mother found out? Had someone seen her with William? But how, in that dark, silent forest on the private land he owned? And apart from that first time, with Ambrose it had been in the haunted woods on the other side of the common, where no one else dared to go. *So, how then? How and who?*

Blindly, she hurried down the lane past the cottages - many with crosses now daubed across their doors. The plague had spread from town after all, the crops had failed, and the hungry, frightened villagers were no doubt looking for a scapegoat. Had they sacrificed the wrong girl and displeased the gods? That's what they'd be thinking. Fear clouded her mind, stabbing at her urgently. Ambrose. Should she go to him? Surely he would put them right and deny these vicious rumours? It would be in his interests to do so. Yes, he had to. If he didn't she could be hanged. The mob would come for her and surely he didn't want that? Not if he felt a shred of affection for her? He could say she had been attacked in town and made with child, that he was taking her in out of religious compassion...there would be some story he could concoct: the villagers believed anything he said.

Yes, yes, that would work.

His cottage was the last one in a row, next to the church. With her head down against the prevailing storm she hurried up the path to his door and banged with her fists. "Ambrose, it's me! I need to speak with you."

The downpour was now intensifying, bouncing off the path, forming puddles around her feet and she gasped from the force of it, water streaming down her face. Why wasn't he answering? Was he not in?

Picking up her skirts she tramped over to the window and from there could see him clearly – relaxing by the fire with a glass of mead. She banged on the window. His little Jack Russell sat up and whined, yet still he gazed into the flames without turning to see who it was causing such a commotion.

"Ambrose! Ambrose!" Why did he not hear her? "Ambrose!" She ran to the back door and hammered on it until her knuckles bled, rattling it against the bolts. "Ambrose! Ambrose!"

Running back to the window she banged on it repeatedly. Still he did not turn round, but continued to sip his mead as if stone deaf; calmly and deliberately ignoring her.

Finally, she understood. Stopped. Her palm flat to the pane. The bastard had thrown her to the wolves.

Retreating from the soft glow of lamplight, her thoughts raced. He would save himself, would he not? Laying the blame at her door for all the disease, starvation and poverty in the village – convincing the villagers she had bewitched him in order to save her own skin. And look what happened to witches. The witch-finders were in the north now and no lone woman was safe from persecution: her only course would be to marry quickly. The plan had always been to wed William – his wife was sickly from miscarriage after miscarriage, so it had only been a matter of time, of waiting. Alas, that time had run out.

Real fear gripped her stomach. She must get to him. He would help her, take her in. Soon Lisbet would die and everyone knew it. Then when she was his wife no one could touch her. Between them they could do this – have what they both wanted so badly. Only Lisbet stood in the way. Yes, she must get to him, he would know what to do – he loved her. He loved her…

Carrions Wood faced the church and she sprinted across the lane towards it, darting under cover of the dripping trees. The instant she stepped in, the ancient woodland enveloped her within its quiet tomb, rainwater trickling from the leaves in splashes as she hurried along the path. With no moonlight or stars to lead the way, she grasped at sodden branches, stumbling over tree roots as the fullness of the storm circled overhead, closing in. Although it was the same journey she took almost nightly to meet her lover, this time the darkness was total, and underfoot treacherous. Slipping sharply onto her hip, she was forced to slow down as she picked her way through the undergrowth, rainwater now coursing down her face, her hands muddy and bleeding. Some twenty minutes later, panting with exertion, she stopped to listen. Yes, the rushing brook could just be heard over the rhythmic drumming of the rain. Almost there…Feverishly she picked up pace again. How his dark eyes would glitter when he realised she had come to him, could be under the same roof…maybe in the guise of a nurse or maid to his wife until… Oh, her death must be hastened. She had power over this brutal, angry man; had something he needed more than life itself.

Overhead, blue flashes lit up the craggy rocks on the moors as the edge of the forest gave way to fields. Breathlessly, blinking away raindrops, she leaned against the great oak – their oak - looking across at Tanners Dell. What a place. Excitement fizzed somewhere deep inside, swelling her heart…*and she could be mistress here.*

If only Lisbet would die. Why wouldn't she die? Last time, right here by this very tree, he'd said he could do nothing about the fact she was pregnant because he had a wife. But if he didn't have one, what then? She had put the question teasingly, sucking her finger before slowly extracting it from her moist, full lips, then tracing it down her neck to the top button of her dress; watching the lust blacken his eyes, the thin lips twist into a grimace. He had pushed her down again roughly, hitching up her skirts once more. "But I do, you conniving little witch. I do have one."

For the longest time she stood with her back to the tree. The pounding, racing brook had burst its banks, spilling onto the grass in a tide of foam, turning Tanners Dell into an island with three sides now surrounded by swirling water. And most of the windows were in darkness, apart from the lower one, where William would no doubt be sitting by a fire, maybe with a candle at his desk, scratching away at the endless accounts he complained of?

She would tap at the window. He would hurry to the door, pull her inside holding a finger to his lips so as not to wake the wife upstairs, peel away her wet clothes in front of the flames, then lay her down to love her with all the force of that uncontrollable passion she found so exciting. The ache deep inside her swelled and pulsed. Perhaps even now his thoughts were of her, on how the storm would keep them apart tonight? Would he come out looking with a lantern held high like he had before, throwing stones at her bedroom window because his lust was up?

The storm was directly overhead now. Staccato flashes of jagged electricity broke through thunderous clouds, illuminating the mill. With the urge to run to him overwhelming, she sprinted from the cover of the trees just as another crack of thunder ripped through the night sky. And with her back to the stone wall, a smile picked up the corners of her lips. Oh, the sweet anticipation. Would he love her while his wife slept on upstairs? He was hers she was sure of it - as confident of that as she had ever been about anything. She had one power and it was time to use it.

Peeping through the window, she cupped her hands. Candlelight flickered along the walls but the fireside chair was empty. She turned round again. Perhaps he had gone out of the room momentarily? A boom of thunder shook the ground and static filled the air, followed by the sound of a tree splintering not too far away. Her heart was galloping… The night sky lit up with forks of silver, the rainfall now so violent it was pummelling the earth, bouncing off it in sprays.

As the thunder grumbled in retreat she ventured another look inside. The fire was crackling healthily in the grate, flames licking high. Magda frowned. He would not have left it like that, and it was far too early for him to retire.

So where was he?

Her gaze was drawn to the floor then. And for a good few minutes she stared, unable to comprehend. Looking at the bodies entwined on the hearth rug. At his fingers coiled around his wife's long, red curls; and the small, white hands clinging to his naked back.

No, this could not be. He didn't still do this with her, he couldn't…

As the rain continued to pour steadily down her face, dripping from her hair, saturating her cloak and pooling around her feet, she began to back away.

76

He had used her. Lied. Taken what he wanted then treated her like nothing, casting her out to starve or be hanged as a witch – leaving her out here to die.

***

<u>Chapter Eleven</u>

Ruby
Drummersgate Forensic Unit
September, 2016

"Dear Lord, please protect me while I talk to Spirit. I ask Spirit only because I have no other way and I badly need help. I mean no harm. Please protect me from all negative forces. Thank you Lord, Amen."

She comes to me quickly. She is a feeling, a presence. And we talk silently in my head; without words.

"Celeste, thank you. There's something very wrong, I know there is. Please will you show me what I need to see?"

As always, the impression of what she conveys is vague and tinny, transmitted in waves on a weak radio signal. She is asking about Alice. *Is it about Alice?*

"Yes, yes – the higher purpose, what they want with her."

My head is thumping; the others don't want me to do this and leave them alone again. It is a risk, I agree, but I have to find out. God will protect us. The younger ones are trembling, whimpering, running down the corridors and slamming doors; our body lying on the bed swathed in a grid of moonlight. Just a girl – a mad girl – on a single bed made up with white sheets; a girl no one knows and who no one can predict because she's fractured into many parts. But she has a soul. She has a spirit. And she has a reason. We all have a reason.

Celeste is shushing me – it's time – lifting my spirit to show the way, to where I can see…it's like falling but she has me now and… Oh, it's very sudden. Instant.

The image is at once of night. A full moon shimmers over a large Georgian house squatting darkly behind wrought iron gates. It's still warm but there's a nip, and wood smoke lingers in the air, decaying leaves…perfume…

Something is happening at the house…

The image flickers and dies. *No!*

"Celeste, please help me. Is this where they took Alice?"

It is.

"Do they bring other children here?"

Yes.

"Did I come here?"

No.

"So this is recent?"

No.

"Celeste, please show me, please, please…"

I don't understand. My conscious mind keeps cutting in and I sense Celeste's impatience. I have broken the trance, and now a vivid dream hovers on the periphery of my mind and I can't get it back. "Celeste, I have to know, I have to–"

Child, do what you've been taught.

I close my eyes once more, breathing slowly and deeply, relaxing each muscle from the top down…distancing myself from all thoughts and emotions, standing still in time…until finally it comes. The dazzling, brilliant light of Spirit streams in like sunshine through a cathedral window….its beauty and power breath-taking…And this time, when the vision comes it is with a voltage that wipes me blind.

Immediately I'm back at the house – inside now – with candlelight dancing across dark walls. It's a spectacularly opulent dining room with floor to ceiling mirrors. The women reflected wear sparkling, plunging evening gowns and elaborate headdresses. But I appear to be sweeping through at a brisk pace, whisking past hundreds, if not thousands of flickering candles. Flames leap from candelabras and chandeliers, burning fiercely on great iron pillars, lighting the way from room to room and multiplied in a dazzling corridor of black glass. I am the light chill breezing past people hiding behind masks; the shiver making them touch the back of their necks - this strange brew of eclectic folk who imbibe from goblets, smoke from pipes and murmur excitedly.

Something is happening…Something is coming. The atmosphere pulsates with it.

But I am in a rush it seems…leaving the heady, incense-fuelled rooms to waft out of patio doors…now sweeping down a silvery lawn…blowing through trees in a flutter of leaves along a dark, snaking path. Until all at once it is before me. What I am here to see.

A black lake glitters with flecks of starlight, whispering oaks mirrored in its depths. And to the side, shrouded by forest, a stage has been set.

I am the draft blowing torch fire sidelong, causing the hooded men to shudder and turn. I do not pause, though, to see what lowlife is here. That is not the purpose. Here is the purpose: a large pentacle has been etched into the ground, lit at each fifth elemental point with a flame; and at the head of this is a magnificent altar set either side with six foot candles on stone columns. On the altar table a black Bible awaits. And a long, silver sword.

I recognise this. I'm falling.

No, Ruby, you wanted to see…

"Marie, help me."

The scene shuts down faster than a plug being pulled. And now there is nothing but the reality of the bars at the window, and the stars so very far away.

I hear Marie asking repeatedly if this is for Alice.

But our energy has drained and we are freezing. There is a brief flash, just a feeling, of Alice in her bed looking out of a window at the same sky as me.

Alice…I will find you…

For the most fleeting of moments the soft blue of her eyes meet mine. And then she's gone.

***

Chapter Twelve

Toby parked outside Amy's house and checked his reflection in the rear-view mirror. He'd actually slept last night, thank God. Probably unburdening himself to Becky had helped. Well, it was reassuring to know he wasn't going crazy, anyway. Now it was just a question of getting a grip. Yes, there was something rotten to the core at Woodsend but they had closed that down; and any member of the sect who dared to show their face would be banged up. That was it. Fear was contagious and it had got to him in that sodding vault. Well, no more. He was young, fit as fuck, and it was time to get over it.

Amy was standing at the porch already, beckoning him to come in.

As usual she was scantily clad, this time in miniscule black shorts and a leather bra top with tassels dangling from it. When he first met her in a bar a few weeks ago, he'd tried not to stare but she clearly enjoyed the attention so he let his eyes drink her up – from ponytail to killer heels. "Wow!"

She kissed him full on the lips before running upstairs to her room. "Come on up – I'm nearly ready."

He knew what that meant and eagerly followed. The second he kicked the door shut behind him she had her top unclipped and was reaching for his zipper. "Steady on, Amy."

She laughed. "You don't mean that."

"No," he said, shrugging off his shirt. "I bloody don't."

Later, as they lay panting on top of the bed, he asked, "Do you think your mum and dad know what we're up to?"

"Who cares?"

"Mine would go ballistic."

Stifling a yawn, Amy turned to her iPod and flicked on, *A Good Day* by Ice Cube, then racked up the volume with bass. "We'll not be going to your place then."

She wasn't a normal sort of girl, he thought. The bedroom was painted in deep burgundy; her choice of music mostly misogynistic rap; and the photographs on her walls, not to mention the DVDs stacked up, were of the hard porn variety, although in the semi-dark he couldn't see them too well.

"Do you still want to go out later?" he shouted over the music.

"Yeah, course. Do you?"

"Where do you wanna go?"

Amy strutted across to the en-suite, and not for the first time he lay agog at the fact that a) she had a private bathroom in her five star super-deluxe bedroom, and b) she walked around stark naked without a hint of self-consciousness. There was a spider tattooed on her arse. He grinned. Well, whatever blew your hair back.

Grabbing a couple of beer cans from the fridge, she snapped one open and threw the other over to him. "I know. Why don't we go to that place you were talking about the other night?" She was ambling back to the bed giving him a good view of what she had tattooed at the front as well, her scarlet lips curving into a salacious smile.

His voice sounded syrupy even to himself. "What place?"

"You know – the house in the woods that's supposed to be empty but had a light on?"

"Woodsend? Are you nuts? I wouldn't go there in full daylight with the entire police force in tow, let alone at night on my own. Fuck off. No way."

She jumped onto the bed, kneeling over him so that her nipples grazed his legs, and started to kiss the inside of his thighs, flicking her tongue in and out as she worked her way up.

"But it's what I'd like to do."

He was gazing at the top of her dark head just as she glanced up and opened her lips to take him in. He groaned. "Oh my God, Amy."

For a moment the dark glitter in her eyes took him aback. And then she laughed and threw herself down on the bed. "Come on, it'd be a laugh. We could take the Ouija board."

"What? Aren't you going to–?" He pulled the bed sheet up abruptly, aware she was taunting him. "Look, I'm serious. I'm not going to bloody Woodsend and no way would you want to mess with a Ouija board – you can't dabble in that kind of stuff, believe me. I've had enough of the dark side thank you very much - it's not a joke."

Her smile died in an instant. "I'll go on my own then," she said, lighting up a spliff.

"Girl goes into the woods on a dark night on her own with a Ouija board – don't be so bloody daft. It's every teenage horror movie ever made. Stupid idea. You need your head looking at, you do."

She blew smoke into the air. "I thought you liked me?"

He softened his voice. "Sorry Amy, it's just that I've been through some pretty horrible stuff recently and this is the last thing I need. Meddling in the occult isn't a game, you know? It's not just a bit naughty. There's a lot we don't understand and it gets out of hand; people get hurt, lives get fucked up. I've been off work for six months because of it."

"You said it was depression."

"Yes, such a bad one I couldn't get out of bed."

She offered him her spliff but he shook his head. "Anyway," he said, looking down at his erection under the sheet. "What am I supposed to do with this?"

Ignoring him, Amy took a long drag, exhaling the smoke in coils. "You were involved with Satanists but I'm not talking about that. I'm a spiritual medium and I can find out what happened there using the board - tell you why it's such a bad place. That friend of yours, Becky, she said it attracted evil and she's probably right. I'm not a stupid teen going into the woods - it's to tap into the negative energy there. I'm going anyway now because I'm intrigued." She started to sit up. "There's nothing to be scared of – you can come or not, it's up to you."

Swinging her legs over the edge of the bed, she then appeared to have a change of heart. Looking down at his erection she smiled again. "Or we could do a deal – you take me to Woodsend and I'll sort that out for you? Unless you don't want—"

In an instant he was inside her, one hand holding her by the hair, the other the headboard. His senses swam, the torrent of words spewing from his mouth no longer his own.

"You're not going on your own you fucking, stupid bitch."

She reached over to rack up the music as high as it would go, as he thrust into her so hard she bit her tongue. "Harder," she hissed, licking the blood dripping over the brim of her lip. "Harder, harder, harder…"

***

It was nearly eleven o'clock by the time they parked at the bottom of Ravenshill. The late summer night was velvety warm, the river low – barely trickling over the mossy rocks. And ahead lay the forest – gloomy, still, and lifeless.

"I can't believe I'm doing this," said Toby. "After all I've been through."

Amy linked her arm through his. "We could have sex in the cottage."

"Is that all you ever think about?"

"It's all *you* ever think about. I wasn't like this until I met you. Come on, this is exciting." Amy pulled him along the path like a child going to the fair. "All that happens is I connect with the spirits and they tell me what I want to know. We can ask them what happened in that circle you went in. Don't you want to find out? The curiosity would kill me."

His feet were leaden, every instinct pulling him back. "Not really. It's enough to know they had satanic rituals here. I don't need to know anymore."

"Don't you? But what about for your report? Wouldn't it help to have some insight? Police use mediums all the time you know? They just don't tell the public."

They'd reached the stile leading into the woods. Dead and grey, its chill breezed onto his face and Toby stopped. "Amy, come on, let's go back. Let's go to the pub instead. This is a seriously bad place. I don't need this shit."

"Oh, no, you don't. I let you have your wicked way with me so now it's my turn. Come on – do it for me." She glanced over her shoulder at the dark, sparkling water before turning back and locking her gaze with his. "Or we could go skinny dipping?"

In an instant a full, rushing river engulfed his senses; sun warmed his back and birdsong filled the air; the light dazzling as seductively she walked towards him with her long hair dripping through the thin, white cotton of her dress. Static filled his ears and time stood still. Pulling the sopping garment over her head she gently eased him down into the grass, rolling on top of him, easing off his clothes, working her tongue, her lips, her fingers…until he was crying out, spent, exhausted and soaked with sweat for the third time in as many hours.

When he opened his eyes again, moonlight was filtering through a canopy of trees and a blurry image was walking towards him. Had he blacked out for a minute?

"What are you doing?"

Naked and dripping wet, Amy was striding out of the river. "Having a wash," she said, stepping into her shorts.

"Someone might have seen you."

She stood over him, wet hair spotting onto his face. "Your point? Anyway, you're not exactly shy and retiring yourself – shouting obscenities like that. My mum and dad would've heard you earlier, as would people for miles around just now."

Toby shook his head. "What do you mean?"

She laughed and held out her hand. "Come with me now, Toby."

***

Woodpecker Cottage was not easy to get to, being off the main path and standing in total darkness. Shreds of mist caught in the dense thicket as they waded through ferns and pushed aside branches, every step hindered by heavy undergrowth.

"I can't see a thing," said Amy.

From behind her he flicked on the small torch he kept in the car, and the cottage lit up in the beam.

"I wonder how long it's been empty."

He caught up with her, slightly out of breath after the uphill climb, and they stood looking at it. A small stone building, its windows were black and soulless, a mass of wayward ivy blurring the line between cottage and forest.

"The last legal occupants were still registered in the late nineties: Mr and Mrs Blackmore. Their son's in a psychiatric unit in Leeds. We don't know where his parents went – even the hospital doesn't have contact details. We wanted to interview them." He stopped to catch his breath again. They were standing on an overgrown path that ran around the cottage in crazy paving. Weeds sprouted from every crack; and on closer inspection, twisted creepers had cleaved into the walls between the stones of the house, obscuring windows and prising off gutters and roof tiles.

Amy rubbed her sleeve against a ground floor window and peered in. "I can't see anything."

He shone the torch through.

The room was or had been a lounge by the look of it, and whoever had been here last had left their furniture behind: dining table and chairs, sofa, bookcases, even pictures on the walls. Over the mantelpiece hung an ornate, oval mirror, and curtains still hung from plastic rails at the French windows to the back. In the far corner it looked at first as if a boy was standing there. Toby nearly dropped the torch, then looked again. It was just a standard lamp. God, he was jumpy. This was such a stupid thing to do.

"Do you think someone's still here?"

He shook his head. "No. The owners must've left in a hurry, though. I wonder why they didn't take their stuff?"

They picked their way round to the main door and tried the handle. "Nothing doing," said Toby. "Let's go. I can't break and enter, you know I can't."

"No, but I can," she said, searching the ground for a stone.

Toby grabbed her arm to stop her. "No. There's been a light on here so a tramp or traveller must have found a way in, which means there's one we could use if you're so determined."

"Okay, Sherlock," she said, dropping the rock. "Let's go see."

It seemed every window, both upstairs and down, however, was intact; the doors securely locked. He had a quick scout around the back to see if there was a coal cellar but there wasn't.

"Come on, Amy. Let's go now. It's nearly midnight." He looked around. "Amy? I said come on, let's go."

His voice echoed around the small yard. Shining the torch into the trees he called again, "Amy?"

In the absence of a reply he began to retrace his steps to the front of the cottage. "Amy?"

An owl hooted from deep within the forest and a quiver of anxiety crept up his spine.

"Amy?"

Pointing the torch towards what had once been a garden but was now mostly long grass scattered with saplings, he noticed a tree swing, creaking slightly as if someone had just been on it. He walked towards it. "Stop playing games, Amy."

Her giggle came from behind his shoulder and he swung round.

"Oh, look," she said, spinning around and around with her arms spread wide. The moon was now directly overhead, floodlighting the small garden. "We don't need to go inside, after all. I think we could do the Ouija out here."

***

87

Chapter Thirteen

Looking back, the whole scene had been surreal, as if it had happened to someone else entirely. What a fool he'd been - how utterly, utterly feckless. Regret didn't cover it.

It was bang on midnight when Amy said, "We have to do this now – right now. Sit down. Come on, sit down."

Reluctantly he'd slumped to the ground. "Why? Why at all?"

Her eyes were glittering. Tossing a curtain of long, raven hair over to one side, she sat with her legs crossed, eyeing him from beneath Bambi lashes. "Because the moon is directly overhead – can't you see? Now put your hand over mine on top of the planchette. Let's ask the spirits what happened here."

Everything he'd learned from Becky about prayer and white light vanished from his thoughts, the futile strands of his mind as flimsy as waving tentacles on the bottom of an ocean floor as he sat with his mouth open and did exactly what he was told.

"Is anyone here?" said Amy.

Her hand was deliberately moving the planchette. "Stop doing that, Amy. I can feel you moving the damn thing."

A tinkling giggle came from somewhere behind, as if a child was peeping round the corner of the house.

He checked over his shoulder. "Was that you? Amy, was that you?"

Her eyes were focused on the board and she shook her head impatiently. "Is anyone here with us?"

"What will you do if it says, 'yes'? Have you thought about that? I really don't like this one fucking bit."

She lifted her gaze to his, her voice thick and slightly slurred. "Shut up. Listen."

The surrounding forest appeared to darken, closing in by degrees, just as it had in the ring of stones. He squinted into the gloom. Something or someone was watching.

"Concentrate." Amy snapped.

It was boring into his back, whatever it was, and the urge to look again was irresistible. He began to turn round.

"Shh!" said Amy. "Did you hear that?"

There had been something, he realised, and it was getting louder: a low whistle, like a soughing in the trees. A wisp of cloud floated across the moon and the treetops quivered. "I don't like this. I'm going."

Once again she fixed him with a stare that riveted him to the spot, her voice deeper, not quite her own. "Shut up. Wait. It's coming."

A knot of fear lodged and twisted inside his stomach. What was coming? What the hell was coming? That whistling was getting louder by the second.

Suddenly the temperature plummeted, and a howling wind whipped up from far away, rapidly increasing in speed…hurtling through the woods like an express train, flattening branches in its wake…before suddenly roaring across the lawn in a blast of leaves and flying twigs.

Amy held the board down, her long hair blowing wildly around her face. "Hold the planchette," she shouted. "Don't let it go."

Every instinct told him to get up and run, yet still he sat there. *It's just a gust of wind and no stupid girl is going to freak me out.*

"Who is with us?" she called out excitedly.

She's bonkers – absolutely, stark-staring bonkers.

Yet there was absolutely no doubt in his mind, either at the time or in retrospect, that the planchette was whizzing round the board of its own accord. Amy's hand was small and delicate, and that piece of wood felt like it had the fist of a heavyweight boxer behind it. Not only that, but it was shooting from one letter to another with unnatural speed and force. Even Amy's eyes were widening. She was most definitely not doing this.

Words were clearly being spelled out on the board: 'I CAN SEE YOU THROUGH THE KITCHEN WINDOW'.

They both swung round.

A light was on in the cottage.

Toby upended the board. "Nice trick. You're fucking with my mind, Amy. Thanks a lot. You knew what happened to me. Well, very fucking funny." Blind with rage, he charged towards the door of the cottage, smashed the glass with a half brick and flicked the catch. "If you're one of Amy's mates you can come out now, you little snot," he shouted into the hall.

My God, I've been made such a fool of...

What had this girl done to him? What else had her little friends witnessed tonight? And what the hell would be doing the rounds on social media tomorrow? He could lose his job over this. "Come out. Come out now, you miserable bastard! Don't fucking hide from me. You've fucking had it, I'm telling you." Wrenching open doors, slamming and kicking his way in, he fired torchlight into every corner.

From the tiny kitchen he stomped into the living room. "Come on then - I know you're in here."

The room reeked of damp and hissed with silence, caught in a time warp. Although the lamp had been switched on, everything else appeared to be untouched – no footprints on the dusty floorboards, and no signs of life.

Still breathing hard and shaking with humiliation, he walked towards the fireplace and crouched down. No ashes in the grate. The place was so small there were only these two rooms and a few cupboards downstairs. So that just left the bedrooms.

He stood up and stared into the age-spotted mirror hanging on the wall, just in time to notice a tiny movement at the foot of the stairwell. Nothing more. A fleeting shadow was all. Was that Amy or the mate she had helping her?

"Amy?"

Taking the stairs two at a time he bounded up to the landing, flinging wide the first door he came to. A single, cast-iron bed lay swathed in moonlight, still made up with sheets, a row of faded, stuffed toys eyeing him silently from the bookshelf. A flowery dress had caught in the wardrobe door, its sleeve sticking out. But there was no one there.

Apart from the bathroom the only other door was to the second bedroom, which was slightly ajar. He kicked it back so hard it hit the wall.

Amy was standing with her back to him surveying the garden below. Silhouetted against the night sky, her hair hung long and dark, and she appeared to be hugging herself, rocking slightly to and fro.

"Alright," he said, more softly now. "You've had your fun, Amy. You spooked me out. Your mate must have got out behind my back but this is it – we're going home now. Well, you can stay if you want but I've had enough."

It was then he realised she wasn't laughing.

Slowly turning from the window to face him, her eyes had altered in shape so they tilted upwards at the outer corners, and her lips were fuller, redder. "I can feel her in me."

"I said that's enough, Amy. You're scaring the crap out of me."

With her arms out in front she glided towards him, half-smiling – reaching out. "William!"

"What? No, I'm not..." He stumbled backwards, realising there was something horribly wrong with her eyes. "Amy?" They seemed to have rolled back in her head with only the whites showing. "Fuck. Oh fucking hell..."

Her hands were almost on his shoulders now and with a jolt of shock he noticed they were cadaverous, the skin decaying on her bones.

He shook his head in disbelief... "What the–" and was about to turn and run, when she threw herself into his arms.

***

Chapter Fourteen

Woodsend
September, 1583

For hours Magda sat in the mud leaning against the old oak, staring at Tanners Dell while the rain came down in sheets and the storm rolled over the moors.

A hard, cold downpour had set in. Thousands of tons of water scrambled furiously down the brook to the river below, bursting into surrounding fields and isolating trees. Already the ground was saturated, puddles were several inches deep; and branches still heavy with leaves periodically cracked and splintered under the additional weight, hanging like broken limbs.

How could he have deceived her so?

How could he?

The pain was a sharp blade cutting into a tiny, soft place somewhere in her breastbone – the place connected to her eyes, her lungs, her heart and her soul – making them bleed red-raw. It lodged as flint – every thought, every breath, every memory making it dig in a little deeper, extracting a little more pain and a little more blood.

Oh God, the smell of his skin, the taste of him, the crush of his iron grip...

They were not raindrops streaming down her face anymore, she realised, but stinging hot, salty tears dredged from a well deep inside her, one she didn't even know she had until now, here, in this moment.

Life is over. It's finished...there's nothing left. Oh God, please help me...please take this pain away...I cannot live with it...

The hours passed in this way, until exhausted, with all her energy drained, she drifted into a sequence of bizarre dreams;

only to jump awake again moments later. To her it was seconds. But the light had changed.

She looked around.

The deluge had relented considerably, the waterlogged forest appearing to float in a murky swamp – branches bowed and weeping, their leaves dipping into the quagmire. Inside her boots, her feet swilled and she bent to undo the laces. There was no going home but she'd better get moving and find somewhere to dry off, form a plan. These were perilous times.

It was either that or die.

As she wrung out her cloak and tipped out her boots, rage began to shake through to her fingers and blind her eyes. How dare they leave her to die. And how dare God. How dare He? Why did he not help her and her unborn child? Was her time over? Was this it? While those bastards lived on? The bone-cold seeped into her skin, now mottled, numb and shivery. All that time in church and this is what it came down to…cast out to die like an animal in the woods.

Damn the lot of them in their warm beds…no…fuck them.

Carrions Wood wore the wintry morning like wet, grey rag; and her boots squelched and sucked in the mud, making progress slow. But she kept up a pace, alert for signs of life, for anyone who might be looking for her. When the path ended and the steep lane to Bridesmoor came into view, she hesitated, listening for muffled footsteps in the foggy dawn. No, there was no one around.

Keeping close to the edge of the forest she hurried downhill towards the river. Mist clung to the hedgerows, spiders' webs spanning the brambles with white crochet lace. Hopefully, no one would yet be afoot to see the dark-cloaked figure of a woman half-walking, half-running through the grey dawn. If word had got out it was her fault the harvest was ruined and they were dying of the plague, there was no doubt in her mind she would be hanged for a witch.

Sickly with hunger, she scanned the bushes. Alas, all the blackberries had turned to pulp, squishing into purple juice between her fingers, prickling the ends with thorns. There were apples in the churchyard, of course, but only the unripe green ones that gave you bellyache, and besides – going back was too much of a risk.

Magda's long, black cloak flew behind her now as she hurried along the river path towards Woodsend. There were no longer any inhabitants on this side of the common, apart from the nuns at the abbey, the forest having a reputation for being haunted. They were nothing but old wives tales passed down through generations, but it kept casual visitors away and it would be safer here for a while – allowing time, at least, to hole up and think about what to do next.

She stepped into the dark, chilly forest. With her back icy and damp permeating her spine, hunger hollowed out her stomach. There was a place in here though, where she could dry off. A place no one else dared visit.

Well more fool them. More fool the lot of them – terrified, brainless vermin who blamed and murdered lone women for their own misfortunes – they should rot in hell.

Pressing on up the path she and Cicely had taken barely five months before, she paused halfway to get her breath. Woodpecker Cottage should be around here from what she remembered. The fog was almost impermeable in the middle of the woods, tree trunks looming in blackened stumps. There was, though…she squinted… yes, a faint outline of a chimney stack…the cottage was there…that was it.

With renewed purpose she plunged through the undergrowth. There hadn't been anyone living here for decades: Woodpecker Cottage was supposed to be haunted by the spirit of a witch hanged many years previously. It was said that on a full moon she flew around on a broomstick and if you saw her or heard her whistle, she would bring the grim reaper to your door within a month.

The story went that the village parson had taken to visiting the woman, but she had rejected him, sweeping him off her doorstep and cursing the old man with the pox, from which he later died. Whispers of witchcraft soon followed, with reports of her keeping a toad as a pet, and sending a red-eyed owl to follow people home at dusk. Just one look from her caused God-fearing folk to drop down dead with convulsions, right there in the street, or certainly before nightfall. That didn't stop people from visiting her for poultices or potions though; or local women asking for love spells. Well-known for working magical cures, she had been a common sight for years, often by the river harvesting herbs, whistling as she went. It was only, however, after a well-to-do-lady from town had brought her sickly child for a cure, and that child had screamed at her on sight, calling her a witch and dying of fever a matter of hours later, that the mob turned up.

They arrived one night – led by churchmen and doctors - carrying torch flames, dragged her outside and stripped her to expose the mark of the devil. Finding a birthmark on her back they charged her there and then with carrying out his work, after which they strung her up by the neck from the old oak at the bottom of the garden, leaving her swinging body to rot until it fell into the dust and was eaten by wolves.

Magda pushed open the cottage door. Dust carpeted the bare floorboards and cobwebs, glistening with dew, netted the windows. Weak rays of ethereal light stretched across the walls, the air musty and stale; and the only sound was that of a bird scratching in the flue.

Beside the dead woman's empty hearth was an old armchair, its stuffing ravaged by rodents, and above the mantelpiece hung a large, heavily ornate, oval mirror.

Magda dropped her wet cloak over the stair rail and took off her boots, tipping them into the small kitchen sink. Her skirts, she thought, stepping out of them, could be hung outside when the sun rose. She looked around for something, anything to wrap herself in, teeth chattering uncontrollably, hugging herself as she wandered from room to room.

There had to be something left of the old hag's property – a shawl, a scarf... But there was very little, she quickly realised, creaking open cupboards, and wrenching open drawers powdered in dust and reeking of mould. The place must have been ransacked too.

At the back of a large, surprisingly elaborate sideboard though, there was a stub of beeswax candle with a piece of flint; and in the kitchen, behind a grubby curtain under the sink unit, a small, brown phial containing what looked like sludge, together with a boline for cutting herbs, had been jammed behind the wall. Upstairs there were only empty rooms, save for some creature scratching around in the attic; and discarded on the floorboards, a damp, discoloured shawl half-eaten by moths.

Standing in her petticoat she wrapped the shawl around her shoulders as best she could and went to sit by the black grate. It would be madness to try and light a fire. As kids she and some others had played here in the woods, daring each other to look through the windows, so today's children might do the same, might they not? No, that would be far too dangerous and besides, a plume of smoke would be noticed for miles around. Oh, she'd survive. A shot of pink burned hotly in her cheeks along with a recurring sharp blade in her breast.

God damn them all to hell.
William Miller, I loved you...

Groaning and light-headed with hunger she stood up and glared into the mirror, her dark eyes flashing. Things had not gone to plan. How could this have happened? Gently her hands stroked her swollen tummy.

Where are you, God, when I need you? Why are you letting this happen? Why are you letting people here starve and die agonising deaths? Making girls like me take all the blame? Where are you? And how in hell am I supposed to feed myself and this child, with winter coming? Damn sitting on rock hard pews every week in a freezing church begging for forgiveness... What about now?

Her reflection eyed her angrily and she moved in closer, compelled to gaze steadily into her own eyes. There was such power in them. Such life yet...The mirrored stare continued to bore into her own until she found she could not look away again; even as the light lifted into morning and dust motes began to dance in the air…She gazed at the image before her, swaying, unable to move…*How beautiful we are…*

Transfixed she continued to stare into the mirror even as her face began, very slightly, to change. Her heart picked up a beat…the lips were picking up at the corners…as if by an invisible puppeteer…and then without any warning the face of another woman appeared…And rushed towards her with great speed, flying out of the mirror. Magda gasped and stepped back, still mesmerised by the image, and still unable to look away.

A rasping, guttural voice bellowed into the room. "God doesn't love you, you low-down bitch-whore. God hates you. God has forsaken you. You bedded men twice your age. God detests you. He hates sluts and he hates meddling witches. And you are both."

Shock paralysed her.

The eyes in the mirror now sparkled feverishly. This was an illusion. Hunger and tiredness made it so. She spat out the words with scorn. "Who the fuck are you?"

The voice changed instantly, to that of a kindly female. "I am your friend, Magda. I'm the one who's here for you."

"What's your name?"

"Lilith."

"Who are you and what do you want?"

"Lucifer's bride. Lucifer is the only one who is here for you – the only one who will help you now."

Magda sneered at the reflection. "You are a fantasy. A lie. A delusion. A dream…a–"

The temperature plummeted to ice and Magda screamed.

"Come on then, Lucifer," she shouted into the mirror. "Take me as your witch and give me what I want. If you're here for me then show yourself. I am not afraid of you. I will dance with you and fuck with you because my life is over, anyway. Just give me what I want. What I need. Because God is going to let me and my child die. It seems He has forsaken us so where are you? This is just a fucking dream…you are nothing, not even real."

Her voice echoed around the freezing room.

"Are you here? I bet you're not, you miserable fucker."

A tiny movement, a glint in the glass, caused her to glance down for a fragment of a second. Someone was here. Right in this room. About to climb the stairs.

She stood absolutely motionless. Watching the spot. Listening. No, there was nothing – how odd. Her gaze flicked back up to the reflection.

What in hell's name is this? What kind of nightmare am I in?

She leaned forwards; then recoiled in disbelief. A shard of ice passed through her. These were not her eyes anymore. An empty stare of blind whiteness looked back at her.

"I'm here now, Magda," said a deep male voice. "God has gone."

***

She woke with a kick to the heart. It was dark – a glitteringly, cold night studded with stars. Tree-shaped shadows swayed and bounced along the walls and the door was wide open.

Still half-dreaming, Magda struggled to make sense of where she was, breathing in the damp air that cloyed sweetly with the aroma of wet earth and burning wood. Her pounding forehead was scorching to the touch and clammy with sweat. Slightly dizzy she tried to stand but found it impossible, such was the pressure inside her head and the heaviness of her limbs. How long had she been asleep? It had been morning just a moment ago, and there had been such strange dreams. Again she tried to stand, this time noticing the scratched circle she was sitting in the middle of, the remnants of the beeswax candle, which had burned down to a stub, and the line of footprints leading to and from the kitchen door. Small prints made with bare feet. She examined her soles. Filthy. Stared at her fingers. Stained with juice.

What dark tricks were these?

Flickers of the troubled dream she had woken from flashed back disjointedly, scattering around the edges of her mind and already fading fast. A woman's deathly stillness…an ebbing flow of dark liquid oozing onto white sheets…a feeling of watching this from the corner of the room, a glass or a mirror…willing it to happen…

Almost, she thought, kneeling up and rocking with the unbearable pain in her head – almost as if she had dreamt a death wish.

***

Chapter Fifteen

Jasmine Cottage
September, 2016

The darkness took her by surprise. It seemed the long days of summer would last forever, then whoosh – suddenly it was autumn and evenings were closing in. Becky switched off the laptop and heaved herself up from the sofa. Ouch and ouch. This pregnancy business wasn't funny. Holding onto Molly with one hand, she pushed herself upright with the other. And still two months to go.

It might be an idea to take the holiday she was due before maternity leave because at this age, describing it as being weighted down with a sack of sand while wading through water would not be exaggerating. And it was only eight-thirty. She couldn't go to bed at this time. Could she? Oh hell, why not?

In the small kitchen, still warm from the range, she leaned over the sink to close the window, having one last scout round for Louie in the hope he might be trotting up the path, meowing urgently with his tail held high. It seemed so wrong without him. You could, she thought, feel his absence in a cut-out cat shape. He had been content here, stretching out on the sun-baked terrace or coiling round her legs when she cooked; bursting crazily up and down the stairs with his ears back when the mood took him. More like a dog than a cat, Cal said, the way he followed you round the house and slumped next to you when you were reading. Sometimes he even put a paw on your arm. Yes, it had felt more of a home with him in it. She frowned. Hadn't he disappeared the same night Lilith appeared in the mirror?

Oh, don't be ridiculous...Well, he had...

She allowed herself a wry smile – since when had she taken to arguing with herself? It was almost a shame to close the window, actually. Wild honeysuckle mixed with old English roses scented the evening air with sweetness. Even the sheets smelled fragrant when they'd dried outside. Simple pleasures, but oh, how wonderful to find happiness in them. It was such a shame Cal was working again tonight. He'd been sent here there and everywhere recently, even to other counties; only to arrive and be told he'd not been asked for. Oh well, like he said, all she had to do was keep safe and hold the fort when he wasn't here.

Why she had such a feeling of disquiet, as if something was going to happen, she really couldn't say. It was spooky, though. And whatever it was seemed to shadow her – as she climbed the creaking, wooden staircase, washed in the bathroom, brushed her hair, padded across the landing...

As always in the bedroom, she kept both the window and the curtains open: there was no one outside here on the moors, and the shining harvest moon was a stunning sight. It seemed too large to be suspended in the sky like that – much more dominant than at other times of the year - the wisps of yellowy-grey cloud drifting across it somehow quite haunting. The barn owls were out hunting again too – savage screeches piercing the night air.

She lay back against the pillows, eyes wide open. What a thing it was, to be so tired you couldn't read or concentrate on anything, yet not being able to sleep either - your mind constantly chattering, on alert for something it couldn't identify but was, at some level, innately aware of.

Moonlight spread over the room in a creamy layer, bright as daylight. The old flocked paper had peeled in places and a tidemark of rising damp stained the walls. She made a mental note to tackle this room next after decorating Molly's.

Somewhere in the house one of the old floorboards creaked loudly, and the pipes banged, followed by a prolonged juddering. It was just the wood constricting after the heat of the day, she reassured herself, and there'd been hot water running so of course the pipes would make a noise. Even so, her heart was fair racing along.

The old couple at the far end had gone to Bridlington for a fortnight, which meant she was the only occupant out here until Callum came back at goodness knew what time. Mentally she patrolled the house again. Yes, she had locked the front door, bolted the back, closed all the windows…except this one because once again, although there was a chill at night now, inside it was close and airless.

God, she needed to sleep. What was it gnawing away at her – this thing of worry inside? Sandi? Noel? Perhaps it was simply the fact she was pregnant at forty-four? Or maybe it was Toby and what he'd told her the other night? No, not that – it was obvious he'd suffer trauma after all he'd seen – totally understandable. But once he'd got the reports all tied up he would move onto other things and recover. He was young and smart, would put it behind him. So what was nagging her then? Noel was drinking but he'd promised to get help, to go and see Harry. Not Noel. Alice? No, Judy was watching Alice. Sandi, then? Was it Sandi?

Talk about paranoia. Sandi had thirty years of competency behind her. Originally a ward sister she now worked for an agency on short-term contracts, in both general and psychiatric nursing. Sandi was, at a guess, in her mid-fifties, with wild, woolly grey hair, which she kept in a short mop of curls that flopped over one eye; had protruding teeth; and a pinched, yoga-toned body with tree-root veins creeping up her arms to prove it. She also possessed a sharp tongue. Nothing though, to elicit concern. She had the place running like clockwork, was always on time and definitely took no nonsense. Old school, was Sandi. Bit odd Ruby didn't like her, but then it took Ruby ages to trust anyone. No, it couldn't be that.

There was just this feeling of being watched that she couldn't shake; of a presence willing her to acknowledge it – so real it was almost touchable. If she stared long enough into the empty air she'd see it…something…it would come…

The bedroom was brilliantly lit, the moon now in the centre of the window, beaming into the dressing table mirror. After the other night she'd moved the cheval mirror to the spare room to avoid a repeat performance. No, this was all perfectly normal and there was nothing to be afraid of. There were no shadows in the mirror and everything was exactly as it should be. The wardrobe door was locked with a key and the coat hangers were not rattling of their own accord. It was fine – all absolutely and totally fine.

But what if a voice called her name? Or shouted in her ear? Or something horrible materialised in front of her? They watched you while you slept – it was happening to all of them – external, and proven like Toby said...not madness at all... but real...real...real...

Silently she cited the Lord's Prayer. 'Our Father who art in Heaven...' and ended with a plea for relief from the paralysing fear. Still her eyes were wide open as yet again the mental process of assessing every tiny thing that might be keeping her awake began; until as night progressed, the shadows shifted and lengthened, and the lights in the dressing table mirror were extinguished, sleep finally came.

Moments later her eyes snapped open.

There had been a breath in her face.

With her heart banging hard she scrambled for the lamp, knocking over the clock as she pressed the switch. Nothing happened. She pressed it again. Checked the socket beneath it. *Hell!*

Panicking, she sat up and swung her legs over the side of the bed. The room was totally dark, the sky now awash with a galaxy of stars. She touched her cheek, almost crying with the fear of it. It was no use, all the lights were going on.

On her way out of the bedroom she flicked on the main light, silently thanking God it worked, and padded across the landing to the bathroom. It had been a bad dream, it really had. All her fears piling in the moment she lost consciousness.

She used the toilet and began to wash her hands, glancing into the mirror at the eye bags she now had. All this nightmare business was no good for beauty sleep that was for sure: maybe a decent eye cream? She rinsed off the soap, and still thinking about eye creams inadvertently looked into the mirror again.

Fuck!

A woman was standing directly behind her.

She stared aghast. Eyeball to eyeball. Blinked and stared again.

The woman vanished.

Half-crying, half-screaming, Becky shot onto the landing and switched the light on there as well, then with the whole of the upstairs lit up like a football stadium, turned the dressing room mirror round to face the wall and leapt into bed.

Molly lurched and she stroked and soothed the child inside her.

She must not convey her fears to the child...it was a night terror, part of a dream...*No it isn't...she's watching you...waiting for you to accept her...* It isn't real... *it's real...*

"Fuck! Fuck!"

Wide-awake in the full glare of electric light she made yet another recce of the bedroom, checking everything was the same as it had been before: wardrobe, chair, dressing table and mirror, stool, lamp, clock, book, jewellery box, chest of drawers...over and over and over. There was no way anyone could have got in. Once more she mentally checked every window, door, lock and bolt in the house. *No one is in.* The incident in the bathroom had been a nightmare, she'd been half asleep, still in a sub-conscious world – her obsessions with the bloody mirror and all the images she'd stupidly gone and looked at replaying like a stuck video. It was a fear demon eating away at her sanity again. Spirits could only travel through the dark, that's what Celeste had said. So if all the lights were on she would be just fine and dandy.

She stared into the brightly lit bedroom, listening for the slightest sound, shuddering as cooler air now circulated behind her neck.

This was bonkers, crazy. Shivering and bone tired she recited the Lord's Prayer out loud this time. "Please take away my fear. Please keep me safe in my mind."

Whimpering, she hugged herself. If only Callum was here and not away so damn much. She had to have sleep, there was work tomorrow. She mustn't replay what had been in that mirror, mustn't…to do that would be to re-conjure those bulbous eye whites in that skeletal, mottled face. Do not, she told herself look at her again even in your mind's eye or she will climb inside.

This is no dream – it's real.

Think of other things…think, think, think, for Christ's sake.

After an hour, with chattering teeth and dizzy with tiredness, she slid tentatively under the covers and pulled them over her head.

What if something tugs at the sheets, though? Or strokes my hair? No, no, stop the thoughts…stop them…stop them now. Or whispers in my ear? Taps my shoulder…Oh, God…I have to stop these thoughts. I'm going to go mad…

In desperation she threw back the covers and rummaged in the top drawer for an anti-histamine tablet, which usually did the trick of knocking her for six in about half an hour; then pulled the blankets back over her head, curled into a tight ball and deliberately decorated the entire cottage in her imagination.

The hours must have passed, albeit in a half-awake, half asleep kind of way, because the phone ringing jolted her awake and the birds were twittering. For a moment, disorientated, she struggled to recall where she was. The mists of early dawn had crept into the room like silent ghosts and on the bedside cabinet her mobile was furiously vibrating. Stretching out a hand she picked it up. It was four in the morning.

"Toby?" it sounded as if he was crying. "Toby, what on earth is it?"

"Becky, something's badly wrong with Amy and I don't know what to do. I'm scared."

She gripped the handset, barely registering what he was saying.

It was misty in the room.

Misty with no lights on.

She had never switched them off.

***

Chapter Sixteen

Drummersgate

Noel was coming off the night shift when Becky walked onto the ward next morning.

"Jesus wept, Becky, you look like shit."

"Ah thanks, aren't you lovely?"

He preceded her into the office for the handover meeting, holding open the door. "Can't you sleep? Do you think you should be working? We can get Sandi to take over now if you want."

"No! No, I'm fine. Sorry, that sounded snappy. I need a coffee, that's all. So for the love of God would you please put the kettle on?"

"Well, you don't look fine."

"Nor do you. In fact you look like the walking dead – a zombie fresh from the crypt...no, wait...a vampire ready for its coffin–"

"Alright, I get the picture." Noel switched on the kettle, keeping his back to her, praying she hadn't caught a whiff of the whisky on his breath. *Thank God for Red Bull and spearmint gum, not to mention the uppers bought outside a club the other night. Dodgy ground, really seriously, sackably dodgy.* "You know I've always struggled with nights," he said. "I've never been able to sleep in the day. Anyway, that means I can't be a vampire, can I?"

She smiled, taking the mug of steaming coffee from him. "Thanks. Yeah, that's something I'm not going to miss for sure – bloody night shifts."

She took a sip, watching him slump into a chair by the desk. "You're still drinking, aren't you? You can't get past me you know? Are things no better?"

He looked up, bleary eyed, his face grey. "What? I just had one before I came in last night–"

"One? Who are you kidding? I'm going to have to open a window – fumes are coming off you so strongly if I had a match we'd all combust. Noel, if this was anybody else I'd be on the phone right now but I've known you a long time and you're one of the best nurses I've ever worked with, not to mention my closest friend. For goodness' sake, get yourself home and not on that suicide bike either. Call a taxi and get gone. Are you on tonight?"

"No."

"Good. Right then – go now before anyone else sees you, or worse still gets a whiff. You need help and you mustn't come back until you've got it. I'm saying this as your best friend."

One of the buzzers was sounding on the ward and she fixed him with one of her notorious stares. "Noel, I owe you my life, and it's because I understand exactly what you're going through that I know you need to go and see Harry. Now. Today. Because it's my guess there's no doctor on earth who can help you with what you've got – and believe me it will get worse and it won't go away. If it's any consolation, and by that I mean you're not losing your mind, there are things happening to me too."

He raised his eyebrows. "Like?"

"No time, I'll fill you in later. That old baggage, Brent, will be in soon for a ward inspection and she can't see you like this. Go on now, please." She bustled him out of the door and once in the corridor, locked it behind them. "I'll get agency staff to cover – now go."

He watched her scurrying towards the buzzing light, shame washing through him. With Becky off soon on maternity leave, this ward would need him, or Sandi would be left in charge…and there was something about that woman…he ran his hands through the lank strands of his hair and tied it back with an elastic band before turning on his heels for the stairs.

"Will you ring a taxi for me, mate?" he shouted to the security guard. "I'll be ten minutes – just getting changed."

***

There was no point going home to try and sleep – it never came – and if it did it was fitful. The taxi trundled over moorland still blanketed in an early morning haze. He ought to be powering across here on his bike not sitting in the back of a cab feeling sick and empty with a throbbing head. He must look awful too – sunken-eyed with days of stubble. Becky was right, he had to get this sorted.

"Drop me in Doncaster, will you, mate?" he shouted to the driver. "Wellbeck Road."

The driver nodded, obviously not one of life's talkers. Well, good. Noel leaned back and closed his eyes. Harry had said to drop in anytime, but it had been eight months, nearly nine, since they'd last seen each other. Pray to God he would still be at the same address.

He must have dozed because when his head lolled onto his shoulder, it was to jolt him into a world of too bright colours and too loud voices. Someone was shouting, "Eleven pound fifty, pal!" A stream of cool air wafted onto his face and he blinked repeatedly, momentarily confused. A ruddy-faced man with a beer belly and a grey beard was standing with the door open, holding his hand out for money. "I'm stopping 'ere for breakfast."

"Oh, right, yeah, sorry." Reaching down into his pockets for cash he almost fell out of the car, and for a good few seconds afterwards, stood in the street trying to recall where the hell he was. *God, yeah, Harry...*

Cars were fizzling past, the chilly air a mix of exhaust fumes and fried food. As he walked he rubbed his face to force colour into his skin, and chewed a fresh roll of gum. He really had no right turning up like this first thing in the morning, or at any time without so much as a phone call, but if he didn't go with this now, he never would. *Oh dear God...* The nerves quivered inside his stomach. *Will Harry understand? Will he be able to help me? Why did I let this get so bad?*

109

Desperation drove him on and ten minutes later he was standing outside the address Harry had given him, ringing the bell before he could change his mind.

The terrace was the only one not occupied by students by the look of it, with the curtains open and an absence of weeds and piled-up rubbish at the front. Sturdily built houses lined either side of the street: handsome Victorian terraces with sash windows and high ceilings that would make comfortable family homes if they weren't on a busy thoroughfare jammed with parked cars, book-ended with fast food outlets and noisy at night with thumping music.

A strange choice for a man like Harry. Noel looked around as he waited on the top step. Well, it was near the church, he supposed, so at least it was convenient. Or maybe just temporary? Anyway, no one was in so he might as well just go now, thank you…

Harry swung the door open still holding a towel and a toothbrush. "Good grief. Noel, isn't it? Long-time no see… Come in, come in…How are you?"

"Hi, Harry! I'm so sorry to just turn up like this."

"Not at all, not at all." He gestured towards his state of undress. "Look, just go through to the kitchen, will you? Pop the kettle on and make yourself at home – I'll be with you in two ticks."

"Sure, no worries. Thank you."

Funny that. Harry hadn't missed a beat.

After filling the kettle he waited as instructed, while the other man clambered about upstairs. The back garden stretched out in a long, narrow strip of grass, droplets of dew sparkling in the early morning brightness, and at the end of the lawn lay a small orchard, windfalls scattered around the apple trees just waiting for kids to scale the fence and grab them. Pity they didn't, it seemed a waste.

"Now then," said Harry, striding into the kitchen. "I need breakfast, I don't know about you? Ah good, you've boiled the kettle."

Noel nodded, suddenly famished. "Thanks, that'd be great – only if it's no trouble, though?"

"Not at all." Harry set about pouring juice, frying bacon and eggs, microwaving waffles and making coffee. "I never know when I'm going to eat next, so I start the day well," he said, rummaging for cutlery and plates.

Harry, it seemed, was an expert at multi-tasking and in a whirl of admirable domesticity plonked an English breakfast in front of him in no time. "Get stuck in, you look like you need it."

God, did he ever? It was like he hadn't eaten properly in months, hadn't nourished himself, taken care of his health, his body or his happiness. The sorrow welled up inside as he finished and pushed his plate away. He could have cried.

Harry was watching him. "Better?"

"Guess I didn't realise how hungry I was."

"Have some more toast. Help yourself. Then in your own time tell me what's been happening to you, Noel. I'm going to need all of it, I'm afraid."

Signs of life began to stir around them - a radio was flicked on in the adjoining terrace, someone dropped a leaflet through the front door, and a car door banged in the street.

Still Noel stared into his coffee, not knowing where to start. "Harry, I…I…just don't feel well," he stuttered. "I'm drinking. I can't sleep. I get night terrors like you wouldn't believe."

"Yes."

"I've tried to block it out. I've done everything I can think of but it's getting a whole lot worse."

"And drink isn't the answer, is it? In fact, isn't it making it worse?"

Noel looked out of the window. "I can't go on like this."

"No, of course you can't."

His eyes burned with tiredness. Squeezing them shut so he didn't have to see his shame reflected in the other man's face, the truth burst out. "I know it's just fear talking, Harry, I do know that it can't be real, but there's nothing I can do to stop these bloody nightmares coming, except to stay awake. I go to bars – gay bars in Leeds – I've even taken coke just to keep me upright. And turned up for work straight after. Claire and one or two of the others have noticed I smell of booze, I can see it in their eyes–"

"Smell of booze? Well that's an understatement if ever I heard one – you're bloody saturated in it man, pickled. It oozes from your pores. Yours is a body that wouldn't decompose in a heatwave, and the last time I saw eyes as red as that they were Dracula's."

"Oh, don't you start, I've already had Becky tell me I look like a zombie ready for its coffin."

"When did all this start? After Kristy's exorcism?"

"I wasn't too good after what happened with Becky, to be honest – that's when we first met Michael. I took her to church last Christmas when she was convinced there was a man trying to possess her. We all thought she'd had a bump on the head and was suffering from psychosis – even she thought that for a while. Well anyway, maybe it got to me a bit more than I thought?"

Harry nodded.

"We'd all seen what happened to Jack too, running around giggling, barricading himself into the office. And then there was Kristy – seeing her like that, the way she was, well it's like... I don't know how to explain it... I just haven't been able to shake off this feeling of menace, like a malignant presence is following me around, watching me all the time even when I sleep. I keep checking over my shoulder because I think I hear something, or see dark shapes skitter across the floor. But there's never anything there, you see? Of course, it could all be depression and psychosis, me just going mad–"

"And do you think that's what it is - that you're going mad?"

"I don't know, Harry. All I'm sure of is that I haven't slept in months, not properly, and the longer it goes on the weaker I'm getting, the less resistance I have and the more I need to sleep. Only I daren't because that's when it comes for me."

"Okay, now this is the difficult bit, but I need you to tell me if you can, what it is that 'comes' for you when you're unconscious. Take it easy, top line is all I need."

Noel took a deep breath. "Harry, I have serious difficulty even talking about this because it conjures it up again, makes it real, like I've acknowledged it in some way; and then I see it all day long – in mirrors, in my mind's eye, on other people's faces instead of their own–"

"Like it's taking you over? Wearing you down? I should say at this stage, well done, because you haven't given in, but I can see you're getting physically and emotionally drained; and it's time to do something because it's my belief you're definitely under psychic attack, and it will kill you rather than give up. It doesn't matter anymore about rationalising this or trying to debate what can and can't happen. I'm telling you straight that demonic possession does exist because I've seen it and it ruins people's lives and everyone's around them. So, tell me exactly what happens and what it looks like to you, then we'll see what we can do."

Noel nodded miserably. "If I describe it this thing will be here in this room...I..."

"Trust me," said Harry. "Just trust me or I can't help you."

"Sorry, okay – well, the second I fall asleep it happens. The mattress bounces slightly as if something has just landed on the bed, something light like a cat...but I'm only half aware of it. I want to stay asleep because I'm so tired, but then a bass, male voice whispers softly into my ear, 'Hello, Noel. It's show time again.'

That's how it starts. And I know that if I open my eyes it will be there – looking down at me from the ceiling - a girl with empty eye sockets and dripping black hair, only not a girl – more like a creature – skittering around on four legs with a head screwed on back to front, its movements crab-like and jerky, scuttling sideways... pitter-pattering round the ceiling... I can hear a rattling chest and a hideous squelching noise. And although my eyes are shut tightly I just know they're going to snap open against my will. And that's when it rushes at me – right into my face. I'm screaming but no sound comes out. And I still cannot wake up and I cannot move. It's shaking the bed, jumping up and down on it, mocking me. And inside my head I'm shouting at myself to wake up, bloody wake up, that it's just a dream, a nightmare. But it won't stop, it goes on and on and on saying the same thing, 'Let me in! Once you let me in I'll stop…it will all stop. Let me in, let me in, let me in–'"

Harry came over, stood behind his chair and rested his hands on Noel's shoulders.

"Okay, that's enough. It's enough for anyone. And we can put a stop to it right now, starting today, but you have to trust me one hundred percent and do exactly as I say."

"Anything."

"I'd like to say a prayer first and then we'll talk."

Noel's shoulders sagged under the other man's hands while the prayer was said, after which Harry crossed himself and then Noel.

"Okay," said Harry, pulling out a chair. "You alright now?"

Noel nodded. This was his nadir; the outside world now utterly irrelevant; the moment right here and right now, pivotal.

"Good. Now, we must work together and we must work quickly. I need to cover two things with you. First of all, I need to know more about the events up at Drummersgate that started all of this, and then I need to know more about you yourself. I can and will administer deliverance but there's no point if we don't deal with these issues first. You have to be very, very strong inside because what's attacking you now is powerful and without mercy."

"Well, I can tell you about Ruby Dean and where it all started, how it affected the whole team; and I can tell you about the satanic sect in Woodsend, but I'm not sure my own history is anything to write home about – it's pretty boring."

"Let's start with what's easiest for you. Let's begin with Ruby."

114

While Noel brought him up to speed, Harry made more coffee and periodically asked some questions, nodding to himself. "Yes, I'd read a lot in the papers and of course Michael filled me in as best he could."

"Michael said he'd helped you once?"

"Yes, yes that's true. I'll tell you the story because I'm going to need you to level with me in a moment, so if I disclose this, which is very difficult for me personally, I'll need you to do the same in return, okay?"

"Fair enough."

"Michael and I met on a Christian deliverance course in Rome. Michael was in a bad place emotionally because one of his closest friends had recently committed suicide and it had made him extremely vulnerable doing exorcisms. Dangerously so. Not only was he bereaved he was also riddled with guilt – there was a lot of negativity there. I think your friend, Becky, was one of the last people he helped, actually."

"And look what that did to him."

"Yes, I know. And I'm not sure I'll ever fully get over it, but that's what they do, you see? It's not just about upside down crosses and orgies; not even the repulsive abuse of children or live sacrifices, which is something we know is real and the police can act on. I'm afraid it is the darker world we have to worry about now – the one most people won't even acknowledge as existing let alone do anything about - because they can't see it. Try getting people to believe an inhuman force is attacking us and see what reaction you get. We're bonkers, deluded, religious freaks…and while we're arguing amongst ourselves, demonic desecration with all its vile perversions is busy deconstructing our very humanity. Which is why I have to ask you to simply trust me."

Harry got up to switch the kettle on again. "You know Michael told me as much as he could when we were driving to the hospital to see Kristy that night. He was convinced those idiot Satanists in Woodsend had opened a floodgate, you know?"

Noel shook his head. "Floodgate?"

115

Harry suddenly spun round, his eyes alight. "Oh my word, of course – why didn't I think?" He put his hands to his face.

"What? What is it?"

"Oh dear Lord, a few things might be clicking into place."

"What do you mean?"

Harry poured the coffee out. "I'll come back to it... Oh, now that has given me a turn." He sat down again, putting two mugs of coffee on the table. "Let me just finish what I was telling you though, because it's relevant and then we can get on and help you quickly." He glanced at the clock. "Time's pushing on. Right, where was I? Yes, when I met Michael I'd been a priest for a while but it would be fair to say my faith had never truly been tested, and I guess, in the end, that it just wasn't strong enough. I performed an exorcism, albeit supervised during the course, and it went badly wrong. If you don't do these things correctly, you see, to the letter, and you leave a door open then the demons will just keep coming back. Anyway, the woman I tried to help ended up in an asylum. Before slitting her own throat."

"Oh man, that's terrible."

"Noel, it was worse than that: she was a woman of God and what happened was a violation of everything she stood for, had worked for and held precious. I will carry the burden on my conscience for the rest of my life."

"Can I ask how it went wrong?"

"The demonic force possessing her wouldn't go. I was there for three days to the point of exhaustion. And then on the fourth day she persuaded me it had gone and threw her arms around me. I hugged her back, too slow to realise she was attempting to seduce me. And–" Now it was Harry's turn to look away. "I am ashamed to say my body betrayed me."

"You didn't actually do anything?"

"No, I didn't act on it, but the demon inside her knew I had physically responded, and the horrible laughter still haunts me. She, or should I say the demon, then delighted in telling her family, all the medical people, and my colleagues about the incident and I was suspended for a while, told to take a holiday. Michael was the one who took time out to explain deliverance to me a little better. You have to prepare people, you see, including yourself. Man alone cannot drive out demons from a person's soul – that can only be done by God. Satan wants man to believe he is as powerful as God, which, if we believe that, leaves us defenceless – we are subsequently weakened because the reality is the only power that can ever drive out Satan is God himself, and the devil knows it. I don't do this for you, you see, God does. But if you have barriers up against Him it may not work."

Noel shook his head. "But what have I done wrong? I'm just an ordinary guy who works hard and does a job he believes in, trying to help the most vulnerable people on earth – those who've lost their minds. What have I done to deserve this? Don't tell me it's because I'm homosexual so the church won't help me?"

Harry held his hands up. "Wait, no, no, no! First things first. I am part of the Catholic Church but I am now part of a national Christian deliverance group too. I'm up all hours of the day and night and you may not believe it but we've never been busier. We rely on charity and I've sold almost all I had to do this. It's my calling, if you like. So none of this is judgemental, Noel. There is no hidden agenda. My job is to alleviate your suffering as you have asked, and in order to do that I need to prepare you for deliverance to the Lord. If you want me to. If you wish to fully open up. And then I can help you."

"What do I tell you?"

"Tell me about you, your parents, your home, why you're alone, if you harbour any thoughts that are depressive or angry or rebellious or resentful. These are the negative energies the demonic entity will feed off to grow stronger, you understand."

"Okay, I get it, I think. Actually, I had a great childhood – middle class home in a nice area, good school, loads of friends. Then aged about thirteen, maybe fourteen I realised I didn't fancy girls and went through a bit of a difficult time–" He stopped mid-sentence.

117

"Did something happen around that time, Noel? Something significant?"

"Yes. It's just come rushing back to me... Oh God, I thought I'd successfully forgotten about this. Oh man, this is hard."

"Take your time."

"I'm gonna have to just blurt this out because it's awful...embarrassing... I suppose I had a crush on a particular boy in the sixth form. He was well-built, stocky really, a bit rakish – funny and stunningly good-looking. Well, one day he caught me eyeing him in the changing rooms and the next thing he got me by the hair, dragged me into the showers and beat me to a pulp, stripped me. All the lads were laughing and shouting like it was a fucking gladiator ring, calling me a shirt-lifter, a dirty faggot... Shit, I've never told anyone this." The colour rose in his neck, spreading hotly up to his hairline. "I got moved to another school and my parents started being – how can I describe it – slightly less physical with me."

"You felt rejected?"

"Christ, yes. And certain church-going members of the family told me in no uncertain terms that homosexuality was a sin. I suppose I rejected a church that didn't want someone like me in it."

"And that left you with a legacy of anger and pain?"

"God, I'm so tired, it's like all the energy drained out of me just this very second...Um...yes, I suppose it did. Although I have to say I think those people are bigots and I feel sorry for them. I have forgiven and moved on though, I really have."

"But you still carry the pain and rejection?"

Noel's bloodshot eyes met Harry's focused, blue stare. "I guess."

"Thank you for telling me. That took guts. Now, will you let me help you?"

"Yes, yes I will."

Harry looked at his watch. "Blimey, lunch time already." Outside the promise of sun had clouded over and light rain spattered against the window. "I've got some calls to make but how about you – can you stay here today? Do you have to go to work tonight?"

"Yes, I can stay if that's ok – I'm not working tonight."

"Good. I'll put the fire on in the front room and you can lie on the sofa, try to get some rest and think about the things we've talked about. Be absolutely clear in your heart and soul about your feelings, Noel. Face up to them and be honest so there's no negative energy to block your healing. And then we can start giving you that help you need as soon as possible."

Noel stood up. "I feel absolutely exhausted. I can hardly walk."

Harry had started clearing up, busying himself with checking messages and filling the sink with hot, soapy water. "Get some rest. Shout if you need me."

"Thanks, mate. Can I ask you one thing though?"

Harry looked over his shoulder. "Sure."

"What was that you said you'd come back to, about Woodsend having opened a floodgate?"

Harry resumed washing out cups. "I'm not sure – just that we may have a problem in the church. It may be nothing, but I don't think so. I really should have put two and two together before now."

***

Chapter Seventeen

Drummersgate

After Noel had gone, Becky flew around the unit picking up the pieces from the night before. It was so unlike Noel to leave handover notes unwritten, drug charts unsigned, and phone messages unreturned; not to mention a ward full of patients kicking off. The list was endless.

It was almost time for the afternoon shift to take over before she had time to shut the office door and grab a sandwich in peace. What a nightmare. Anyone else and they'd get it in the neck, but Noel...well, if he was going through anything like her own experiences last year he had her full support and more. Massaging her lower back, she grimaced. Hopefully it wasn't anything like as bad as that; and with Harry's help he'd soon be fine and could confidently be left in charge while she took maternity leave. Sooner rather than later though, please God, because this was stressful - really physically and mentally tough.

Cramming the sandwich into her mouth, she quickly tidied the desk and set about filling in the patients' notes; after which she called in one of the students to double check the drug cupboard with her.

"It doesn't add up," said the student, a male nurse with a goatee, who slopped around with his hands in his pockets.

Becky frowned. There was indeed a mistake. They went through it all again. Pharmacy would go ballistic. "I think it's probably a case of someone needing a tramadol and whoever it was forgetting to sign for it."

"Haloperidol, as well."

"Yes."

"Someone's had too much."

"Indeed. Right. Well, if you'd just witness my signature, Ewan, I'll report it this afternoon."

He stared at her for a moment too long, one eyebrow raised ever so slightly, then scrawled his spidery autograph with a flourish and sauntered out again.

Becky slammed shut the cupboard door. Little prick, looking at her like that.

Outside it was the kind of golden September afternoon the great romantic poets had eulogised about. She should be relaxing on the terrace back home, drifting off with nothing to do but flick through a magazine and let warm sunshine melt into her skin.

She began to wash out cups, and when one of the buzzers sounded yet again, this time from the dayroom, she opened the door and yelled for that lazy article with the goatee to go and answer it.

"Ewan!"

He was leaning over the reception desk chatting to Security, deliberately ignoring her. She made a hand gesture through the glass pane, along with the mouthed words, "Get that, please." He took his time, finishing the conversation before ambling over to the day room.

Becky closed the office door, exhaling slowly through flared nostrils. "Count to ten, Becky, count to ten… Nope can't do it…Just too sodding tired."

After Toby's call in the early hours of this morning – four o'clock to be precise - she'd fallen into a comatose sleep, the kind she would have killed for seven hours previously, only to be woken again an hour later when the alarm clock shrilled into her brain. Dazed and muggy-headed, she showered and dressed, made breakfast, then walked to the bus stop for the hour long trek to work. Tired didn't begin to describe it; this was chronic insomnia with a jet lag level of fatigue.

Now sick and dizzy, she sat down at her desk with a thud. Toby, frankly, had been an idiot. How he'd got himself tangled up with a silly girl like Amy, she'd never know. After all he'd been through, and off he goes into the woods to play the Ouija board like one of those vacuous teens in a horror movie. You couldn't make it up, and frankly it was hard to decide whether to be furious with him or concerned.

She put her hands over both eyes just to rest them from having to see things in colour, almost enjoying the stinging relief.

The story about how Amy had managed to persuade him to go to Woodpecker cottage was vague to say the least – he'd been adamant he couldn't remember a thing, from the moment he arrived at her house to finding himself outside in the moonlit garden playing Ouija.

"Do you remember driving there?" she'd asked, still half asleep as she sat up in bed trying not to panic because the lights were off. *Did I switch them off before I went to sleep? Did I? Because I just do not remember doing that!*

"No."

"What? Erm, okay – well do you remember her asking you to take her there?"

"No."

"So from the time you entered her house to finding yourself in the middle of Woodsend at midnight, you are completely blank?"

"Believe it or not, Becky, yes, I am."

"What can you remember then – anything?" She hadn't meant to snap, but distracted by the fact the lights appeared to have been switched off, and having had less than four hours sleep, she was going to have to forgive herself.

"I arrived at her house. She answered the door in this sexy outfit and then we got a bit frisky. She lit a spliff and that was it. I don't remember anything after that."

"A what? A spliff? Did I hear that right? Are you for real?"

"I know, I know, but it was nothing really, just a bit of weed and I only had a couple of drags – if that."

"And then you drove a car? Oh, for pity's sake."

"But that's just it. I wouldn't have done that if I'd been in my right mind, would I? You've got to believe me, Becky, please. Anyway, the next thing I know I'm sitting in the middle of the forest and it's really windy, like gale force, and the whole thing is like some kind of crazy nightmare – like it's happening to someone else–"

"That'd be the spliff."

"Yeah, well maybe, but this next bit definitely wasn't the spliff, not the kind I've ever had anyway. We were upstairs in one of the cottage bedrooms – that's where I've just come from – and no, I have no recollection of how I got there. I just remember suddenly coming out of this weird dream and panicking because Amy's eyes were all funny, like rolling back in her head so you could only see the whites – it was horrible. Then she collapsed on me, fitting with all her limbs jerking. I carried her out and turned her on her side into the recovery position. I didn't know what to do and there's no phone signal out here either, but thankfully she's come round. I asked her if she was okay to make it back to the car and that's where we are now – by the river at Woodsend."

"And she's ok, is she?"

"Yes. She's asleep in the passenger seat. I'm going to take her straight home. She's got the sort of parents who let her do what she wants. She goes out all night to clubs and stuff and they don't bother so I'll just get her back and then that's it. She's freaked me out, I mean seriously freaked me out. I don't think I'll see her anymore. I'm sorry I rang, Becky. I just got scared. I thought she might need to go to hospital."

"No, but she may have epilepsy by the sound of it, so you'd best tell her mother if you can. At least let her know. If you want my advice though, Toby, I'd lay off the bloody spliff and vodka and get a girlfriend who's a bit less wacky. You don't need this."

And neither did she. Not at four in the morning anyway.

Toby was another one, though, another friend she'd do anything for. It wasn't his fault she was in her mid-forties and pregnant with a husband who was always away, or that she had a high-stress, under-staffed job.

There came a tap at the office door and she looked up sharply. If it was that arrogant, lazy little snot with the goatee…

A tall, blonde woman dressed in jeans and a white shirt walked in carrying a toddler.

"Amanda! Oh my God, how wonderful to see you."

Amanda grinned. "Just popped in to say I'll be at the staff meeting tomorrow. I start back next week."

Becky heaved herself up, waddled over and threw her arms around the other woman. "Oh, thank God. I am so, so happy to see you I could cry. I can't tell you how relieved I am you're coming back. You seem like an angel."

"Ah, you're really at the end of your rope, aren't you? Sit down, Becky – I'll make us some tea and we can chat for a bit. You've got bedlam in the dayroom, by the way, did you know?"

Becky grinned. "Oh, I'm sure Ewan can handle it. I don't suppose you've got any–"

Amanda rooted inside her copious tote bag and plonked a packet of chocolate digestives on the table. "Of these?"

"Ooh, I did kind of hope."

"Thought you might appreciate them – I know what I was like. Becky look, I want to apologise for not being able to cope before when Jack was ill. I had Ellie to think of and frankly, it got way too scary. I heard about it though, when Tanners Dell was raided, and well, I did feel bad about abandoning Ruby. I know she needs me and Claire can't do everything, and I do love my job. So, well, I've had a long discussion with Isaac and he says the job's mine if I want it, so here I am."

"I heard you were coming in for interview. I have to say I'm thrilled, I really am. Noel will be too."

Plonking a mug of tea in front of her, Amanda nodded towards Becky's bump. "When are you taking maternity? Not long now by the look of it."

"I want to go soon. Next week if possible. Thing is, Noel's a bit unwell, but I think he'll be back in a few days and I've been training up an agency nurse who seems very competent. More than competent. She's a general nurse too, and she did midwifery

– early sixties and very old school. She'll keep them all in line for sure."

"Wow! Sounds good. Although I'll miss you being here. This place is you and you are this place if you know what I mean?"

Becky laughed. "I've had enough of it, though. I am so tired you would not believe."

"I'm not surprised; you've been through a hell of a lot in the last year, and pregnancy can take it out of you at any age. No, you go as soon as you can. Enjoy it, you and Callum."

"I would if he was ever around, but it seems like the CID is short-staffed too – he's all over the place. He's got to go to Crawley next week. Anyway, as soon as I'm happy everything's in order here, I'll take the holiday I'm due and go."

"If this agency nurse is as capable as you say, why worry?"

"True. She's called Sandi, by the way. The only thing is Ruby doesn't seem to like her. Still, she's got you now so I feel happier about leaving."

"Maybe it's just because Sandi's new? It takes a while and if she's a bit officious it could be off-putting. Oh, I just popped into to see Ruby and she remembered me like I'd never been away. She looks like a different girl – so much healthier. You've done a brilliant job. Although I did think she seemed rather anxious and jittery. I thought she'd be on less haloperidol not more. Anyway, we can catch up tomorrow at the team meeting."

Becky frowned, about to respond when the phone rang.

"Hello. Riber Ward, Sister Ross speaking." Her frown deepened. "Hold on, hold on. What do you mean, 'an incident to do with Alice'?"

***

125

Chapter Eighteen

Ruby
Drummersgate

It's so quiet in here tonight – no one's shouting and moaning, or banging their head against the wall. That's a first. It lets your mind be peaceful. And it's nice just lying here looking at the sky with all the stars glittering. Every few minutes a meteor bursts across it with its tail on fire, shooting over the moors…I wonder what happens at the end? Does it explode mid-air or does it land somewhere and burn everything? God, I don't know. I don't know these things at all. The world is made of magic yet people like me don't get to see or understand any of it; sitting in our little cages in case we go and hurt someone, I suppose.

Oh, look, my legs are twitching again like they're being electrocuted… No, really, they are literally jumping about.

I need to think but it's not coming to me; everything's in a haze lately. Something's not right, though – not right at all - something to do with that bitch, Sandi. Her face in mine, that sly smile when she whacks in a double dose of fucking haloperidol like I don't know what she's doing; like I'm stupid; like I can't see my own limbs twitching like a junkie's; like my own neck doesn't jerk round in spasms that hurt like hell. *Fucking bitch, fucking bitch, fucking–*

His face is shown to me without warning. Only to fade away again in an instant. A man – the face of a man. Why? Who is he? Why is Spirit showing a man to me? I need to know about Sandi, not this bloke, whoever he is. So is he something to do with Alice, then?

Whoosh. The visions are coming. Celeste is nearby, I can feel her …yes, yes… Got to get to work, sit down and ask for help… *Oh please, please, show me…*

"Dear Lord, I ask you for protection for what I am about to do. Please guard my soul while I am gone. I do this for the greater good and for the love of my child. I mean no harm and I ask for protection from all negative entities. Thank you and Amen."

This time I do as exactly as I was taught, opening up the energy channels and imagining the most powerful divine light flooding into me. Celeste does not always show herself but tonight her presence is extremely strong, radiating power and something that feels like determination. Something is going to happen now and happen quickly.

And when it comes, just minutes later, the violent surge of energy practically picks me up, projecting me into the unknown… For a moment fear flutters in my stomach, but it's only a moment; this trip mustn't stop – it must take place. None of the others are coming. They are safe inside.

But I am flying…

Our body is left lying on its side, childlike in the blue-tinged light, as my spirit floats away. When I first did this I made the mistake of looking down at the bed and panicking. Would I get back in? But now I know I'm well protected and besides, there is no choice – my spirit is being taken to see something they want me to see.

But where is this? Not the house. Not where I was before. No, this is a dimly lit corridor with a linoleum floor. The air is stale in here, with a lingering smell of over-boiled vegetables, and there is crying, whimpering, from some of the rooms. It's a sad place, confusion imprinted in an atmosphere heavy with rejection, anger and fear. At the end of the corridor a light flickers and the soft murmur of a television programme filters out…

Footsteps…

I am the shadow that makes him do a double take.

He shrugs off the ghost shimmering over his skin, pausing now to observe the occupants of the dayroom, his tread on the linoleum creepily soft. This is the man whose face I have just seen. Yes, a neat, sharp profile. He wears glasses, I see that now, the lower lip wet and protruding. Devouring his charges with large, watery eyes he stalks the ward, observing all, missing nothing. It is a thin disguise. And my heartbeat slams into my throat because the door he finally stops at is Alice's. He peers through the glass as she lies there in bed with her back to him, staring out of the window at a small yard enclosed by a high concrete wall. Something has been written on that wall and it worries her greatly. She thinks of little else.

He lingers still, and my eyes bore into the nape of his neck. I would laser holes through it if I could. Abruptly he swings around, rubbing the skin as if stung; but moves along all the same, a tad uneasy.

What is his interest in my child? The suit, the deference from the nurse at the desk who nods goodnight... *Alice's doctor.* *Fuck*!

The bumpy landing back into my own body is a nasty shock.

For a minute my head pounds sickeningly and my heart's galloping. The moon is halfway across the window now, and someone down the corridor is calling out, deranged and disconnected, as if they just woke up.

The loud pulsing inside my head and chest finally starts to subside; and I hear the other parts chattering. How long have they been doing this? They're not supposed to without me. They should be asleep. This matter alone is disconcerting – I am the host and everything must go through me or anything might happen.

"What is it? Why are you up and talking?"
Sandi.
"Yeah, yeah, I know about that bitch."
She's doubled the haloperidol.
"Yup."

128

What's the connection?

"Don't know."

Immediately the agitation I felt earlier is back, but this time my body is too sedated to move and lies exhausted instead. It's often the way after using spiritual energy, but this is worse than usual.

It's what she wants. To keep you looking mad. To keep you down. She doesn't want you speaking to Becky or Noel. Soon there will only be her and we're scared.

"I know. Keep everyone in. Keep them locked up. Marie, don't let Eve or Dylan come out or she'll have us in the straitjacket. Keep the little ones away. One of us is a snitch and she'll prise it out, make them tell her what she needs to know."

Why? What does she need to know?

"Jesus, Marie, I don't know."

What does she want with Becky? We don't get it.

"They've got plans for Alice. They must have. They don't want Becky or Noel liaising with me about her. It's something they need her for. It's all linked but I don't know how. My brain's foggy. I can't keep awake, can't keep the energy going to talk to Celeste."

She's knocking us out.

"I know."

Noel's fucked, have you seen him?

The other parts are kicking and pounding around inside me. It has to stop or I'll get migraine and stomach cramps and then they'll drug me up again and it'll be worse than ever. I need to talk to Becky about Alice before Becky goes away. But Becky told me Alice was doing well with her therapist, and that we might even be reunited someday. But that doesn't make sense. Nothing is making sense. I know there is something badly wrong yet I'm being told there isn't.

Ruby, someone is blocking us. We can't see. It's dark in here.

Celeste is calling into my right ear, interrupting. Her voice, as usual, sounds like it comes from across an ocean and it's difficult to hear, so faint. We all stop chattering. Strain to catch the words…

Tell Becky to watch Sandi.

"Why? Celeste, why? How?"

Lilith.

"But what does she want with her? How? I don't understand."

For several minutes the static crackles in my ears, but there is nothing more tonight; just a grid of shadows crawling slowly across the sheets.

***

Chapter Nineteen

October, 1583

There was a blood moon that October night, staining the sky in a palette of scarlet, orange and amber. On hearing a murmur of voices beyond the abbey walls, Magda shrank into the shadows, the shivering heat of fever now coursing through her veins.

Just a few short months ago she and Cicely had waited in this exact spot before stealing roses for the May Queen's crown. A fragment of memory lingered – Cicely's long golden curls coiling silkily in her fingers as she held her frightened sister with all the comfort of Judas. But this was no time for guilt. She did what she had to do to survive; and so it was again.

As the voices on the other side of the wall faded, she pulled the dark hood of her cloak down low, and crept around the side to where she and Cicely had found the low-roofed log store. An oak tree marked the place, its branches extending almost as far as the main archway separating the kitchen garden from the manicured lawns. It wasn't difficult to climb and turned out to be a good vantage point from which to observe the scene.

A file of black-clad figures appeared to be gliding towards a church next to the abbey. Ornate in design, the little, stone church was intricately adorned with carvings and gargoyles, surreal against the flame-red skyline. And to the side lay a tiny graveyard ringed with iron railings, its tombstones small and neat, set in lines. The nuns' soft chanting was simultaneously haunting and hypnotic as they floated towards it…and Magda watched, mesmerised. It was the first time either she or anyone she knew had ever actually seen the sisters. With the name of the abbey being 'Five Sisters' it was a surprise, therefore, to see so many of them…thirteen in all…

Seamlessly, the nuns merged into the dusky scenery, fingering pendant crosses, heads bowed in prayer. When finally the last of the blackbird figures had been swallowed into the dour interior of the church, pulling the solid wooden door behind her, Magda jumped down into the shrubbery.

All was quiet. The abbey windows eyed her darkly - inviting the imagination to wonder about the occupants and the daily life of these reclusive women. Rumour had it the sisters took in orphans from town who'd been found diseased or abandoned on the streets. Did these children lie behind the long line of narrow windows upstairs? Did they ever recover from their fevers and poxes? Or die in those dark dormitories, listening to the owls and foxes in the forest, knowing their imminent fate lay in the cemetery mere yards from the window?

Perhaps they were observing her now? She looked up sharply, half expecting to see a row of small, sickly faces. Alas, there was nothing but the dead-eyed stare of unlit glass.

Dusk was descending rapidly now in a smoky chill; shadows from the huge oaks and horse chestnuts spreading across the lawns. Cautiously, Magda emerged from her hiding place. Anyone peering out of those windows would glimpse little more than a fleeting movement, she decided, darting over to the kitchen garden. This was about survival and besides, what else was she to do?

The eyes behind her own instantly recognised the layout; and with the new intrinsic knowledge of where and what to harvest she set to work quickly, expertly snipping herbs and tugging up root vegetables. There was everything here she needed to heal herself, and more. Her eyes grew wide as she moved along the walls and down to the stream – deadly nightshade for the picking, hemlock and wolfsbane. What would the good sisters want with this kind of magic? Because there was an abundance.

The taffeta-rustling of the autumnal leaves and tinkling of the brook had muffled the voices but on hearing them she stopped and straightened up, listening intently – the sound like nothing she had ever heard before. A soaring requiem filtered into the perfumed air...the singing so high and pure...a choir of angels...

Candlelight had spilled onto the grass through the stained windows, the blood moon behind the church spire a deep, ruby red in the darkening sky: the whole, a scene of such heavenly beauty that it held her captivated. Although a wind had got up, she lingered, wandering around even as her throat prickled and her limbs ached. This was an affluence of staggering proportions – a picture painted in Sunday School of the Garden of Eden. Here was a fresh, clear stream edged with wild garlic, a duck pond, a well, and an overflow of chickens nesting in coops lined with fresh straw.

She eyed one of the coops, glanced briefly over her shoulder at the abbey windows, then reached inside the nesting boxes one by one until she found a smooth, warm egg underneath one of the brooding, grumbling hens; and dropped it into her cache. Sweat had surfaced all over her body in a fit of shivering, the fever now bedding in. She leaned against the wooden frame, nauseous and dizzy. It was time to leave.

Abruptly the singing ceased.

Magda looked over at the woods; at the grim, silent wall of trees. From within came a long, low whistle; the wind sweeping up a whirl of coppery leaves. She should not have left it so late. Something was wrong. Although itching to make an escape, instinct cautioned her to wait. There was another breath on the air. Someone else was afoot. She shrank further behind the chicken coop, praying she had not been seen.

At first it wasn't clear whether it was man or beast who hovered beneath the archway leading to the abbey. But with the blood-red moon lighting up the lawn as if it was a stage, whoever was there had little option but to sprint into its full glare, albeit fleetingly.

It was enough.

Magda's heart gave a sickening bump of disbelief.

What in hell's name would he be doing here at this time of night?

Inside the lead-crossed, upper windows of the abbey candles now flickered, and from her hiding place some of the occupants became visible. Her hand flew to her mouth. There were faces. Lots of them. Children. Maybe a dozen, maybe more, with their palms pressed to... no banging on the glass. At the same time as the man was running up the steps.

The evening was now damp and cold. She flew through the first archway to the rose garden, the scent heavy and cloying - a few creamy heads drooping like sad ghosts in the eerie light. Then with one last backwards glance she bolted under the next archway, across the lawns to the log-store, and scrambled over the wall.

Once over the top she lay on her back breathing hard, her head thick and muggy. Again there came a faint whistling from deep within the trees. What was that? Not an owl. Nor any creature she could make out. Nor was it human. But a constant low whistle that blew through the bones like an ill wind.

She hastened to her knees and ran flat out. The forest was not a safe place to be at night. Everybody knew that.

***

Chapter Twenty

Present Day

Four in the morning and Toby was driving Amy home from Woodsend. "Amy," he said. "I know you're half asleep but can you hear me?"

She nodded, keeping her eyes shut.

"Alright, well listen, okay? I'm dropping you back home and then that's it – I can't see you anymore. Firstly, I'm a copper and tonight I've seriously crossed the line. And secondly, to put it bluntly, I think you're fucked up and you need help. Girls your age should be out drinking and dancing and going to parties and stuff, not summoning up the dead in haunted forests and getting possessed by demons."

A sudden belt of thick fog hit the tarmac, reducing visibility to almost zero and he slowed right down, frowning with concentration. Inside the vehicle it was warm and drowsy and initially it sounded like Amy was snoring.

It was a shock to realise she wasn't. She was laughing, snorting with it.

He shot her a brief sidelong glance, reluctant to take his eyes off the road for so much as a second. "What's funny?"

She hadn't even opened her eyes, still semi-reclining and snuggling into the travel blanket he'd covered her with. "You. Like you think you can just finish with me."

The reflective glare of headlights in fog was blinding. Gripping the steering wheel he changed down through the gears until the car was crawling along. "Do you know something, Amy? I was seriously worried about you back there. I thought you were ill or you'd gone mad. Now I see it was just another bloody prank to creep me out because of what I've been through. You're an evil little bitch, do you know that?"

She threw her head back and laughed raucously, thumping the seats with her palms.

"Fucking hell! You're as mad as a shithouse rat."

Amy wiped her eyes with a manicured finger, still smirking. "You are like, so easy to wind up, Mr PC Plod. So, so easy. But no, actually that's not what's making me laugh. Take the next left turning by the way, it's a short cut."

He took the sharp fork as indicated, the fog now a dense cloud as the climb steepened. For a while there was a feeling of time standing still, the car no longer moving – being locked into a special zone of hell with a scary, crazy girl he barely knew. She oozed malice, sitting there chuckling to herself. God, how he'd love to just tip her out right here and now.

Why had he automatically done what she instructed and taken this road, anyway? The main drag might be longer but they'd have been dipping down by now. Yet without question he'd just bloody done it.

"What is it then?" he said. "What is it that's so hilarious you've made yourself cry with it?"

"It's just that you think there's a way out. There isn't, you see? You can't just drop me off home and that's it. You're one of us now."

Obliged to concentrate on the road, he struggled to comprehend. "What the hell are you on about?"

"I mean, that you will be escorting me to a party tomorrow night. You will arrive at nine so we can have sex and a few drinks first; then we'll go down to the party. And, oh yes – you will come. Do you want to know why you'll come?"

He laughed drily. "There's no way I'm going anywhere with you ever again, Amy. Dream on. God, I'll be glad to get off these blasted moors."

"You'll come because if you don't I will make a phone call and tell a PC Plod at the desk that you raped me tonight. I've got the bruises to prove it and I've already sent the incriminating pictures to a very close friend, who will vouch for how traumatised I was. There was also a video camera in my bedroom. Do you remember smoking that joint, drinking, then jumping into your car afterwards? Oh, everyone saw you…my parents have quite a house full at the moment."

The car veered wildly into the oncoming lane as he almost lost control. He could no longer see the road at all, not even the white lines up close at snail speed; but it would be even more dangerous to stop – especially with her as a passenger.

He tried to find the words, "Hang on a minute – raped you? What the… That's not the way I remember it, Amy."

"Really? Well it's all there on tape – how you leapt on top of me calling me a whole load of disgusting names."

"My God, you nasty little–"

"Bitch? Yes, along those lines. All documented, Toby. And I was so upset about it, as you can imagine; what with you being twice my size and me not being able to do a thing about it after you spiked my drink. You really took advantage of me and that was unforgiveable. Wait a minute, would you like me to sob and show you how I do this? I'm the most amazing actress – super convincing."

Her words knifed into his reality. Without doubt she would carry out her threat. He was finished.

Putting her feet up on the dashboard, Amy casually lit a cigarette and blew out smoke rings. "Bet you'd love to punch me in the face?"

"You have no idea."

"Have you ever hit a woman?"

"Of course I bloody haven't."

"Have you ever killed anyone?"

"What? What the fuck is this? Of course not."

At long last the road levelled and soon began to dip. He wiped the sweat from his forehead. "Amy, why would you do this to me? What did I ever do to you to deserve it? Surely you wouldn't want to be with someone who doesn't want to be with you? Can't we just leave it here?"

She answered in a sing-song voice, "Oh no, sorry. No can do."

The T-junction caught him by surprise and he slammed on the brakes. "Which way now – left or right?"

"Left."

The signpost to her village swirled into view. Good, thank God. Less than half a mile to go before he could drop her off and never see the loony cow again.

"I don't understand."

"Oh, you will. Like I said – come over at nine tomorrow and then you'll see. Hang another left again here, that's it. And you will come because if you don't I will sue you for rape and assault, and I do have a whole lot of evidence as I said, not to mention friends in very high places. So don't risk it, sweetie. Go straight over at the junction. You'll know where you are then."

Seconds later he drew up outside the imposing wrought iron gates to her family home and jerked the car to a halt. "Get out."

"See you soon then, lover boy."

He watched her saunter towards the gates before turning to stare directly at him, her dark eyes gleaming in an alabaster, white face he now saw as monkey-shit insane. Christ, she was scary. What in the devil's name had he ever seen in the mad bitch?

She waved, then turned and sashayed down the gravel driveway to the mansion her parents owned, as if she'd had a perfectly normal night out.

***

You're one of us now...You're one of us now... You're one of us...

Five hours later he jump-started awake, looked at his watch and leapt out of bed. There wasn't even time for a shower.

"Take some toast with you, love," his mother shouted down the drive as he ran to the car. He darted back and grabbed it. "Love you, Mum."

"Love you too. Just take care now – you're tired–"

In his rear view mirror he saw her waving and raised a hand. Ten minutes – just enough time to brush his teeth, use the loo and get dressed. Madness. That bloody girl. Just his luck to meet a total psycho! And what the hell was that about being one of them? One of who? And why? What did she mean?

Snarled in traffic, he thought hard. What he had to do was keep cool, treat this like an investigation and look for clues, going right back to how and where they met. Look at it objectively; outsmart her, because something told him he hadn't walked into this by accident. So...he narrowed his eyes... stroking his hair back over and over... he'd been targeted then? And maybe she was just a puppet?

They'd met at a bar in town: one he and his mates frequented because after the pubs closed it was one of the few places that played great music but didn't charge the earth to get in, or hike up the drink prices. Another bonus was the kind of girls who went there. The club was underground, painted black and thumped with rap and base. She'd appeared at his elbow when he went to buy in the next round, gazing into his eyes while they talked, and he'd found it impossible to look away.

She was into dance, she said, shouting into his ear. "You heard of flexor dancing?"

He laughed, gulped down a whisky chaser. "Eh?"

"It's like African voodoo music – where you send yourself into a trance?"

"Oh yeah, trance dance?"

She shook her head, grabbed his hand. "Not like you mean. Come on, I'll show you, you're so gonna love this."

The traffic was inching forwards and he glanced at the clock. Shit he was going to be really late. "Come on...come on... the bloody lights have changed, you dozy fucker! Step on it!"

There hadn't been any clues she was into dark stuff, though. In all fairness to himself, he could not have seen this coming. He sifted through the memories of that night: the club had been dark with strobe lighting; the dancing frenetic, animated, and exciting. At four am they'd snogged outside in the gennel before she'd run for a lift with friends, and he'd dawdled happily to the taxi rank. After that they'd been out for a drink a few times and, yes, he'd told her a little about what he'd been through, but no names, no details... In fact, it really wasn't until the dinner date at Becky and Cal's that she'd shown the slightest interest in anything 'spooky' as she'd called it. God, that seemed light years away now.

Someone blasted the horn behind him and he jumped. There was quite a gap in front – he must have drifted away - something he continued to do all day: operating in a daze of taking calls, attending meetings and filing reports, while trawling through his memory bank. Was there anything, really, the tiniest of hints that could have alerted him to this? But there was nothing before that night at Becky's, and even that was just a bit inappropriate, nothing serious. Maybe she was one of those possessive, jealous bunny boilers, threatening him in order to get her own way?

That could mean having to move away, get a transfer…

For the zillionth time that day he glanced at the clock. Only this time the hour had come. Six o'clock. He grabbed his jacket. In three hours' time he was supposed to be at her place. Was she being serious, though? Should he take a risk and call her bluff? Who was she anyway – just some nasty little piece he wished he'd never met.

He had a good reputation - people who would vouch for him; hell – people who owed him. Cal and Sid would back him all the way. Maybe, just maybe–

His phone signalled a text had just come in. He picked it up.

'DON'T EVEN THINK ABOUT NOT COMING TONIGHT LOVER BOY OR YOU WILL SERIOUSLY REGRET IT!'

***

Chapter Twenty-One

The second he pulled up outside the house it was obvious Amy's parents were throwing one hell of a shindig. Well, if all he had to do was have a few drinks to save her the embarrassment of telling them she'd been dumped, then maybe it wouldn't be too much of a hardship? The more he thought about it the more he convinced himself that's probably all it was – a spoilt brat manipulating others to get her own way.

Well, think again, Amy!

He got out of the car, deliberately leaving it on the lane rather than buzzing for access through the electric gates. It was imperative to have his wits about him tonight because she could have something seriously horrible in mind, and a rapid escape route might be needed. A sudden vision of himself handcuffed to the bed buck naked made him shudder. He wouldn't put it past her.

Perhaps, he thought later, when he had so much more time to think than expected – he had been concentrating too hard on Amy herself, prematurely concluding she was just a problematic drama queen he would have difficulty extricating himself from. Whatever the reason, he cursed his own stupidity because he sure as hell plundered right through all the warning signs. And despite the night before, not to mention everything he'd witnessed at Tanners Dell, the fact that the outside of the house was lit up with red flames, giving the illusion it was on fire...passed him by. The fact that the woman who opened the front door was dressed as a dominatrix also passed him by. And the unusual interior of the hallway, criss-crossed in cobweb lace through which guests had to disentangle themselves, also passed him by. The party, he thought with contempt, was nothing more than an extravaganza for eccentric rich people who'd been at the dressing-up box. *Wankers, the lot of them.*

Until he was shown into the lounge.

He stood in the doorway with his mouth open, staring into a dark, candlelit room lined with mirrors. Good God, this was one hell of a freaky vicars and tarts do! The costumes were at best outlandish, at worst disturbing. There were women dressed as nuns but with bits cut out to reveal intimate body parts; some wearing plunging evening gowns with mad hatter headdresses crafted to represent birdcages or tropical gardens; another had a pair of horns on her head and very little else to cover her modesty. Mostly the men wore bondage gear. Some wore nothing at all. And every single person in the room had their face hidden by a mask. Masks which turned towards him as he stood there with a bottle of pinot noir in his hand, staring.

Perhaps he could, at that point, have turned around and fled? He would never know. But he walked into the room all the same, intent on finding Amy, having that one last drink, and then leaving.

A plastic face with a rictus grin swung round to face him as he passed through, the mask disconcertingly face-on even as he moved further in. Yet the man had not moved. He looked more closely, realising the guy was wearing four different faces, one for each side of his head. Nor was he the only guest to wear a multi-faceted mask – the same features but with different expressions – it seemed multiple personalities were all the rage; alongside masks resembling cracked dolls with an eye missing or a chunk of flesh gouged out. *What a fucking sick kind of party!*

One drink and he was going. That would be it. Amy could get over herself. Whatever she threw at him he'd handle.

Standing by the fireplace he scanned the room. 'Let's just get this done, Amy,' he was thinking. 'One drink and then I'm out of here.' Dumping the wine, he accepted an exquisitely presented cocktail in a long-stemmed, frosted glass from one of the young waiters. The colour of black cherries with a syrupy consistency, it slid congenially down his throat.

"Thanks, mate," he said, replacing it and taking another. Anything to lubricate the awkwardness of the evening. Anyway, they could afford it.

It really was one hell of a place, though.

That Amy's parents were well-off he'd been fully aware of; that the lounge opened into more and more candlelit, mirrored rooms, each darker than the previous one, was interesting. God, there were even mirrors on the ceilings; every wall covered in them; the whole giving the impression of a never-ending corridor filled with flickering flames and ghoulish masks. On previous visits he'd been whisked straight upstairs with only a cursory glance at what looked like a normal living room, albeit a large one with a marble hearth, a fully equipped bar and a cinema screen; but wow, this really was something else. The house must be colossal. Curious, he wandered further in, weaving through the hum of the crowd, accepting another sweet cocktail along the way. This wasn't so bad. Just wait till he told the lads back at the station about it. How the other half lived or what?

The adjoining room was long and narrow, painted dark red and adorned with the now ubiquitous mirrors. Chandeliers heavy with flickering candles had been hung in a row of three over the top of a polished rosewood dining table, set with a bizarre feast.

Toby stared so hard his eyes nearly popped.

Suddenly too hot, the murmuring chatter too loud, he swayed slightly. This was no feast. Lying down the length of the table on a bed of roses was a naked woman. She lay as if deceased, her skin a shiny, white porcelain; and her eyes not only closed but devoid of lashes and stitched up, as was her mouth. With thick black thread. And all around her lay dolls. Some of the dolls had been beheaded; others had their scalps removed, and some had the hair pulled out or fingers missing.

He whirled around to the sound of an outbreak of laughter, stunned to realise he was drunk as a skunk, giggling and unsteady. He shook his head as if to clear it. He'd only had two or was it three glasses of that stuff, but the floor had turned into a tightrope. *Whoa...time to go. Bloody hell – what had they put in those drinks?*

He scanned the room again. No, none of those were Amy – no spider tattoos on their arses. He giggled again, hand to his mouth like a schoolboy as he lurched from chair to table, and table to door. Nope, she wasn't here.

Going...going now, please...He'd turned up seeing as he'd been threatened, but no way was he going upstairs to find her.

Staggering back the way he came, he was, however, forced to an abrupt halt. That was funny - the doors were closed. He winged round again, disorientated. A cool breeze beckoned him through to the patio doors the other way. 'Presumably,' his muzzy brain thought, 'this would lead onto the lawn?' Good idea. Okay then, out we go this way instead...

"Excuse me, thank you, thank you..." Edging his way through the kinky bondage gear and nudity he walked towards it, candle flames dancing in the draught, and music now straining on the night air. It sounded like drumming with discordant strings over the top. *This was one weird freaking party...* He was giggling again but couldn't stop; lunged for a table to put down his empty cocktail glass but missed, and it smashed onto the wooden floor. He was giggling uncontrollably; vaguely aware now of a hand under his arm, steering him into, 'the garden room' as someone was referring to it.

The garden room. He stood swaying.

Well, that was funny because it was bloody dark for a garden room...There weren't any plants in here either. He smirked, spurting with laughter. It was totally dark so how the hell could this be a bloody garden room? Not very good for the begonias, was it?

The hand underneath his arm suddenly let him go and he slumped onto the floor in a heap. Ooh, no call for that...Now on his knees he tried to stand; and then it gradually occurred to him that it wasn't simply dark in here – it was totally black. Not only that but it appeared he was the only person in here. It took a minute or two for his eyes to adjust.

And when they did it was to see three silhouetted figures framed against the moonlit lawn, waiting for him to acknowledge them. Cloaked in black robes, their faces were hidden by hoods.

Behind him the double doors shut with a firm click.

"Hi, Toby," said a voice he recognised. "So glad you could make it."

He wheeled around to find Amy, a spectre in a sliver of moonlight.

"Awww…you came."

"What the hell kind of party is this?" he slurred, pushing her away.

Someone laughed nastily.

"Toby," said Amy, grabbing his hand. "You're just in time for the ceremony. We're almost ready."

And it was then, at that precise moment, it hit him. Game up. Snap.

Lumbering through the patio doors into the crisp evening air like a drunk falling into the street, treetops zoomed in and out of focus and he clawed at thin air in an attempt to stay upright. The drumming was louder out here, its rhythmic intensity increasing. Hands were shoved under his armpits, lifting his feet off the ground as tree trunks reared into his face and bestial creatures with horns danced in and out of focus like something from a medieval banquet. He laughed again, tripping over roots. *Wheee, he was flying, flying through a forest…*

Oh, it had come to an end.

So soon…

He stared out through a drug-induced fog of incomprehension, head lolling, vaguely aware his kneecaps had been slammed into something hard. A glimmering lake swam into view, moonlight rippling across its glossy surface. In vain he tried to keep his eyes open, registering vaguely that some sort of stage had been set. A play? A macabre kind of theatre?

"You're going to love this," said a female voice he thought might be Amy's.

His head swivelled around at the sound of her voice, in time to see a grim army of black-cloaked figures marching behind them. He tried to stand on his own two feet but couldn't - every attempt resulting in falling sideways - and something was cutting into his ankles. He looked down, realising with a stab of shock they had been bound together with rope. *When did that happen?*

Somebody wrenched his head back by the hair.

"Toby," said the same sugary female voice. "This is your initiation, darling. It's all for you. So you see – you really can't leave us now, can you?"

***

Chapter Twenty-Two

The Child and Adolescent Unit

It was late afternoon when Becky rushed into Reception to see Alice. Already the bedside lights were on, and the distinctive waft of chips told her evening meals were being served.

"Who asked you to come?" the receptionist asked. "Only there's nothing down here about a visit."

"Judy Harper."

"The receptionist frowned, tapping at her computer keyboard. "The psychologist? No, she's not left a note. Sorry, I can't let you in." Eyeing Becky over the top of her bifocals, she added, "And she doesn't work here anymore – she left. Didn't you know?"

"Yes, that's why she asked me to visit Alice. Well, could I have a word with the ward sister then, please?"

The woman shook her head. "I doubt it. Do you have an appointment?"

"No, but I really do need to speak with her urgently. Could you just ask her, please? Tell her Judy called and asked me to come over?"

The receptionist began to shake her head again, when Becky erupted. "Okay, look, I'm heavily pregnant, I'm dog tired and I've come a long way on public transport. I am Alice's mother's nurse, and I've been working closely with Judy, who rang and specifically requested my help. I have to talk to the nurse in charge."

"I'm sorry—"

"Would you mind just asking her, please? I wouldn't insist if it wasn't important. Please, at least give her the option."

The receptionist pressed her lips tightly together.

Becky stared her down.

"Right. Well. I'm sure she won't have the time, so don't say I didn't warn you. This is not hospital procedure, it really isn't."

Becky held the stare, slightly raising her eyebrows until the woman finally picked up the phone. "I don't suppose you've got a moment to see a lady in Reception have you, Isobel? She says it's important but… Oh, you have." She put down the receiver. "She won't be a minute."

"Thank you."

Shortly afterwards a petite blonde bobbed her head round the door from the ward. "Is it Becky? I've been expecting you – come on in."

"Blimey," said Becky as they marched down the corridor to the office. "I thought she was going to have me escorted from the premises by the gestapo."

The other woman laughed and showed Becky in. "Bit of a dragon, that one. Don't worry about it." She indicated an armchair by the window. "Take the weight off. Tea?"

"Oh lovely, thank you. Yes please."

"I'm Issy by the way. I saw you with Judy the other week and wanted to come over and introduce myself, but I got caught up with a problem. Sugar? Milk?"

"Just a tiny drop of milk thanks. I don't suppose you have any biscuits or anything–" She patted her bump and grimaced. "Sorry, I'm absolutely ravenous and I've had nothing much all day and then the journey up here straight after work and–"

Isobel laughed. "Yeah, sure. Chocolate Hob-Nobs do you?"

"Oh thank God, yes please. Honestly, I'd kill old ladies for them at the moment."

"No need." She passed her a new packet. "Take them - I'm on a diet and you know what it's like? You don't get a break, the canteen's closed and there they are – looking at you. And you can never have just one, can you? Anyway, I take it Judy told you what happened?"

"Only that she'd been suspended. She said Alice kicked off and she was blamed – something to do with her making things worse and encouraging Alice to produce false memories? She's extremely distressed and very worried, as am I. We'd only just started working together, pooling information and hoping to bring mother and daughter together."

Isobel handed her a mug of tea. "Hope that's okay?"

"Thank you." Becky took a sip. "Ooh yes, that's lovely. So what happened to upset Alice so much? Do you know what triggered it? Did she switch?"

"Well, a few weeks ago Judy said she'd seen a woman in the courtyard at the back of the unit. She described her but none of us knew who she could be and as you know, no one can access it without permission. We brushed it off, I suppose. But then yesterday she was apparently there again; only it wasn't just Judy who saw her this time. Alice saw her too. None of us knew anyone fitting the description but it sent Alice into apoplexy – screaming, tearing at her hair, running round knocking chairs over. According to Judy there was something about the wall - something written on it. In the end Alice had to be sedated and she's still up in Isolation."

"Was there anything... I mean, did you see anything significant on the wall?"

"Well, that's just it – only the usual scrawl – something any of the kids could have done."

"Can I see?"

"It's dark, Becky."

"Aren't there any lights outside? I'm sorry, I just really need to see."

"That's what Judy wanted to do as well, only first she went up to Isolation with Alice, which is where she bumped into Dr Mullins. They had quite a set-to – you could hear the shouting from here. He was having her removed from Alice's care immediately. She was in tears. To be honest with you, I felt really bad for her because she was the first person Alice had actually started to trust. It's a huge shame."

"Hmmm…interesting…so Judy never actually saw what was on the wall? Can I start there, do you think? Honestly, I know you're busy and I wouldn't ask but I think it could be important."

Isobel, Becky noticed, was one of those people who made sudden and definite decisions. Whipping a set of keys out of her desk drawer, she stood and motioned Becky to follow. "Come on then, let's go. Will you want to see Alice, too? Are you going to help Judy get reinstated – is that it? Or do you just want to reassure her Alice is okay?"

"The latter really. I'm not sure I can help her get reinstated unless she takes the matter further and I could put a word in. I'm here for Ruby, as well. I'm the only link she has with her daughter, you see, and I promised I'd look out for her, especially before I go off on maternity leave."

Isobel was clattering ahead down the corridor and onto the unit, ignoring cheeky comments from some of the teenage boys. "No, it isn't a bun it's a baby she's got, Gavin. It'd be a flipping big bun, wouldn't it?" She spoke over her shoulder to Becky. "We'll go out this way and lock the door behind us."

The outdoor courtyard consisted of a high-walled, small patio reached through a locked and bolted door to the side of the art room.

"Going dark early now, isn't it?"

Becky nodded. As far as outdoor recreational areas went this was pretty dismal, but someone had planted out a few tubs, and along with tables and chairs there was also a hammock swing and a tiny summerhouse with cushions inside. She walked around the perimeter, trying to work out what could be seen from where Alice would have been sitting behind the glass. The facing wall was red brick and clear of any graffiti. It wasn't until it tapered towards the window in an alcove that anything written on it would be seen, and that too appeared to be clean. She glanced back to the window to where she and Judy had sat with Alice that day, then back again, imagining a line of vision. There. She bent down. Yes, there was a smudge of what may have been chalk. Something had been written and then erased.

"Over here," she called to Isobel.

The two women examined it closely. "How long ago did this happen?"

"Three, maybe four hours?"

"Can you see anything definitive?"

"It looks like a few loops...but...yeah, scrubbed out. A leaf? Or is it a flower?"

"Hmmm, could be...There was definitely something there, though, wouldn't you say?" She looked Isobel in the face. "Okay, look, I'll admit I'm very worried and I need to bring you up to speed fast so you know why. And then I have to see Alice. I'm sorry, Issy, but I do – it's incredibly important."

Isobel regarded her intensely for a second or two, then nodded. Another quick but firm decision made, Becky noted. What a gift. She couldn't even decide if she needed a haircut sometimes.

They sat in the alcove, tucked into the shadow of the high security walls while Becky quickly told her about Woodsend, after which she confided her recent suspicions about certain members of the sect still being at large. "It isn't over is what I'm trying to say. There's a lot more I could tell you, but there just isn't time. The important thing is you've got to be on alert for any underhand tactics because I think Alice is still in serious danger. Judy was making progress and now she's been removed. That's what happens. Someone, somewhere, orchestrated this, I'd bet my life on it. All I'm asking is to be able to check Alice is okay from time to time; and if anyone strange comes to see her that you let me or the local police officer on the case know about it." She gave Isobel Toby's card.

Isobel turned it over. "Yes, I read about all this in the papers, of course – spoke with the child protection officer myself when Alice was first admitted. And I know Judy was of the belief Alice had suffered RSA...that she has DID and not post-traumatic stress–" She flushed, looked away.

151

"But?"

"But I'm as guilty as anyone for agreeing she go to foster carers."

"Oh, you mustn't blame yourself, Issy. It's hard when you've got a consultant over-ruling you. What's he like anyway, this Dr Mullins? I don't think Judy rated him."

Isobel lowered her voice to a whisper. "Oh, he's quite nice actually, charming you know? New. The other one, Dr Lowry, retired suddenly about six months ago and in stepped Leslie Mullins. He'd been working out in America and Australia - by all accounts at the top of his game. Come to think of it the problem between him and Judy was no doubt exactly that - a clash of egos. He's very ambitious, you see, and my guess is he didn't want someone else taking over Alice's case, someone with more specialist knowledge and experience than him, especially with it being so high profile. Anyway, he's of the opinion that Judy was forcing false memories to surface and it was dangerous. According to him Judy destabilised her when she should have left this to him. I don't know what to think – I'm just trying to keep the peace."

"Isobel, Alice was doing really well with Judy, and her memories are very similar to Ruby's so I'm not at all sure why Leslie Mullins would say they were false? And how is sending the child to a foster home in the village she came from, not dangerous? I think I'd better tell you a bit more–"

***

Ten minutes later Isobel was bounding up the stairs to the isolation unit, with Becky gasping for breath behind her. Neither spoke. Both kept checking over their shoulders.

Alice was in a padded room, heavily sedated and bound with restraints to stop her from hurting herself. When the women walked in, she opened red-rimmed eyes swollen from crying, her focus entirely on Becky, who had knelt down next to her.

"It's okay, Alice," she said gently. "You've had a scare and I understand that – I would have been scared too."

"You okay for a bit?" Isobel said. "Only I've got a situation on the ward. I'll be back as soon as I can." She threw Becky the room key. "I'm trusting you, Missus."

"Thank you." She turned back to Alice. "Shall we take off these horrible things from your wrists?"

Alice stared back.

"Are you with me, Alice?"

Almost imperceptibly, Alice nodded.

"You don't have to trust me, or anyone you don't want to, okay? But I have a very good idea of what you've been through because I know someone who's had similar experiences. I've been her friend for a few years now. She's funny and she's clever. I like her ever so much. You remind me of her, do you know that?"

For a while Becky chatted about ordinary daily things, reassuring Alice that she'd just been talking to Judy, and that Judy was very well and had asked about her.

"Shall we have something nice to eat? Would you like one of my biscuits? I've got them because I have a real baby coming soon and she's making me hungry."

Alice took one but let the chocolate melt in her fingers.

"Alice, I haven't got a lot of time to talk to you today, but I did want to tell you that I understand how scared you are. Sometimes we need to be scared in order to be aware of danger and you've been very, very clever, just like the friend I was telling you about, in dealing with that. But I can tell you this – whoever you think is trying to get to you will not succeed. They are not in here. They are out there and we will find them. I promise you we will find them."

"Find who, Miss…er…?"

He had not made his presence known with even the slightest pad of a footfall and her heart almost missed a beat.

For a moment, however, Becky did not turn around to answer because the look on Alice's face told her something more important. The man standing behind her was not to be trusted.

His tone hardened at her lack of response. "I said—"

Becky pushed herself to her feet, giving Alice's hand a small squeeze. The child's grip was like a vice so she kept it there, letting her hold on. God, what she'd give to be able to sweep this girl up and run out with her in her arms.

"I heard you," she said over her shoulder. "Just give me a minute, I'm struggling."

Silhouetted in the doorway he cut a slight figure as he stood coolly waiting, impatiently observing her discomfort.

"I'm the consultant here - Dr Mullins. And you?"

She got to her feet in a rather more ungainly fashion than she would have chosen.

"Mrs Ross - the ward sister up at Drummersgate."

"And your business here is?"

"Just a moment, let me say my goodbyes." She turned round and bent so that her face was skin to skin with Alice's cheek. "Alice," she whispered, acutely aware of Mullins' frustration that he couldn't hear what she was saying. "I'll get rid of him. And I will see you again very soon."

Alice began to cry and work herself up, the nails gripping into her hand so hard it hurt.

"Do you see what you're doing?" Dr Mullins snapped. "We had her calm and under control. You and that other woman are doing nothing but harm. In my office. Now!"

Alice's eyes suddenly rolled back into her skull, guttural noises croaking from her throat. *God, where was Issy?*

"And get those restraints back on."

Just who did he think he was talking to?

In the absence of any professional authority, Becky decided to ignore him and stay with Alice until Isobel returned. "Alice, it's alright. Alice, it's okay."

It seemed like an age. Alice had clearly switched - a pretty nasty alter now in her place.

Dr Mullins had started to creep forwards, his shadow looming. Still Becky hung on, guarding Alice, holding both her hands until at last Isobel's scurrying footsteps could be heard rushing up the stairs.

"Issy, she was okay but–" The words died in her throat as her eyes met Mullins'.

His expression bore no emotion whatsoever. "My office," he repeated.

With one last glance Becky handed over to Isobel, then turned to follow him down the corridor.

Leslie Mullins' office was at the opposite end of the building in the old Victorian quarters, and he set off at a pace with scant regard for her condition, leaving her little option but to trail after him like a naughty schoolchild. Passing through several sets of double doors he shot down a flight of concrete steps to the basement, with Becky struggling to keep up. Breathless and annoyed she scurried behind his long, flapping coat as he strode through the connecting corridors past the laundry and various store rooms, eventually emerging into an empty tile-floored reception area marked with the chipped paint of neglect. This had clearly been the original psychiatric unit, now housing offices and typing pools; all deserted at this time in the evening. Overhead fluorescent lighting buzzed and flickered on low wattage.

As she stood behind him, out of breath, waiting for him to unlock the door to his office she looked around. They were quite alone down here.

He let himself in, holding open the door for her to follow with one finger.

"Come in, come in – take a seat."

He didn't take off his coat, but sat down at his desk, neatly crossing one long, thin leg over the other, and folded his arms. "Tell me again why you're here, Miss…whoever you are–"

Odd accent. She couldn't place it. Ignoring his instruction to sit, she towered over him. "Allow me to educate you then. I'm Alice's mother's key worker. I've been involved with Ruby

Dean for over two years and she's extremely concerned about the welfare of her daughter, who as you know was recently rescued from a satanic cult–"

"Allegedly a satanic cult – nothing proven, eh?"

"Hell of a lot of evidence though, Dr Mullins, and both mother and daughter suffering from DID. It's taken me six months to get any decent kind of contact here and finally Judy and I met to discuss the case and were making excellent progress. Now I find Alice has been distressed by something she saw in the courtyard, where she should have been safe, and Judy has been suspended. That is why I'm here."

"Ms Harper has been suspended for reasons other than Alice becoming distressed by something that is not there, Miss–?"

Becky saw his mouth twitch with annoyance as she deliberately began to scan his office, looking at certificates and photographs.

"Ms Harper was suspended for professional misconduct; for what is known as inducing false memories. And my staff are doing an admirable job of keeping Alice Dean calm and helping her with her speech. In my opinion she does not have DID but that, frankly, is none of your concern. You have no rights, absolutely none, to be on my ward and I do not expect to see you here again, do you understand?"

Becky's gaze settled on a family portrait. The house in the background was a serious Georgian pile by the look of it - Mullins grinning at the camera, one arm around a tall, dark-haired woman so bizarrely dressed she had to be in the fashion world; the other around the waist of a pale, skinny teenager in a crop top – presumably his daughter. Her focus flitted back to him as he finished speaking. A sense of deep unease crept under her skin: there wasn't a shred of humanity about him.

"I don't think we have anything more to say to each other," she said. "Good-bye."

Leaving the door wide open she hastily retreated down the tile-floored corridor, enjoying the loud click-click-click of her echoing heels and the slam of each door as she left the building through the main exit at the back, and out into the car park.

That girl.

Once safely outside she stood among the parked cars, grateful for the nip of autumn air cooling the sweat on her face. If she wasn't mistaken and she was pretty certain she wasn't – that was Toby's girlfriend, Amy.

***

Twenty-Three

Noel woke to the full heat of an electric fire on his face.

Disorientated, he pushed away the blanket that had been pulled up to his chin and swung his legs over the side of the sofa. A carriage clock ticked steadily on the mantelpiece. He stared at it. Was that the time? Seriously? A wide grin spread across his face. It was six in the morning, which meant…Oh, thank God and all his angels…that he'd slept since yesterday afternoon. *Slept...*

He turned off the heater, watching the orange bars fade, click-click-clicking as they cooled, before standing and stretching…still smiling…*He'd slept*…How bloody fantastic was that? God, how we needed sleep – and how utterly wretched we were without it.

The house was silent as he padded into the hallway; the streets outside still glistening with last night's rain – a blank canvas waiting for the paint of daily life.

Hoping not to wake Harry, Noel softly closed the kitchen door behind him and switched on the kettle, assuming the other man wouldn't mind if he made tea and toast. Starving didn't cover it. But, oh man…he couldn't keep the smile off his face…And not a single bad dream, nightmare, demonic voice in his head; nothing. Why, though? What was different about being here?

As he poured bubbling water onto a teabag, the question was uppermost in his mind: *why*? Had it been the fact there was a cross on the wall? Or that Harry was a priest? What was it? Because for some reason he'd been totally free of the terror, which had plagued him since the night they'd exorcised Kristy. A terror which had escalated to the point where he craved the oblivion of annihilation; had started to feel anger with a god who could leave him to suffer like this; and had even, almost, been prepared to surrender to the one who promised both relief and reward.

"Caught you!"

He jumped, swinging round with a piece of toast in his mouth. "Bloody hell, Harry - I didn't hear you." He laughed, whizzing round the kitchen finding plates and setting the table. "Want some tea?" He gestured towards the kettle. "Just boiled."

"Yes, please. Just let me flick the heating on."

Ambling back a minute later as the antiquated boiler clunked, groaned and reluctantly fired into life, Harry said, "The one problem with these old houses is they take a king's ransom to get warm. I take it you slept well, then?"

"Magnificently. I feel almost human – amazing - thank you. What happened? Did you slip something into my drink?"

Harry laughed. "No, nothing like that. I said a few prayers for you, that's all."

"Magic. And frankly I don't care what did it because it worked. I feel like me again. Really, it's incredible."

"Yes." Harry sat opposite him, buttering a slice of toast. "But Noel you need to care what did it, because I can't be here all the time and you have a life to get on with. The minute you leave here you will be attacked again, you do know that?"

"It was just such a relief, I'm sorry – it's sheer elation."

"They'd like you to think it's over, that there's no problem anymore, but I'm afraid what you're feeling is a false sense of optimism. You badly needed a night's sleep in order to have the strength to face what's ahead, but the danger – similar to only taking a day or two of antibiotics instead of the full course - is that you will feel miraculously cured so you don't need to do anything else. But you aren't. We have a huge amount of work to do yet, and if we don't do it the demonic will return; probably ten-fold."

"I'd give anything just to walk out of here and go back to life as it was, but yes, I know you're right. Okay, so what happens next?"

"Well, you know what they say? There's no time like the present. While you were asleep I organised something for today, later this afternoon if that's okay? I've got a full service this evening but we need to do this before then and it will take a few hours. I have a strong feeling we mustn't delay."

"A few hours? Really? That long? It's not like what Kristy had, is it?"

"No, but we have to start getting you prepared. Your job is to be in as good a shape as possible, remember? Because you will need to be – by that, I mean well rested, strong and determined. I have people coming out of their way to help us and so I'm asking you to do your bit, Noel." He stared directly into his eyes, the piercing blue steady and focused. "You must be one hundred percent on board with this, so any doubts you have about going ahead, let me know."

Noel nodded. "There is no doubt."

"Sure?"

"I swear."

"In that case I need you to do exactly what I ask. Firstly, stay here and get plenty of rest, drift off, sleep if you can and eat well. Also think hard about what we talked about yesterday. You have to fully want deliverance and you have to fully repent of any residual negative feelings you may harbour; and most of all have faith in our Lord Jesus Christ that He has the power to do this. I can't do it, no man can, only God can deliver you."

"I do have faith, yes. I saw what happened to Becky and I saw what happened with Kristy. Nothing will ever be the same for me again. It's shaken me to the core, shattered me."

Harry nodded. "You don't have to be religious or follow any particular teachings, I should be clear on that; just be in touch with your true spirit and believe in the power of God."

Noel nodded.

"Good, well we're halfway there. I'll need to give you some instructions but I have an overwhelming feeling of urgency. There's something really nagging at me…To be honest it was my turn to sleep badly." He drained his tea, put down the mug and stared hard again at Noel. "You haven't dabbled in the occult, have you?"

Noel frowned and shook his head. "No."

They sat in silence for a few minutes, until Harry suddenly stood up and pushed his chair back. "Right, best crack on. I've a few errands to run first. Then when I come back we'll have lunch and a little chat about exactly what happens before we pop down to the church."

"I'm going into the church for this? Oh, I thought it would be here?"

Harry sat down again. "Does that worry you?"

"No, of course not, I'm just surprised. I thought you would do it here, privately, like a kind of therapy or counselling session."

"No one in their right mind would perform a deliverance on their own outside a church – it's far too dangerous. There needs to be three of us, and we'll have an entire team of people in another room praying throughout."

Harry's gaze had fixed on something above his head and Noel glanced over his shoulder. "What? What is it?"

The other man looked uneasy.

"I'm getting a headache. I don't feel well. What is it? What's going on? Can you see something? Oh my God."

Harry was transfixed. Without taking his focus off whatever it was, he answered slowly and carefully. "Noel, because of what we've been through together and because of what you do for a living, I'll tell you if you insist, but I wouldn't advise it."

"Yes, too right I insist. What is it? Can you actually see something? What's happening? Harry, I'm scared."

"You have a dark shadow behind you, Noel. These things can attach themselves physically like creatures doing piggy-back – weighing you down, affecting your thoughts and your feelings – but you can't see them because they're on your back. We must not be afraid, though, because they are as nothing and we can and will cast them out. Have faith."

Abruptly he stood up. "Right, it's nearly seven already – got to make a move. Feel free to use the bathroom and have a shower. There's a new toothbrush in the cabinet - just make use of whatever I've got."

He turned to leave, got as far as the door and then hesitated. "Noel. Promise me you will not go anywhere while I'm out? Don't let this thing win. You are a good man and we need to do this. Hang on in there, okay?"

Noel nodded. "If I hadn't seen what happened to the others I'd probably be legging it by now, you're right. I'm not daft, though. I'll stay here, I promise."

"Good man. And hopefully when I come back you won't be smelling like a farmyard animal anymore, either?"

Noel laughed, stroking his overly long stubble. "I'm so ashamed. This could not be less like me. I'm known for being so scrupulously clean I squeak."

"Exactly."

Sobering in an instant, Noel searched Harry's eyes. "I don't think I realised how bad it was. You don't, do you? You cope and keep going for as long as you can until–"

"Until you either give in, or stand and fight?"

"Yes."

***

It was four in the afternoon when Harry's key turned in the lock. Noel sat up from where he'd been dozing on the sofa; startled to find the bright morning had been replaced with the insipid greyness of a dull afternoon.

Harry strode in. "We're going to have to get our skates on. Sorry, it's been one of those days – laden with fools' errands; appointments made and cancelled, waylaid at every turn, and two of our prayer team struck down with the flu. The main service is at six as well, but come on – we're ready for you now, me lad."

Soggy yellow leaves clamped to their ankles, a cacophony of bells chiming through the chilly air, as the two men hurried down the stone steps towards the church.

"Have you had a good think over what we talked about yesterday?" Harry asked.

"Yes."

"Did you find yourself rebelling at all? Trying to justify any of your feelings?"

"God, yes. Sorry, I mean–"

Harry laughed.

"Yes, I did get a surge of rage when I thought about the bigotry, the high-handed piety and sheer hypocrisy of what my own family said to me. But then, you know, what others think or say isn't anything I can control. Anyway, I've truly let it go; and to be honest, bearing grudges or trying to change other people's attitudes isn't going to help me now."

"Exactly. So there's no lingering anger?"

"No, none."

"What about bitterness? That you were excluded from family events and didn't get what most people take for granted? Do you still feel cast out? Isolated?"

"I feel sad about it sometimes, but not bitter. It's their loss." He laughed.

They had reached the old Gothic church where Noel had waited in vain to see Michael at the end of last year; the one he'd brought Becky to when she needed him most. The lych-gate creaked on its hinges, above it the inscription, 'Grant O Lord, That Through The Grave And Gate Of Death We May Pass To Our Joyful Resurrection.'

As they passed underneath, the traffic noise became markedly muted. There was, Noel thought, an unearthly stillness about the place. Lichen-coated tombstones stood in the damp, autumn afternoon exactly as they had for centuries. And again there came that crawling feeling in the nape of his neck. Instinctively, he glanced over his shoulder towards the oldest part of the graveyard, to where a cluster of moss-coated Celtic crosses was slowly sinking into the earth. A row of yews lined the perimeter, the branches bowed and heavy with rainwater; and abruptly he turned back - remembering all too vividly the night a ghostly figure had been standing there with a black dog, observing him intently.

Harry pulled a ring of keys from his pocket and opened the wooden door to the vestry.

"We'll go in through here."

Behind him, Noel's steps slowed and Harry looked round. "Are you okay? What is it?"

Noel was drained of colour. "I don't know - I feel rough – really rough, like I've got the flu or something. Maybe when I'm better – next week?"

"Don't let it win, man. We have to do this."

Noel's stomach twisted into knots and his legs dragged. "I don't think I can."

"Keep coming. Have you got any pain?"

He put a hand on his stomach to indicate where it was, finding he couldn't speak. Then to his abject horror, on sight of the members of the prayer team waiting for him inside, a tirade of profanities flew out of his mouth. "Oh, my fucking, good God! What's this then? The fucking, happy-clappy band?"

"Start now," Harry instructed the others, reaching to pull him through the door.

Noel clung onto the frame, gagging with nausea, the muscles in his face contorting with spasms.

"Come on, Noel. This isn't you, we know that. You must not be afraid. Trust in God. He has more than enough power for this; and just think how well you'll sleep and how good you'll feel when you are rid of this parasite."

Noel stood in the doorway, soaked now in sweat, fighting down an overwhelming feeling of vertigo and sickness.

"One more step, Noel. Come on. Make your body do it."

He nodded. Then threw himself into the church and immediately crumpled to the floor, the hard parquet slamming into his hip.

"Somebody help me get him on a chair."

He came-to for a second, finding himself bent double with his head between his knees. Someone was telling him to take deep breaths.

"I'm going to be sick."

The world turned black.

When he came-to again Harry was a blurry figure in front of him holding a cross. Noel's head lolled as he lurched in and out of consciousness, sweating profusely, his heart banging too hard and too fast - the caustic stench of vomit and urine searing through his senses. Something was digging into his wrists – had they tied him to the chair? He tried to stand, an animalistic roaring resounding in his ears.

"Noel, stay with me. Look directly at me."

His eyes burned, unable to focus. "I–"

"Look straight into my eyes no matter how difficult it is and don't speak unless you need to tell me something. If you feel anything rushing up from your throat let it come. If it's full of profanities don't worry, we've heard it all before. Just let it come out and then let it go. Nod if you're with me."

He nodded.

Harry then began the rites of exorcism.

A tiny part of him, the essence of his soul, immediately shrivelled into a tiny shell somewhere deep inside as the storm raged around him. Silently he prayed – reciting over and over, The Lord's Prayer. *Please God, please bless and save my soul...*

Miles and miles overhead, coming as if from the surface of a vast ocean, voices that were not his own screeched and roared, screaming around his skull in a chorus of scathing hatred. The chair on which he sat rocked violently, slamming repeatedly onto the floor. Still he clung on. Still he prayed. And still he trusted, hoped and kept the faith.

Until all concept of time had vanished; and it was dark; soft, velvety and quiet.

He opened his eyes. A tiny light flickered in the distance and he focused on that until it made sense. Candlelight. It was a candle. And he had died. Had he not?

***

Chapter Twenty-Four

Ruby
Drummersgate

It's the time of year that seeps under my skin, reawakening the old things…that smell of decay and chimney smoke mixed with damp leaves…still grey days, candyfloss mist wrapping round the trees...That's all it takes – the turn of the season – and I'm back there. Crouching behind the ring of oaks, tiny as a mouse, watching the hooded ones dance and chant, torches aflame… wanting to see what they do… needing to know, keeping out of sight, out of mind…

But she smells me on the night air, turns with a smirk on her lips.

"Bring her out!"

Think of something else, something else, something else…

The waxing moon is travelling across my window in a ring of radiant gold; eventually reaching the right hand corner, swallowed then by clouds. Tonight is one of those bonfire-scented nights, shrouded in fog, dampness heavy in the air. Curtains are drawn early, lamps switched on. We must keep the darkness away.

It's coming, though.

She feels it too, I know she does. A prickling urgency.

"Did you lose time again, Ruby?"

What?

I see one of us is blinking, trying to make sense of the moment. Who am I? Where am I? Isn't it dark? Wasn't it dark just now?

This room is painted stark white with colourful pictures on the walls. It's hot in here – too hot – overheated, and blinds filter out the light of a sunny day; the sky such a deep blue you could dive right into it and somersault with joy. Too beautiful, too exquisite. It causes pain.

I'm aware now of vacantly staring at the woman opposite. My hand is holding a paint brush.

"It was nice of Jes to send you a red rose, wasn't it? Was it Jes? He was your boyfriend, wasn't he? How lovely! Is it a special anniversary for you two or something? Ruby? Are you with me? Am I speaking to Ruby?"

A rose? What rose? What's she talking about?

She is right though, whoever she is, to ask if she's speaking to Ruby. I think it might be a while since I was in the driving seat. The chatter has been nonstop inside here because we've been discussing the message – the one from Celeste – but we can't remember it exactly. Have we given it to this woman? I know her well, don't I?

"I'm Amanda, Ruby. Don't you remember me?" She smiles slightly, a cool, elegant blonde with slender hands and a nose slightly too long for her face. The white shirt threw me. For a second there I thought she was an official, but it's okay, I recognise her now. God, that took a moment.

She passes me a fresh piece of paper. "Show me again, Ruby. What is it about the rose? I don't quite understand."

There is something about this rose then. I'm blank on it. And then whoosh…my hand flies across the paper.

"What's this?" She frowns and picks up the drawing.

One of the others must have done it - sometimes I don't understand what happens - but we know, we know about this rose, don't we?

Suddenly there is an interruption. The door behind clicks open and a shadow falls across the paper, blocking the light.

"What the hell's she doing?"

The very sound of her voice makes me flinch, and just as my hand reaches out to snatch back the paper, Amanda smartly folds it in half.

Thank you… thank you… Amanda can be trusted. We can trust Amanda… It filters down, my words echoing through the system.

The fear of her, though, triggers a switch. Too late. It happened the second that bitch came into the room.

No, not yet, it isn't safe.

"Will someone stop her doing that?"

"Ruby, Ruby, come back to us. Sit down, please. Ruby, it's okay."

But it is not okay. *When you get a rose… has she had the rose? Someone sent us a rose…*

They know where we are. That's it. They know where we are and what we are thinking. And they know where Alice is. There is no escape, not ever, and now they have sent in this spy, this bitch from the coven. They are coming for us. It's started.

Stopping dead, I suddenly realise I'm in the middle of the room staring at two people, one sitting down and one standing up. Who are they? A blonde lady and another one – the one with eyes like flints of coal.

"It's all right," says the blonde lady. "Ruby, you are safe now."

"Ruby's not here," says Eve.

The one with the hard eyes is watching us, her lips forming words only I can hear. The voice is deep, echoing far back in time like a slowed-down record. "It's time to go home now, Ruby. We've found you. You didn't think we'd let you go, did you?"

I have to go away now. I have to go to the park.

"You know what happens if you betray us."

Four and twenty blackbirds baked in a pie… hmmmmmmmm…

The blonde lady fades to a dot - down there from my bird's eye view - clearing away the desk, glancing at her watch, throwing things into a large bag. She shares a quip with the other one, laughing as if she cannot see what she is, as if she cannot see the sludge-dark aura around her and the empty pit of her eyes.

"Ugh, that infernal nursery rhyme..." says the demon. "She's off with the fairies again, isn't she?"

The blonde lady turns to Eve and smiles. "Eve – is it Eve I'm talking to? I'm off home now, love, but I'll pass your message to Noel, I promise."

My head is shaking.

"What message?" says the other. I can see her skin hardening and cracking, the hissing serpent uncoiling inside her.

The blonde lady continues to gather up papers and we hold our breath. Will she remember to do it? Or will she betray us?

The bitch is glaring at her, silently demanding a response, when Eve jumps up and rushes towards the television set, railing at it, shaking her fists and screaming.

It's all she needs - Amanda scoots out of the door without replying. Good. She has the message I gave her for Becky. I did it. She's got it and she knows to keep it from the other one.

But now the doctor is coming into the room for Eve.

"What's she doing on the floor?"

"I think her therapist upset her. Honestly, she's totally unmanageable and we're very short staffed."

"Okay, I'll give her an IV sedative. Then we'll have her in Isolation, I think."

"No, she'll be fine in her room," says the demon. "As long as she's sedated I can look after her."

***

170

Chapter Twenty-Five
October

Toby sat on the edge of his bed in a state of shock.

Suspended from duty following an allegation of rape, he had also been removed from the Tanners Dell case, with no further access to the report he'd been finalising for the trial. In answer to his concerns, the official response was the team had all they needed from alternative sources, the work he'd done so far being sufficient; although he would still be called in as a witness for the crown prosecution. That was it.

On top of that, every attempt to contact both Sid Hall and Callum had been ignored; their respective mobiles either switched off or going straight to voicemail. He'd stopped ringing days ago. No doubt they believed Amy? Or they'd had orders not to interfere. Either way it made no difference now.

He closed his eyes, bowing his head. So what the hell happened next? Maybe this is how criminals felt? Once they'd broken into a house that first time, snatched a purse or even pulled a knife? Once they'd done it and stepped over that invisible line, they joined ranks with a different set of people holding a different set of rules. Life was never going to be the same again for sure.

Downstairs, his mother was clattering dishes in preparation for the evening meal. Even she was terse with him, a hint of suspicion in the brittle atmosphere while she busied herself more than usual. Surely she of all people couldn't believe he was capable of rape? His spirits plummeted.

She'd done a good job on him, had Amy: a tearful, fragile looking thing covered in bruises and nasty scratches, armed with a video showing an indisputably, brutal sexual assault. He couldn't have done that. It could not have been him… and yet his face was there for all to see, and it sure as hell looked like he did.

He put his head in his hands. Well, he was finished then, wasn't he? Totally fucked. There was no coming back from this one. Like, who in hell's name was ever going to believe the good doctor and his daughter wanted him removed from the Tanners Dell case in order to protect their satanic coven? That they wanted to bind him in and shut him up? He almost laughed. Certainly not that fat, fucking judge who'd conducted his initiation at the black mass three weeks ago, raising his fist into the air to hail Satan. The bastard presided over the family courts, deciding who children should live with, how other people should behave and who should have what.

The other problem was that the whole thing sounds so outlandish no one believed it actually happened: these are human beings and humans don't do this kind of thing! And not only are they human, but professional, intelligent, well-bred humans responsible for the welfare and smooth running of a civilised society we take for granted. To ask anyone to start unpicking that, to tug loose the foundation stones of their core existence, was nowhere near as easy as convicting a young police officer of rape, especially when the prosecuting lawyer has a solid base of evidence before him.

Yeah, they'd sewn him up just as tightly as if they'd cut out his tongue. Like poor Alice.

He lay back on his single bed in the room he'd grown up in, watching the rain set in. The leaves were falling steadily now, fluttering from barren branches silhouetted against a battleship sky. It would be winter soon, and somehow that seemed fitting. The colder and bleaker out there the better. He put his arms behind his head and closed his eyes. At least he'd been allowed home: one small consolation hard won by his defence lawyer, and thanks largely to his clean character references and impeccable history in the police service.

Men didn't cry, eh? A single tear dripped down his cheek and he smeared it away, then another, forced to give up as more and more brimmed over until he was wracked with sobs. Even if he got through the trial and came out the other side, he would still never recover from his so-called initiation. Nor could he tell anyone. Not a single soul. Ever. That's what they did, how they tied you in for life. And probably even beyond.

It replayed in his mind on a miserable carousel and probably always would. Every time he relaxed, dropped off to sleep or simply closed his eyes it would be there - waiting; only ever on pause, never on stop.

Dusk snuffed out the afternoon mizzle and the bedroom darkened. Flitting in and out of sleep, the horror movie of his downfall resumed, as it would a thousand times more…over and over and over…As always, the second he slipped into the replaying of it, he tried to wake up - whimpering, pleading with himself not to see it all again…

But once more it is black dark on the edge of those moors, treetops spinning in a silvery kaleidoscope, the intoxicating smell of incense and bonfire… Suddenly pain shoots up his neck…Someone has his head wrenched back; rough hands hauling him to his feet, dragging him along by the armpits towards a stage. Huge flames leap skywards either side of a podium set with an altar; a wooden cross towering at the back.

It is a nightmare. He will wake up. Wake up…wake up…

Pain again – shooting across the side of his head as it impacts with hard earth, thrown to the floor in front of the altar like a carcass of meat. Someone grabs his hair, jerking back his neck. His eyes are taped wide open. Just so, he assumes, there'd be no chance of him missing a darned thing.

No, no…not again, not again…no…

A monotonous humming is rising in strength and volume, boring into his brain, drowning out thought. Fighting to keep his mind both sane and alert, he inwardly cites the words of a song he knows word for word – one his dad used to play when he was a kid, 'Baby we were born to run…' The boy inside sings it repeatedly, determined to stay conscious. It is a nightmare now and he must wake up…must wake up…must wake up…

The searing pain of a needle punctures a blood vessel in his arm, jerking him violently awake. Has he lost time? Helpless, he watches a cannula being inserted into the vein, followed by the contents of a large syringe injected into his system. The blood vessel aches, screaming as if it will burst as the drug now shooting into his circulation burns its way to the heart. The pain is too unbearable to take and someone, presumably himself, is crying out for God.

The world turns black.

Once more he comes-to, his head throbbing, the bones of his skull banging in sickly waves; taped-open eyes smarting and streaming. Flames are leaping into a smoky sky and macabre creatures with the heads of animals dance frenetically on stage, grunting and cavorting in crab-like movements, heads swivelling to unnatural angles on the stems. A tribal witchdoctor's face suddenly looms into his, its body scuttling sideways again, fast as a spider.

There are stars up there somewhere. Gradually, his eyes adjust to the stinging smoke and he forces himself to admit that yes, this really is happening. And no one is coming to save him, either. This is it.

Oh dear God in heaven, please just let me die…don't make me watch what's happening here… I know what these people do. Please…

The atmosphere is now crackling with anticipation; the chanting a clear demand, like a pop concert where the rockstar's name is shouted to get them on stage….yes, they were calling someone, repeatedly reciting a name: *Baphomet… Baphomet…Baphomet…* in a fever of excitement, stamping feet, making hissing noises.

Then abruptly the dance stops. The creatures vanish and a deathly hush falls on the crowd. There isn't a breath on the air; just the faint lapping of water and a silky rustle in the trees.

So intense is the dark silence, it is as if he is alone, staring into flames that are slowly scorching his retinas.

From deep within the forest a bell now tolls: a sonorous tone that resonates through the night with funereal sobriety; a fading echo that falls once more to silence.

Clearly what the crowd have been waiting for is now imminent. They know what it is. He does not. Fear catches in his stomach.

What the fuck's coming?

Several more minutes pass, with the collective presence finely and attentively attuned.

Then he hears it. They all do. A low, ominous growl – something that sounds inhuman - possessing many voices - and which grips his insides in a terror such as he has never known. Desperately he tries to avert his eyes, to not see whatever horror is about to emerge from the blackness of those woods; while the crowd behind gasps, some with their hands clasped gleefully, excitedly.

The growling becomes louder, emanating from every direction; a surround sound in conjunction with a gale force wind now thrashing its way through the forest, flattening branches and snuffing out the flames.

His burning eyes stream. Impossible as it is to blink, he has the misfortune of being able to see someone, or something, begin to materialise from out of the smoke. And as it speeds into its diabolical existence, both pillars of flame re-ignite. Unable to look away, unable to not see - this is the image, which will forever haunt him, appearing in every nightmare, recurring dream and waking thought he will ever have from hereon in.

Before them stands a man wearing a pointed black hood and robe, the shaded face one of such malignant loathing it makes him physically and mentally buck with revulsion – the impact so shocking he can barely comprehend it.

What in hell's name…?

The man placates the crowd with long-fingered hands, a black-toothed grin cracking open a deformed skull much larger than that of a normal human being. There is something else horribly unnatural too – an overpowering smell of a wet dog. The jaw seems to jut out and sideways, his movements oddly jerky, as with a multi-throated roar he lunges for the long, silver sword lying on the altar.

Raising it to the sky the demonic choir of voices roars, "In the name of Satan, ruler of the earth, I command the dark forces to bestow their gifts. Open up the gates of hell. Come forth from the abyss and grant us our indulgences. We have taken thy name rejoicing in fleshly life. Come forth and answer to your names… Baphomet… Mephistopheles…"

With each demon named, the crowd echoes his commands; until finally every demon has been called and the thing on stage summons forth its henchmen, who stand by like executioners. The crowd now breaks out of its obedient reverence with fervent shrieks, as the next set of entertainment is brought forth. A wide-eyed drunk is being led in by scantily clad women dressed in leather bondage. Toothless, unkempt, and afflicted with a red, blotchy complexion, the guy, Toby assumes, is most likely a vagrant.

The thing on stage is breathing so heavily its chest rattles like a bubbling sewer, drool running down reptilian skin to the thick, sprouting hair on its neck. With revulsion Toby notices the hand holding the sword resembles a long claw coated in thick dark fur – just as the hapless victim is flung in front of it.

No, this wasn't going to happen… it couldn't…

The menacing voice rises theatrically into the darkened sky. "Behold…the gates are open!"

A gladiatorial roar goes up from the crowd.

The sacrificial victim appears bemused, half-laughing as if he's a star turn in a comedy, and then he looks up and sees the sword, the masked men either side of him, and at the same time as Toby - the cameras zooming in for a close-up. Realisation sweeps across his face. His entire body bucks and kicks as he squeals in the dirt like a stuck boar, his cries pitiful and painful to the soul.

Vomit gags in Toby's throat, the ropes lacerating his flesh as he fights to save the man. But there is nothing he can do. Absolutely nothing. As the man is tied and hoisted upside down by the ankles onto the large, wooden cross. As his throat is slit and his jugular spurts out pints of ruby-red blood that sprays out in a fountain. And the chosen few dart forwards to fill their cups, guzzling fresh arterial blood like greedy vampires, before holding aloft the dripping goblets, gashes of red seeping down their chins.

"Joy to the flesh forever!"

"Hail, Satan!"

"And let the black slithering shapes of the underworld spew forth slime from hell and delight in this victim I have chosen."

Suddenly the focus switches to Toby. And the henchmen begin to walk towards him with slow, ceremonial purpose.

Is it his turn now? *Oh my God.* Was this what Amy meant when she said it was all for him? He tries to pray, to think of the words…

They pick him up by the elbows and haul him up the steps to face the vile thing on stage. "Dear God, please help me, Our Father who art–"

It is impossible to avert his taped eyes from the creature's hypnotic stare, and his prayer falters, failing in a brain that will no longer work. The cold metal of a sword is rammed into his hand and for the briefest moment his skin makes contact with those claws. An electric charge bolts into his heart. Then one of the executioners kicks him in the back and he stumbles forwards - eye-to-eye with the dead tramp.

The man's face still stares in bulbous-eyed terror at his unexpected fate.

"Pierce his flesh and cut out his heart. You will start the feast. I command you."

The shaking starts in his knees and works its way up, racking his whole body. "I..I..can't…"

"Or we will cut out yours."

His raw, burning eyes focus miserably on the corpse, the stench of defaecation and fear overwhelming; cameras whirring in closer.

"We will feast on flesh this night and then you are bound to us. Your mind will be opened to the power that awaits you beyond this life, beyond this universe. After which you will never leave the path of adversity – the greatest power ever known. Now, I command you in the name of Satan – cut out this man's heart!"

Someone shoves him in the back again; then another grips a hand over Toby's on the sword, forcing it to pull back high into the air, before plunging it into the muscle and bone of another human being.

Immediately the cry went up. "Hail, Satan!"

"Cut out his heart. I command you."

The knife now hacks through the skin - gristle and bone splintering apart as it cleaves into the blood-soaked flesh.

"Now eat."

The flesh shoved into his mouth is warm, chewy and sickening. It sticks in his teeth, lodges in his throat and oozes down his chin.

"Swallow."

Retching, gasping and spitting out globules of human flesh, he is glad of the dark hood then rammed over his head - the rope being tied round his neck, a relief.

"Now take him to the basement and get him ready."

***

Toby lay in the dark. He'd missed dinner. How could you eat when you'd been force-fed a human corpse? How could you watch television like you were normal, listen to music or read… or be interested in anything ever again?

His mobile beeped. He stretched out to see who it was, surprised to see how many calls he'd missed in the last few hours. Maybe he'd slept? That was the thing, it was hard to know if he was dreaming, recalling reality, or making it all up.

Scrolling down the list of missed calls, he frowned. There had been a sudden surge of activity as if his life had just been plugged back in. Becky. Noel. Callum. Sid Hall. Any number of his mates. Becky again. Noel. Urgent. Urgent. Urgent. He tossed it aside. Not that he could reply to any of them; that had been made abundantly clear.

In the first few days following his arrest, he hadn't quite understood that the world as he knew it was finished. But he did now. During those days in the basement he'd been assured there were eyes everywhere on the outside, but he would never know who or where they were. The police. The hospital. The courts. The media. TV personalities. They looked after their own and he could be a part of it. That was his call. He could be a part of it or he could be dead.

For now he would be allowed home to his parents on the clear understanding he would not be writing up any reports and would not be contacting anyone.

He looked again at his mobile. At all the calls from Becky, Callum and Noel, and his heart reached out to them. These were the best people in the world yet he couldn't speak to them or see them ever again. He had to let them go.

The phone lit up and beeped once more but he ignored it, turning away onto his side.

Later he would see it. Much later, in the quiet, blue-grey hours of dawn. That's when he would read the single line that would propel him from suicidal depression into action.

'**ENJOYING THE RIDE**?
Sender: Ernest Scutts'.

***

Chapter Twenty-Six

October, 1583

At three am Magda woke from a feverish sleep to find herself lying in a pool of moonlight on the hard oak floor. Shivering, she swallowed another dose of the pungent liquid she had concocted the previous evening. Both the ingredients and the knowledge had been instinctive; and now as she stood in front of the ornate mirror that hung over the fireplace, she knew without doubt she had been here before. These were not her eyes. Her body yes...but that was merely a vessel now for the power that would come - the power needed. Her fever raged, the pink spots on her cheeks burning a hot, bright fuchsia.

"Show yourself, Witch. Come to me."

Her pupils were tiny, black pinpricks in the moonshine.

"Come to me. I command you – come to me. I do not fear you."

The silence of the empty house seemed to mock her childish voice. She clenched her fists. "Show yourself! Show yourself!"

Still there was nothing. Hushed whispers taunted her from the darkened corners of the room as moonlight moved across the window; and a peal of mocking laughter tinkled on the icy air.

She's going to die...she's going to die...

Glaring into the pits of her own eyes, she shouted, "Where are you?" This had to happen. It must. "Do not forsake me now!"

Images flashed into her mind – of William coiling his fingers through the red curls of Lisbet's hair, of Ambrose complacent by the warm fire...of praying to God with tears streaming down her face, but with no help and no response. He didn't even exist. It was all a big joke. From deep within her a volcanic rage erupted. Picking up the glass vial she had just imbibed from, she broke it over the hearth, slashed her wrist and daubed the blood across the mirror. Then with her forefinger smeared in the name, 'Lilith.'

She stood back. Looking at the unknown name. Her lips flickered into a smile. Then the smile broadened. The words. She knew them now.

They spewed from her mouth, "Ad ligandum eos pariter eos coram me…"

Now… now she would come.

"Ad ligandum eos pariter eos coram me…"

Staring through the blood-smeared glass she kept her eyes focused. Her face had begun to change shape, another one sliding in. A slither of apprehension crept under her skin….*She was coming…* It was real. This would happen. Witchcraft…delicious, wonderful ancient witchcraft…This existed. Oh, those fools. This was all…everything…Without taking her eyes away for a second, the vision now began to alter by degrees…. lips twitching, pupils shifting shape, glittering now with an alien energy sparked with red and silver. Fear licked alongside the excitement.

"Come to me, give me what I need. I see you now. Come to me."

Her stomach quivered, fingertips tingling.

Then suddenly the pupils flooded to limpid pools, rippling outwards to swell the whole eye like black ink spreading over the surface of a well. A surge of power thumped into her heart, sending waves of pure hate charging through her veins."

"Who are you? What is your name?"

As if in answer, a light breeze brushed the hair from her face, pulling her gaze from the mirror, before a violent shove threw her physical body aside.

Slumping to the floor in a pile of sodden rags, Magda's conscious mind was instantly erased. And another world began.

The cottage door inched open to reveal a shaded garden crammed with foxgloves, hollyhocks and lavender. The feet beneath her were lifted from the ground, carrying her out of the door and down the path towards the oak trees at the far end; floating over the style and through the wood in a re-enactment of that evening's steps.

This time it was not, however, to the abundant garden at the abbey. This time she was to climb over the side of a stone wall into a cold chamber that echoed and swilled; the air dank and putrid. Lowered on a creaking winch by invisible hands, she watched the stones become increasingly dark, the surface slimy with moss, until the winch lurched to an abrupt halt and the small pail swung alarmingly into the side. Her long, gnarled fingers were working quickly now, knew what they were doing, blackened nails scrabbling at a crack just large enough for a small vial to be pushed inside; to where no living soul would ever find it.

This is my will… this is my will… so mote it be.

When the dream broke, it left her body twitching on the freezing floorboards; and her soul weighted down with a feeling of endless doom.

She lay blinking in the ethereal dawn, aware in the deepest part of her that the thought was cast and the deed was done. The price though… Ah, the price…

***

A sharp rap on the door roused her. Daylight. Deep blue light shone through the burnt crimson of the sparse leaves still clinging to branches; a blinding sun radiating through the forest.

Magda pushed herself to kneeling position and stared at the door. It was shut and bolted. She tried to think. It must be late afternoon. Stretching out limbs rigid with cold she immediately felt at her forehead. It was cool. She lived.

The rap on the door came again; insistent this time – the person on the other side clearly determined to get an answer.

She frowned. Who could it be? No one had lived here for years and no one knew she was here. *Had she been seen?*

Crawling on her hands and knees to the wall separating the living room from the kitchen, she peeped round the corner. A face was pressed to the kitchen window and her eyes widened in disbelief. Oh no - her mother.

Another pounding on the door and a rattle at the bolt, "I knew it. Magda, I can see you. I know you're there. There's only you mad enough to stay here on your own at night. Magda, I have to speak to you – it's for your own good and it's urgent."

For a moment she sat motionless. Waiting. For what? For the voice inside her to tell her what to do? Nothing came. In the distance, the far distance, the sound of melancholy church bells pealed through the air, plunging the swelling feeling of doom inside her to greater depths. Her mother's voice reached out to a girl she used to know - to a child who had once run home with a bowl full of plump blackberries, the juice smeared all over her face; then later, with the mouth-watering aroma of hot pastry wafting from the range, had sat at the kitchen table with her sister, pressing leaves - Cicely with her tongue out in concentration…laughing at her…

"Magda! You have to know. Magda!"

The door inside her snapped shut and a peevish sneer slid across her features. *What did that infernal woman want?*

Hauling herself to her feet she lifted the bar across the door and faced the woman who had brought her up: the woman whose eyes used to shine whenever she looked at her; but who now reeled back in revulsion.

"Oh my God." She crossed herself.

What the hell did she do that for? "What is it? Where did you expect me to go?"

"Oh Magda, you look awful. I didn't think that… I mean I thought you'd go to the next village and find work or–"

Magda glared.

"I heard you'd been seen in the woods… Look, there's no time – you have to know – Lisbet Miller was found dead this morning and they're coming for you. She'd been hiding in a wardrobe but they say her eyes were almost clean out of her skull with terror. They're saying it was witchcraft – someone who took a handful of her hair; some of her nails had been pulled out too. Covered in scratches she was, like the beast himself had been at her. Magda, some say they saw you."

Magda laughed, about to shut the door.

"No." Her mother rammed it back against the wall. "Listen to me, you foolish girl, it's important. There are things I didn't tell you but you have to know, I see that now."

"You can't help me. You have no power."

"You want to know who you are, don't you? It would do you well to listen, my girl." With an almighty shove the bigger woman muscled into the cottage kicking the door shut behind her. "I'm going to tell you now what happened here, to the witch who lived here all those years ago. You knew it was haunted here, you knew that? I didn't think you'd do this…" Her gaze travelled to the oaks at the bottom of the garden. "They hanged her. The mob hanged her right there, Magda, and all she did was try to help folk with healing."

Lisbet was dead…

"Magda, what's wrong with your face?"

Her hands felt at her features. "What do you mean?"

Her mother's eyes mirrored the horror of what she saw. "You seem to have aged, lost all your colour, your eyes are red raw, and you've got sores… It's only been a few days and yet–"

"Why do they say it's me?"

"Ambrose and William are telling folk this is witchcraft. The crops are blackened. Lily Moorcroft's child fell from his crib and broke his neck after she walked along the river the other day. The cattle have fallen sick and now this. They're saying it's you – that you are the one who should have been the May Queen; and now the whole village has been cursed."

"And I'm supposed to have killed Lisbet? On what grounds? What evidence do they have?"

"That you are a witch and they will have you out for trial. Magda, you have to run."

"What do you care, Mother?"

Her mother glared. "I lost my only daughter, Magda. Cicely was my own flesh and blood and you took her. But that doesn't mean to say I don't care, that I don't have feelings. I brought you up from being a baby."

"You said there were things you hadn't told me, that I needed to know. Is it just that this cottage is haunted by a witch so people are saying I must be one too? Is that it?"

"She wasn't a witch to start with."

"Who?"

"The one afore you." Her mother checked over her shoulder again and then again, listened for a moment, then said, "Look, there isn't much time." She grabbed Magda's shoulders. "I used to come here, to the woman who lived here. I couldn't conceive, hadn't for years and feared I never would. I was desperate but she worked her magic – took locks of hair and mixed her potions, buried them over there by the oaks. When they were coming for her I still hadn't conceived and so I took her child on – out of kindness for the poor babe, who was only a few months old and such a pretty thing. And because of all she'd done for me."

"The child was me, wasn't she?"

"Yes. Your mother's name was Magda so I named you the same in her memory. Her spells had worked, you see? Because only a few weeks after she'd gone, I discovered I was with child. I gave birth to Cicely, and then had my five boys. The Dean family will live on now, and it's all thanks to her."

"So who was my father?"

"Him at the mill."

"What?"

"Yes, that was the scandal you see, the one no one could know? William Miller had his own woman hanged, calling her a witch and a liar just like all the rest…but you could see – anyone could see…You've got those dark, slanted eyes of his–"

185

"But, I don't understand–"

"Magda was one of the sisters at the abbey. It was a disgrace, so of course they couldn't marry. And she was barely out of her teens. He ruined her; taking her to the mill like all those other poor children. Oh, he gets rich on those takings, you mark my word."

Magda sank against the wall, sliding down.

Her mother crouched level with her, on her haunches. "Do you think we don't know how well those nuns live? Do you think we don't know how they're paid and who by? It's him and Ambrose. They take those children and use them for whatever depraved things they do down there in that basement. That's another reason he wanted her hanged - once he found out some of us were going to her, befriending her... thinking she might tell one of us eventually, I suppose? He'd kept her quiet until then." She nodded towards the sideboard and the gilt-framed mirror. "Gave her those from his place. Mind you, she never liked the damn things. Said the mirror gave her nightmares. God rest her soul."

Magda's stomach churned with acid.

"I don't know how they live with themselves mind, those God-fearing women up at the abbey. They should be praying day and night for what they do." She glanced at Magda's bump. "It'll be Ambrose's I expect, that child, will it?"

Magda stared back with hollow eyes.

"You see now why I couldn't tell a young girl this story? What goes on at Tanners Dell is evil, Magda. I had to make you go away once I knew what you were playing with. We can't stop it, though – there's not one of us in the village who could ever breathe a word. So much as catch William Miller's eye and next thing you know you've got the devil himself to deal with."

Magda's voice seemed to her own ears, to be very far away. She watched one of her small, pale hands reach out to take her mother's rough, calloused one. "Why didn't my mother like that mirror?"

The older woman shrugged. "I'm not sure. I came to her one day and she'd changed, said she'd seen a face in it not her own. It was soon after that the folk in the village started gossiping about her. She told me the parson we had back then had been calling on her, that she'd given him short shrift after he'd come looking for what he shouldn't, but they said she'd cursed him and a few days later he died and cries of witchcraft went up. I'm guessing William was too close to the flame and, well, it was him who led the mob."

A twig cracked nearby and they both swirled round, squinting into the glare of the low autumn sun.

"Magda, I have to leave now. Take my advice and run. William Miller is a powerful man – a judge now in Doncaster – and he and Ambrose are stirring up a witch hunt so you need to go."

"Witch hunt? But they can't do that. There's no proof - nothing."

"Oh, my dear. 'Tis enough an area is cursed, that people die of hunger and the plague spreads. You have a mole on your thigh – the devil's mark. And they're saying you've been seen by the orphans in the abbey grounds. One of them, aged five, says he lies with fever because you looked up and gave him the evil eye. There've been a lot of deaths in that abbey, a lot of burials in the cemetery. The word of a small child is ample. These are extremely dangerous times, daughter. You have to run for your life."

"But where will I go?"

"The sisters might hide you. They're your only hope."

She hesitated. "But they would not protect me. They don't protect the children."

"Only because he would hang every last one if they ever breathed a word of it."

"So why would they help me?"

"Guilt. For what they let happen to your mother. The abbess...go to her. But go now. Quickly. She remembers. She will hide you."

"I–"

Her mother stood up, her glance darting back to the window. "Go now Magda. If the mob find you they'll hang you high."

***

Chapter Twenty-Seven

Jasmine Cottage.
October, 2016

The old couple in the end terrace had been having a bonfire, the acrid smoke from burning leaves still lingering in the foggy night air. It was not unpleasant. Becky sat downstairs with the kitchen window open, delaying bedtime and wondering if Louie would ever come back. Probably not now. Once again Callum had been called away and wouldn't be home until morning, so here she was facing yet another night alone. A barn owl screeched close by, and she bent to turn down the range. Well, there was no putting it off; if she didn't lie down soon she'd have to sleep where she fell.

With considerable trepidation she climbed the stairs. Rarely a night went by now without a pulse-racing terror that woke her soaked in sweat. Every single damned night, and it was wearing her out. If it didn't sound so silly and far-fetched she could swear the woman in the mirror had slipped into her mind and was haunting her from within. It happened the second she closed her eyes; at first just an awareness similar to that Noel had described, of a body staring down at her from the ceiling; followed swiftly by overwhelming panic, and an urgency to wake up because the white-eyed witch was sinking towards the bed. She could smell mould, decay, and unwashed skin; would move her head from side to side, away from the fetid breath exhaling in her face, the strands of hair swinging onto her forehead, the fingers touching the sheet, pulling it back...

The entity, floating over her body like a cold mist would then begin to osmose into her body; a feeling of sour malice crawling under the skin with such evil intent it froze her to paralysis. Becoming progressively harder as the fatigue deepened with every passing nightmare, was the fight to surface, wake up, and reach for the light. It left her hyper-ventilating, with her heart racing to near fibrillation. And sure as hell it would happen again tonight.

Exhausted, Becky reached the landing and peered into the moonlit bedroom. What if she didn't wake up in time? If she hadn't the strength left? What would happen then?

Close to tears she admonished herself. Oh, for Christ's sake, she could hardly go to a doctor with this. It would be her pregnancy, her hormones, depression and psychosis. Yes, psychotics thought their demons were real when they weren't... Yes doctor... three bags full, doctor... I'm taking the tablets you prescribed to knock me out, doctor, which means I won't wake up in time to stop her possessing me and now I'm certified insane... Thank you, doctor...

Ignoring the bathroom mirror, she brushed her teeth, cleansed and moisturised, all with her eyes tightly shut. No way was she going to see that woman in the mirror again. No freaking way. Oh dear God, would this ever end? And now Molly was at risk too according to Celeste. Imagine telling the doctor that! Yes, a deceased woman told my mentally ill patient that my child would be attacked by a mythical demon. Wouldn't they just have the baby off her within hours of being born? A single tear dripped down her cheek and she swiped it away. What in heaven's name had she ever done to deserve this? But of course the answer to that was clear as day, wasn't it? Whatever had been sent to attack her had waited patiently, and now Molly's birth was imminent. Her heart skittered in her chest as the full impact hit her... Wouldn't that be the ultimate revenge?

**

Keeping all the lights on, Becky got into bed and propped herself against a stack of pillows. It had been a very difficult day and her mind was still whirring. After the contretemps with the deeply unpleasant Leslie Mullins, the first thing she'd done on getting home was call Judy to relate what had happened.

"I'm not far away, actually," Judy said from her mobile. "I drove down to Sheffield to see my solicitor and I haven't set back yet. Well, to be honest I'd like to have a proper chat. I don't want to drag you out again so how about I come over just for a–"

"Yes, please," said Becky. "I think that'd be a great idea."

In the end, Judy had stayed for hours, the two women thrashing out their suspicions over countless cups of tea followed by one of Becky's signature risottos, after which a picture of the situation emerged that neither had expected, and which shook them both to the point of disbelief.

"If that is the case and our hypothesis is correct," Becky said, "then as the only member of the original team to survive Ruby's exorcism, I'm seriously unlikely to come out of this alive, and nor is Molly."

Judy's frown deepened as Becky told her what had happened that afternoon. "And his daughter's seeing Toby," she said. "She behaved quite oddly when she was here, as well. And now Toby's refusing to take my calls. No, something isn't right – it isn't adding up. There's something we're missing but I just don't know what."

Judy nodded. "Well, I'm determined Alice will not be left alone with Leslie Mullins. Actually, I had my suspicions from the start – not I might add that he was involved in Satanism – just that I didn't feel he was either competent or caring enough. Anyway, as you can imagine I'm taking legal action concerning his wholly false allegations. I have not practised hypnosis. Nor have I asked her leading questions: Alice drew and re-enacted what happened to her totally voluntarily, and was only just beginning to open up."

Becky nodded. "His accusations are without foundation. But why would he do that? I hope to God he isn't in on this sect. Jesus Christ. Do you think he could be?"

Judy blanched visibly. "Alice's programming seems to be more sophisticated than Ruby's, doesn't it?"

Becky nodded. "So as the organisation grew in size they recruited more knowledgeable members? Maybe Crispin

191

Morrow knew enough but people like Mullins specialise in this stuff. He knows exactly how to treat Alice, which is why he's doing the opposite."

"That would be my guess. I think the paedophile ring attracted people involved in various professions, and with the aid of the internet started to include some serious players. So yes, someone knew that children protect themselves with disassociation, and they also knew exactly how to manipulate that. For example, they encourage the child to tell a person dressed up as a nurse or a policeman. That person would have said things like, 'You're safe now. You can tell me everything, I want to help you.' The trusting child would tearfully spill the beans and subsequently be punished unimaginably for the betrayal. We would be talking about having to kill another child; or be locked in a coffin full of spiders and snakes for hours. Maybe days."

"Oh my God."

"So the lesson is learned and learned well: you must never ever trust anyone, especially in a uniform. There are eyes everywhere. We see you. We read your thoughts. We have a micro-chip in your brain that will relay all your thoughts to the Fathers. This is further complicated by implanting codes that will make the victim return home and 'tell' – such as a certain set of numbers or a set day. And this is what got me fired I think. I couldn't say over the phone but I saw a drawing on the wall at the same time Alice saw it. It was a rose on a stem with one leaf. I also saw the girl who did it. Someone must have let her in."

"Was it the same one as before? Did you recognise her?"

"Yes. I'd put my life on it."

"Young. Dark hair. Skinny?"

"Yes."

"Did you ever go into Mullins' office on the ground floor and see his family photos?"

"Once but I can't say I looked at the photos."

"Because that does sound like his daughter, Amy."

"She's probably a victim too, you know? Or a programmer. All of which explains that once I saw what triggered Alice's meltdown and who did it, they would want me the hell out of there."

"But why are they coming for Alice? I mean, what can she possibly do to them?"

"That's what I'm wondering. They certainly want her back in their clutches, which is why of course, she was fostered out. It's obviously a lot harder to get her out of a secure unit swarming with nurses and security cameras. I really must have put a spanner in the works. I still don't see why they would want her back, though? They've made it so she can't talk and put one of their own in to guard her, so as you say she's hardly likely to tell her story."

"I suppose a lot of work was put into her. If she's like Ruby she's a medium too – a channel for all those dark spirits they want to invoke?"

"Hmmm… Becky, I've only skimmed the surface telling you about the work I did with Alice. Don't be… Oh God I'm not even sure… Well yes, yes, I have to. Look, nearly all of what she drew and re-enacted was to do with dolls, hangings, beheadings and blood-letting. I am pretty sure that children kill other children in that sect – that's what binds them into believing they are just as evil as their captors. And I'm also sure they're forced to torture each other. Stay with me on this. Alice's baptism, which you say was foiled mostly by you and Toby, would have been planned for her thirteenth year, and that, I'm afraid, might well include the murder and cannibalism of a new-born. They use them all the time."

The colour drained from Becky's face.

"The thing is, Alice repeatedly drew a picture of a demonic looking woman with bulbous, white eyes; supposedly a demon woman from biblical times who brings death to pregnant women and the new-born. I never believed in all that tommyrot but these people do and that's what's worrying. Anyway, it's just occurring to me that part of Alice is programmed to get out of there for a certain date and she knows where to go and why. A part of her is going to do it and she will be helped. I know she's been told that when she receives a rose it is her call to go."

"Does she have to physically receive one?"

"I've told Isobel not to pass it on if one comes for her. Issy knows how serious this is."

Becky sat in shocked silence, digesting the implications.

Judy squeezed her hand. "I can only guess it's revenge for exposing the cult in Tanners Dell. Maybe the blood of an enemy's child would enhance their black magic?"

Becky's hands were shaking so badly now that Judy clasped them in her own. "I've been successfully stopped from helping Alice. My only hope is that Isobel and her team keep her safe while you and I figure out what to do next. And this is all supposition, of course. You have every right to tell me to leave if I've scared you half to death."

Becky almost laughed. The flesh and blood threats she could cope with. "No. No, stay. There's a whole lot of stuff I think you ought to know, anyway."

After another strong cup of tea – how she'd longed to open a bottle of merlot – she made the risotto and told Judy just what had happened to the team following Ruby's hypnosis at the tail end of last year. "So you see why I don't take any of this lightly."

"All those coincidences people just write off...I can't tell you how many accidents I've had recently , how many calls I've had taking me away from Alice on false pretences, and how many illnesses and bad dreams left me so I couldn't function properly."

"Bad dreams?"

"Nightmares, to be more precise – that there's someone in the room watching me while I sleep. I can smell them. It's like cauterised flesh or extremely strong tobacco smoke, or a filthy public toilet. Honestly, I sometimes think I'm going mad."

"You're not. Judy. Do you want to stay here tonight? I'd be ever so grateful if you were in the next room."

"No, love. But thank you, it's really kind."

"No, it's utterly selfish actually, but I know what you mean – it's nice to wake up in your own bed."

"Becky, all I can do is my level best to get reinstated and offer you my listening ear at all times – any time of the day or night. If you need me, I'm there. It's going to be difficult getting to Alice now, but Isobel's agreed to meet me after work so I'll keep tabs on her that way. What about you? When are you due?"

"Not for ages. November."

"Which hospital?"

"Doncaster. I was only going to take the minimum time off but it's been harder, physically, than I thought, so I've booked annual leave to run into it. I've finished now. Bit of a concern because Noel's not well, but I've hired an agency nurse, Sandi, who seems efficient enough; and our psychologist, Amanda, is back so at least Ruby's got someone she can relate to. Frankly, it's a godsend Amanda turned up like she did."

"Has Ruby continued to make good progress?"

Becky nodded. "Yes, very. She's identified a lot of her alters and they talk to each other inside her – it's quite amazing. A fascinating subject really, how the mind works, how it's protected her soul, the essence of her. She's clairvoyant too. Can you imagine not being sure of who you are, and you've got voices speaking from the inside plus others from the outside? She's a true miracle."

Judy smiled. "You're very fond of her, aren't you?"

"I adore her. I'm worried sick about leaving her for three months, to be honest."

"I think she'll be fine. Does she still ask about Alice?"

"God, yes. Actually, she's very agitated at the moment–" Becky stopped mid-sentence, her mouth dropping open.

"What, what is it? You look like you've just seen a ghost?"

"Something else is bothering me. The thing is, neither Noel nor Toby have been answering any of my calls. I've been ringing them both for days now and left tons of messages. I particularly

195

wanted to be able to reassure Ruby before I went off. But I've had absolutely no replies. Nothing. Nada."

"They're both grown men and probably very busy. Try not to worry about everyone, Becky. Worry about yourself and Molly." Judy stood to put on her coat. "Where's that husband of yours, anyway?"

"Away again and that's what's just occurred to me."

They stared at each other for a significant moment. "Removed," said Becky before Judy could voice the thought. "You know how these occult circles work, you know what they do… someone has been sending him all over the sodding country from one wild goose chase to another. Someone in the police force."

"Fuck."

Becky raised her eyebrows. It seemed odd a word like that coming out of Judy's mouth. "Yes. Oh God, Judy. Do you think they will get Molly from me? I mean, how? Some kind of baby switch while I'm out of it and Cal's in Timbuk-bloody-tu? What if I'm alone when I go into labour? I haven't really got anyone close except Noel and I need him to look out for Ruby."

"You've got me," said Judy. "If he isn't there in time I will be. I promise."

"Thank you." She gave the other woman a hug, watching her hurry to her car, turn to wave before jumping in and reversing down the long drive, the headlamps blurring into the foggy night until they disappeared from view.

***

Midnight, and still Becky lay wide-awake. Despite the comfort of the bedside lamp being on, the fear of closing her eyes kept the adrenalin pumping. Having gone over the afternoon's conversation with Judy but still coming up with no clear answers, she began the now nightly routine of carefully noting every individual object in the bedroom at least three times – from the location of the chair under the dresser, to the position of the jewellery box, and the hairbrushes on the table. Callum's charcoal coloured towelling robe hung on the back of the door and the wardrobe was locked with the key sticking out. Her zebra patterned Kindle cover lay on the bedside cabinet and the clock showed it was one minute past midnight.

She looked down at her white, almost childlike hands clutching the rose-sprigged bedspread as if they weren't hers at all. Everything seemed like a dream; her own existence an oddly, distant thing. Staring into the atoms of the air she wondered what truly lay between her own breathing body and the inanimate items of furniture in the room. Could something see her? Was it staring into her face right now? Someone she could not see in return? Just because human perceptions did not facilitate anything other than the basic five senses did not mean something else wasn't there. Some people, sensitives, picked up these energy vibrations all the time, as did animals. Possibly there were dozens or even hundreds of parallel energies here right now all peering in? The darker, more malevolent ones just waiting for playtime.

Her breathing sounded tenuous, fatigue weighing heavy. Spirits, she thought, drifting off – we are all spirits and this life is but a dream, the wider truth shown to us only in microcosms in case we lose our minds…

The shock of the phone ringing woke her from a bizarre dream involving old school mates she hadn't seen for thirty-five years or more; and her first thought was that it was light and she'd slept without incident. Picking up her mobile, she glanced at the clock. Seven-thirty. She grinned. Fantastic. That was seven hours she'd had. Oh God, though, her neck was cricked.

"Hello?"

"Is that Becky Ross?"

"Yes, who is this?"

It was Judy's husband as it turned out. Hers had been the last number on his wife's mobile and he thought she ought to know. Judy had been killed outright in a car crash on the M1 late last night. She would not have known a thing.

A few minutes later Becky's contractions started.

***

Chapter Twenty-Eight

The roar of the motorbike filled his senses as it accelerated over moors hazy with mile upon mile of dewy, purple heather. It was going to be one of those briefly hot, perfect blue-sky days, ablaze with shimmering coppery leaves. This is how we're supposed to feel, Noel thought – this glorious exhilaration. He twisted the handle further until the bike felt like it was flying. How wonderful, how absolutely bloody marvellous to be alive.

The ward, when he walked in half an hour later, seemed by contrast to be stuck in an institutionalised time warp of daytime television and disinfectant: smaller, darker, and dirtier than he recalled.

Sandi was halfway through the drug round; her back to him.

Sensing an atmosphere, he shrugged, calling out a casual "Hi!" as he unlocked the office door. Yes, he was late for his shift today, but so what? He was here and he'd slept and life was wonderful.

Why hadn't the bloody woman pulled up the blinds in here or stuck some coffee on, anyway? He sighed as he pulled out the patients' notes, missing Becky already. Funny he hadn't had any calls or messages from her. Not a word in days and he badly wanted to speak to her, to tell her what had happened and how brilliant and amazing it was to be alive today, tomorrow, every day....He checked his mobile again. Nope, still nothing. The rattle of the drug trolley sounded like Sandi was moving further down the corridor, so he closed the door, sat on the edge of Becky's desk and picked up the phone.

It rang and rang and rang... echoing, he imagined, around her empty cottage while she was taking a lovely, long walk. Okay, well he'd try again later. It would have been really great to talk to her, that was all. In fact, he was bursting with it. Becky was the sister he'd never had; the one person on earth he could confide in without fear of judgement or rejection – and the one person on earth he now wanted to share his good news with. She'd understand, that was the thing; and it would be good to thrash out one or two other matters too. Like the weird behaviour of the congregation at Harry's service last night. What would Becky make of that? Oh, and his surprise at Sandi's presence there.

He sat thinking about that. He'd never have had Sandi down as a born-again type. He thought she was into yoga and new-age stuff. Yet there she was, seated about halfway back in a throng of people wearing business suits.

After his ordeal, he had woken to find himself covered in a blanket, lying down in a candlelit room. A kindly old couple were washing up and chatting, keeping an eye on him, he supposed. And when he sat up, dazed, wondering where he was and why it was dark, they'd fussed around making cups of tea and asking how he felt.

How long had he been there? What had happened? Had he made a fool of himself? And most of all, had it been successful – would he be able to sleep again?

The old lady pulled up a chair and spoke quietly. He was to ask Harry these questions but yes, he had been delivered to the Lord. She looked so happy, he remembered thinking - her eyes as bright as a young girl's. "Mind you," she said. "Such language!"

He flushed to the roots of his hair, then realised she was laughing. "That old devil," she said. "Doesn't have any manners, does he?"

They chatted for a while longer until it occurred to him they may want to go home. "Oh, sorry," he said, jumping up, then swaying for a moment.

"Don't hurry, dear. Take your time. Do you want to wait in here? We can stay until you're ready. Or would you prefer to sit at the back of the service? They should be finished soon."

In consideration for the couple, who did look tired and must have had quite an ordeal themselves, he opted for the latter.

Besides, hadn't Harry asked him to comment on the congregation?

The desire to go home and sleep was overwhelming, but it was important to see his friend before leaving, and so, offering profuse thanks and even more apologies to the old couple, he slipped into a pew at the back of the church to wait. With the overhead heaters on full behind him, and an aching fatigue from the trial of the afternoon, he'd been a bit slow on the uptake and only noticed Sandi at all because she'd glanced over her shoulder. Recognising her with surprise, he'd been about to nod when, unsmilingly, she simply turned back to face the front again.

He shrugged - strange old broad – and tried to focus. So what was different or odd about the congregation that had so disquieted Harry? It seemed to him they had swayed with almost gospel enthusiasm during hymn singing and contributed extremely generously when the collection box came round. The atmosphere had been formal but rousing, candlelight burning smokily, the abundant offerings of pumpkins and flowers for the harvest festival still in evidence. He'd concentrated hard, trying to do his best for Harry as he sat in the dusty shade of the arches with a clear view of the flock. A couple more had turned round to take a cool look at him; but that was it.

Until it came to prayers. And this is where Harry may have had a point. As Harry read out the Lord's Prayer the congregation recited it with him, as expected in a church service; except some of the suited ones were slightly shaking their heads from side to side. Barely perceptibly. He frowned. No, that had to be his imagination: he was looking too hard, trying to find fault.

Leaning forwards, elbows on his knees, he put his hands together in prayer while Harry administered Communion.

Finally, concluding the service, Harry declared, "Peace be with you."

"And also with you."

Noel remained seated while everyone filed out, realising he actually knew one or two of them – doctors mostly, who he recognised from various local workshops, case conferences and training modules he'd attended over the years. A young, dark haired girl cast a sly, somewhat smirking glance his way as she walked out quite unsuitably dressed in a black PVC mini skirt and fishnets. Ah – typical rebellious teen? There was also a guy who'd been in the papers a few times – a lawyer. And wasn't that the woman who presented the news on local television? It did seem quite a highbrow mix for a deeply unfashionable, inner city church like this one. As he'd say to Harry later, you'd imagine these sorts of people would attend a church with a much higher profile, not one in Doncaster hidden by moss and overgrown shrubs.

Outside, as Noel and Harry watched the last of them leave, they climbed into various Audis and Jaguars, some chauffeur driven. The light rain from earlier had set to solid drizzle, rainwater dripping steadily from the yews, pooling on the bare earth below.

"And?" said Harry.

"I think you've got a new fan base. To be honest the only thing that struck me as odd, and please don't take offence, is why people of that calibre are coming to a down and out place like this? And why now?"

Harry nodded. "Well, it could be we were the one church round here with a regular, loyal following; the operative word being, 'were' because those regulars have now stopped attending. Even Tom, our local news editor."

His words hung in the air between them.

"The Scutts trial is coming up soon, Harry. Smack of anything to you?"

"Well, they could have come to disband the Christian stronghold here, I suppose–"

"What about converting people? Do you think it's that?"

He shook his head. "They've thrown a few fund-raising parties but to be fair I don't think any of the old regulars were converted – there were more quarrels than anything else. It's such a shame. People who'd rubbed along for years organising raffles and coffee mornings, were suddenly at each other's throats."

"What about yourself? Do you feel under threat in any way?"

Harry's laugh echoed in the porch. "I'd be lying if I said I didn't check over my shoulder when I'm locking up at night. But my faith is very strong, Noel."

"It wasn't your faith I was worried about. Your soul radiates out of you–"

"You mean my life? Because they don't want anyone being helped and they know I'm possibly the only person in the entire area who's an exorcist?"

Noel gave his upper arm a squeeze. "Watch your back, mate, that's all I'm saying. We need you. We all do."

"I'll be fine. Don't you worry about that. How are you feeling, by the way?"

Noel grinned. "Shattered but a million dollars, if that makes sense? Thank you, Harry. I mean it - I can never thank you enough – but you know that."

"Oh, it wasn't me," said Harry, raising his eyes skywards. "But I think you know that. You take care now, Noel."

***

It was coffee break before Sandi finally went to the canteen and he had chance to call Becky again.

The phone rang and rang and rang. He tried her mobile. Straight to voicemail. She hadn't left any messages, hadn't replied to his texts; nor had she called the ward.

Something was wrong.

He glanced at his watch. There were at least five hours to go before he could reasonably knock off, and with that infernal woman ruling the unit like a 1950s hospital matron it was unlikely it would be any earlier.

Come to think of it, the atmosphere in here was like a morgue: not a single patient sat in the dayroom, all of them choosing to stay in their rooms and lie on their beds in a daze. He frowned. *All of them in a daze?*

Locking the office he shot past that lazy article with the little bunch of hair tied on top of his head. "Ewan, can you do something for me?"

Ewan stood with his hands in his pockets. "Sure."

"Give Claire a call and ask her to come over, will you? I'm pretty sure she's up in Leeds today but some of these patients are bit too zonked for my liking. We need the doses checking. Something's not right."

Ewan nodded, still standing there as if hankering for a longer chat. "Sure, man."

"Like now?"

"Yeah, right. I'm on it. Jesus – everyone's, like, so stressed."

Noel turned in the direction of Ruby's room.

"Oh yeah, man. Nearly forgot…"

He stopped, half-turned back again. "What?"

"Message for you. Sorry, it was a couple of days ago now. Amanda had to go off – her kid's sick with chicken pox or something. Anyway, she said to call her, that it was urgent?"

"A couple of days ago and it was urgent? Right okay, fine… thanks for remembering to tell me, anyway."

"No worries," said Ewan, sauntering off.

Despite his new-found surge of optimism for the human race, it was a struggle when it came to those like Ewan, and he made a conscious effort to shake off his irritation before knocking on Ruby's door - Ruby's perception was a hot knife through butter. She looked sound asleep when he walked in – coiled into a foetal position, sucking her thumb. Had she had a switching incident? Nobody had said. And it seemed odd she was out of it at this time.

"Ruby?"

He picked up her wrist. Her pulse rate was barely forty bpm*. *What the fuck?*

Turning her frail body onto her back he shook her slightly but she was as limp as a rag doll. "Ruby? Can you hear me?" Pressing the buzzer for assistance he darted into the corridor and grabbed a blood pressure machine, dashed back with it and quickly attached it to her. Only then did the situation hit him full on. She had a systolic* of eighty-two and a diastolic of fifty. By now her limbs were beginning to twitch and her eyes had rolled back in her head; drool oozed from the corner of her mouth and her tongue began to dart forwards in a lizard-like fashion as if she was about to be violently sick.

Ewan trotted up to the door.

Noel shouted, "Have you phoned Claire? Right – this is urgent Ewan – bleep the SHO and bring the crash trolley down, I need an airway. Now!"

"Ruby? Ruby, are you with me sweetheart? Come on, it's going to be alright. I've got you now."

***

In the end he held her in his arms for two hours, long after an IV infusion had been inserted and the medical team had arranged for her to be transferred to the infirmary. Her respiratory rate was dangerously low and the extrapyramidal effects alarming, particularly the spasmodic twisting in her neck. She hadn't surfaced from the coma and artificial respiration would need to continue through the night.

When she was finally carried into the ambulance on a stretcher, tears coursed down Noel's face. He looked away, over at the moors, not realising until now just how much this girl had crept under his skin. And Becky would be devastated.

They'd all suffered part of Ruby's torment but the girl herself had weathered most of it – this slight, bird-like child of a woman.

"Please God, don't let her suffer anymore."

There was, however, no time to dwell on her further because the rest of the ward was in turmoil. Claire Airy was back, tearing from room to room. All of the patients were heavily sedated, not eating or drinking, and some had soiled themselves in their beds, having lost muscle tone in addition to consciousness.

"What the hell's going on? Who was in charge here?"

Noel shook his head. "The agency nurse, Sandi – and it looks like she's fucked off."

Claire's face was ashen. "Noel, everyone's been overdosed. Not fatally but certainly enough to distract us and make it look like Ruby wasn't singled out, which she most definitely was. If you hadn't got to her when you did she would have died. Someone tried to murder her, do you realise that? She was given enough haloperidol plus a cocktail of other drugs to kill her."

She stared at him, wide-eyed. "Noel - oh my God, Noel."

He put his arms around her and gave her a brief, firm hug. "I'll call the police. Meanwhile, let's get everyone stable and cleaned up. Come on, we've got a job to do - we can do this."

It took the rest of the day. Noel called in the afternoon shift to come in early and both sets of staff worked solidly until six; one by one giving statements to the duty officers. By half past, Noel and Claire were sitting upstairs in the staff room drinking strong, syrupy coffee and wolfing chocolate bars from the slot machine.

Ewan sat hugging himself. "Man, I can't believe it. I just can't believe it."

Noel suddenly looked his way like he'd only just noticed his existence. "Shit! I forgot. You said there was a message from Amanda?"

"Oh Noel, let yourself off the hook – you haven't had a minute," said Claire.

"It's unusual though – very - especially since I can't get hold of Becky."

He had Amanda's mobile number on speed dial and got through straight away. "Amanda - I'm so sorry, but I only just got your message this afternoon, and we've had a terrible emergency–"

"Noel, it's fine," she whispered. "Sorry, only just got Ellie off to sleep. No, I couldn't get you on the phone, that's all, and I'd left loads of messages. In the end I had to ask Ewan to–"

"You left messages? Really? That's odd. Seriously, I haven't had any from either you or Becky. None."

"Maybe your phone's on the blink? Anyway, the message is from Ruby and she was very worked up about it so I have to pass it on. She wanted to tell Becky something, but of course Becky's off now and I can't get hold of her for love nor money – she's another one not answering. It was one of her psychic things so I don't know if it means anything to either of you, but here goes: 'Tell Becky she must not be alone at the birth.'"

"What does that mean? Why?"

"I don't know. Look, this is where I need you to bear with me because I don't know what's agitating Ruby so much, but she was getting increasingly frantic – drawing pictures of babies and swords...and a rose – someone sent her one, you know? Anyway, while I've been off with Ellie I've done a bit more research and Satanists *mark* a new-born child by taking his or her blood to use in black magic rituals. Well, what if it's Becky's baby they want? I know it sounds far-fetched but Ruby was extremely agitated, and all I can say is, will you please make sure Becky is okay? Just warn her to watch out. The birth is ages away so I don't think any of this is urgent, but—"

"Amanda, someone just tried to kill Ruby. And after what has happened to the rest of us, I honestly wouldn't discount any of what you've hypothesised; the fact that they believe this and act it out is enough for the rest of us to take it seriously. Okay, I'll speak to Becky as soon as I can. To be honest, though, I've been trying to ring her and Callum all afternoon. In the end I called Toby, the officer who was in charge of the case last year. Apparently he's been suspended for something and he's very upset about it – he wouldn't talk to me - but I know he'd do anything for Cal and Becky and I literally begged him to check on her. Anyway, I've got to get off the phone, Amanda. But thank you. Thank you."

He turned to Claire and Ewan, who both had their mouths open, having heard the conversation on loud speaker.

"Claire you know what can happen with this lot. You saw what happened to Jack, to Martha, to Kristy?"

She nodded. "I just can't believe this is real."

"I'd agree with you, but something they do works, I swear to God."

He was already phoning Becky's house phone again; then tried her mobile, leaving yet another message to call back urgently. Again no answer.

He tried Callum. Again it went to voicemail.

Like a rock plummeting to the bottom of a well, his stomach plunged and kept on plunging. "Something's very, very wrong, Claire. We've been behind the door here – they've got one over on us. Shit! I've got to find Becky."

Claire put a restraining hand on his arm. "The worst thing you can do is go firing off across those moors on your motorbike before you know where she is. Let's ring the hospitals and the police first."

He jumped up while she rung around, pacing, thinking. This whole thing had been sewn up incredibly fast. So it was all about exacting revenge on Becky, was it? Christ, she'd have to leave the country. She'd have to take Molly and bloody emigrate. *Christ!*

Claire clicked off the phone. "Becky's in Maternity. Looks like Molly's coming early."

***

Chapter Twenty-Nine

Doncaster Royal Infirmary

Becky opened her eyes to find a familiar face looking down at her.

"Oh hi! What are you doing in my bedroom?"

"This is the DRI, Becky."

"Is it?"

"Yes, you were brought in this morning, don't you remember?"

"No. I must have been out cold." She looked at Sandi through a haze, trying to make sense of it. "I didn't know you worked here?"

"Jack of all trades, that's me," said Sandi. "Maternity, surgery, lunatics–"

Becky frowned. "God, I must have been really out of it – I can't even remember how I got here."

The room was small, whitewashed and windowless, her bed a trolley with rails around it. Instinctively she checked her bump, rewarded with a healthy kick from Molly, before another wave of contractions started and she grimaced, a fresh wave of sweat breaking out.

As she flopped back against the pillows the mask came back over her face. "That's it, take deep, long breaths. It won't be long now."

Something's not quite right.

Her brain searched frantically through a fog of confusion; crippling spasms of pain frequently axing through her thoughts, leaving her reeling and exhausted. The clock on the wall in front said five-thirty in the afternoon... so she'd been here, what, ten or eleven hours? No, that didn't stack up. A blurred snapshot of memory flitted in and out of her mind – of the wind whipping back the hair from her face as she was carried into an ambulance, of the potholed lane bouncing the van from side to side, of worrying if the cottage door was locked properly, wondering where the hell Callum was... before the world had blanked out.

"Where's my husband? Where's Cal, Sandi? Is he on his way?"

Sandi had her back to her, busy at the medical trolley. Unresponsive, she faded in and out of focus. *Hadn't she heard?* Becky took the mask from her face, biting back the screams as another contraction took hold. This labour had, must have, been going on all day? So where the hell was Callum? And Noel? They were supposed to be here.

She heard her own anxious shout pierce the air. "Sandi - I said, 'where's my husband?' Hasn't he been called? And where's my phone? I need to ring him. Please." She flopped back again, panting hard. "I wanted an epidural. It was agreed way back. I can't take this level of pain. Will you please get the doctor? I need... I need... Oh God, it's coming again—"

Still the other woman did not respond.

All wrong... something was very, very wrong...

Several more long minutes passed with zero response. At last the contractions eased off and she could think again. Why did Sandi have her back to her all the time? Why wasn't she answering? How come she'd been unconscious all day but was now being left in agony? Where were the other members of staff?

Suddenly Sandi appeared to finish what she was doing and swung round to face her.

What the fuck?

The woman's eyes were entirely black. Becky stared in horror.

"I don't understand. What is this?"

As she continued to stare, Sandi's face started to dissolve into the ether – the familiar image of protruding teeth and frizzy 'child's drawing' hair disappearing – until all that was left was a feeling of falling into a black, bottomless abyss.

"It's nice they waited for me to come and see to you personally," said a deep, guttural voice.

"What?"

"There are so many of us now but I wanted to be the one to do it. So, better late than never. Let's get on with it, shall we?"

"With what? Oh, yes – I get it. This is a nightmare, isn't it? I'm at home and I'm going to wake up. I have to wake up...or the demon will get me. I was so tired, you see and I knew this would happen – that I wouldn't wake in time?"

A chorus of voices laughed raucously.

"All I've got to do is wake up."

Another wave of breath-taking contractions gripped and shook her. She screamed with the pain. "For fuck's sake give me some fucking gas. Where's Dr Faulkner? Where's Debbie, my nurse? Where is everyone? Oh my God, Jesus Christ!"

"Isn't going to help you now," said the voice.

Sweat poured from her in rivulets as the pain racked through her body. She gripped the railings and yelled until her throat was raw. When it eventually subsided she flopped back, gasping and crying. "This is fucking real, isn't it? And I'm going to die and you're going to take Molly. So who the fuck are you, then? Tell me."

The other woman seemed to float towards her now, a fuzzy image in a black cloak. Becky fought against the sedatives she'd been injected with. *Oh no, dear God no...* The thing, woman, whatever it was, was holding a scalpel. And it was then, in a sudden flash of understanding Becky realised what was going to happen. Of course, this had been planned ever since 'they' somehow knew she was with child. Something had been sent to watch her so the second Molly was ready to come, they would be waiting. And Callum had been deliberately removed from the scene....

Yes, it was all so bloody obvious now. *Fuck, fuck and fuck...* Tears squeezed out of her eyes. Had these bastards done something to him? And what about Noel? Had he drunk himself to death? Had a road accident? Oh God, no, please no... And now this bitch was going to kill either her or Molly or both of them. Life was over.

The black-eyed thing looming over her shook its head as if it had read her thoughts.

"We're not killing the child. We just need her blood," it hissed, spittle flying out, drool running down its chin as it drew back the blade. "She will be our future high priestess, won't you, my dear?" Its icy fingers stroked Becky's tummy. "Once we have her blood she's marked, you see? We will watch and wait until she's ready to start taking instruction, probably around the age of three. That would be about right."

With superhuman effort, Becky ripped off the mask and frantically tried to unhook the bars of the trolley, which had been pumped as high off the floor as it could go. With her other hand she swiped at the scalpel, but Sandi was quicker and the blade struck her palm, blood spurting onto the sheet. Another series of contractions took hold, forcing her to slump back. They were so close together now the birth had to be imminent. Molly was coming. "No," she whispered to the child inside, "not yet...not yet...." But the baby was coming now, the pain insufferable. With all her strength she kicked Sandi in the stomach, flailing her arms around to keep the knife away, oblivious to the gashes to her hands, screaming at the top of her lungs. "Get away from us, you evil cow. I'll kill you first, I swear to God... aaaargh...Please, God, help us!"

Sandi had jumped back from the kick and Becky's glance darted to the door. Where was everyone? My God, if she was really in Maternity, where were the other nurses? The obstetrician? The receptionist? The orderlies?

In that split second Sandi darted forwards, and an iron-hard shove on the forehead slammed Becky flat to the pillow, the other hand clamping round her throat, constricting her windpipe.

"If you move again or cry out I will slit your throat. Either way we will have this child. No one crosses Lucifer. We have this entire area in a stronghold, and the pathetic bit of Christianity you have left is being taken apart bit by bit. So if you want your shit life back you can have it, but it will be shit, and trust me it's going to get worse and worse and worse. No one disrespects Lucifer. Got it? So lie still now, there's a good girl."

Becky had no option but to watch as Sandi then drew back the lancet. *Oh God, please help us...*

The pain of the next contraction was sudden and violent. Molly was coming and coming now.

The scream ripped from her lungs at the same time as the door flew open, and Toby Harbour burst in. Becky yelled, "The knife!"

Then with her eyes squeezed shut she heaved Molly into the world, vaguely aware of more bodies, shouting, a baby crying...And a horrible inhuman-sounding screech as someone's head cracked against the wall.

***

Chapter Thirty

It was much later – nearly midnight - when Toby and Sid Hall cruised past the Mullins' house. It sat in gloomy silence behind wrought iron gates, not a flicker of light in any of the windows.

"Doesn't look like anyone's home," said Toby.

"Hmmm…Let's take a wander round the back."

With the headlights switched off, Sid drove the car quietly along the lane to the side of the house, hanging a right down a bumpy bridleway towards the rear. Eventually they came to a five-bar gate, leaving them no choice but to get out and walk. A wet, murky fog closed around the two figures as they clambered over a style and proceeded to tramp across the fields.

"I didn't realise it was this foggy. Must've come down quick," said Sid.

"I can't see you, mate."

The older man, stocky in his anorak and boots, waited for him to catch up, his world-weary face grim. "My guess is they've scarpered but we'll take a look round, any road."

"This fog's a right pea-souper."

"Aye, bloody cold an' all. Come on, let's get this done."

"I don't like this, Sid. I've got a really bad feeling."

His words were muffled, and with a flicker of panic he realised Sid had already been swallowed by the fog. His feet were sinking into the mud. "Sid," he said, standing still. "Sid, slow down, I can't see a thing. Where are you?"

His partner's muted voice replied from somewhere to his left, or so he thought. "It's come down bloody quick has this, very peculiar."

"Where are you?"

"Keep coming towards my voice. I think we're at the back of the woods so we should be tracking downhill soon. You with me?"

He bumped into him. "Sorry, yeah. Don't worry I'm not going to hold your hand but I am going to keep touching your shoulder. I hate this. I hate not being able to see owt."

"Suppose it happens suddenly like this on t' moors, specially this time of year. Give it a minute and it'll lift again, you'll see."

"Have we got to do this? Couldn't we just go back to the car and scout round the house from the front?"

Sid didn't answer. Okay, it was a stupid question but Sid had no idea how evil these people really were. Nobody did.

"We haven't got back up if they're still here."

"Aye and we'd look like a right pair of Charlies if we got the place surrounded and there were nowt 'ere but a couple of badgers."

"Fair point." They were dropping steeply now, stumbling down scree, the chill of the trees and the water mingling with damp fog. "Right," Toby said. "Well, I'm definite that when I was here that night we walked out of the patio doors and along a path that led directly into some woods, so—"

"Stop!" Sid came to an abrupt halt, holding up a hand to prevent them both walking straight into the lake.

Already their feet were sinking, muddy water swilling round their ankles as they realised too late they were mired in the reeds.

"Ah, shit, I'm up to my bloody ankles," said Toby.

Struggling to backtrack, they grabbed onto each other's shoulders to try and lever themselves out, lunging for dry land on hands and knees.

"Jesus, that was close."

"Flaming Nora. You could be up to your neck before you know it," said Sid, breathing hard. The black expanse of water lapped gently under a veil of fog, merging seamlessly into a quagmire around the edges. "This fog stops you hearing an 'all. Bloody hell, my poor, old heart's going like the bleedin' clappers. Come on, we'll have to walk round it, see what we can see."

As Sid headed west towards the woods, Toby instinctively hung back. That smell – something heady and sweet lingering in the autumnal air – immediately transported him back the night of the black mass, and the moment another hand had forced his to sink a blade into the heart of a freshly murdered human being. The taste of the man's blood lurched into his throat and he swallowed hard.

"Come on, lad – keep up."

Their boots stuck and squelched, the going hard, until all at once the clearing where the stage had been set was directly in front: a large but empty area of grass ringed by ancient oaks.

Sid turned to face him. "This where it happened?"

Toby nodded, desperately trying to clear his head. "I'm not likely to bloody forget."

There wasn't a sound; the fog so dense now it obscured all but their immediate personal space.

"Seriously, this whole place creeps me out," said Toby. "They could still be here. Watching us." He started to shake, looking over his shoulder, turning round this way and that. We should have had back-up."

"And how do you think I get back-up when people are saying what they're saying about you, soft lad? No one would touch you with a barge pole. I've stuck my big, thick neck out here. So shut up now and listen. These people – what they do is way too dodgy to hang around. They'll know by now that we busted that woman at the hospital. My bet is they're long gone, and my hope is they've buggered off a bit too quickly and left us a nice bit of evidence."

He flicked on his torch. "If there's anything 'ere we'll find it. Mind on the job, and let's get cracking."

It helped, Toby found, to think in those terms. In fact, it took his mind off things more than lying in the safety of his own bedroom. At least there was, in some small measure, an element of taking back control.

They found nothing, however. Two hours of searching and not so much as a shred of bonfire ash, let alone the charred bones of a sacrifice, had been found. The cold damp of an October night had soaked both men through, and Sid stood up holding his lower back.

"You sure it was here?"

"Hundred percent."

Deep in thought, Sid headed off along the path leading back to the house. "Come on lad, keep up, it's bloody horrible out here."

Toby hurried behind. Here was Sid, his sergeant – a man forty years his senior who should have retired by now – and him, the supposed bright young thing, leaner and fitter and better educated, feeling like a schoolboy by comparison. Those bastards had stripped him of so much more than his badge. Rage ignited inside him. How much fear and pain did they have to cause? Did they really get off on it? Lousy bastards. If it was the last thing he did he'd make sure every last one of them got banged up for life.

And it probably would be the last thing he did, too.

As they approached, footfalls soft on the turf, the back of the house lay waiting in darkness. Wordlessly they began shining torches into each ground floor room.

"Yup, they've flitted," said Toby. "Everything's covered in dust sheets."

"No sign of life, that's for sure," Sid agreed. "God, that's knackered me, has that little jaunt. I could do with a pint."

They sat down next to each other on the wet patio floor, staring into the impenetrable gloom. Spectral outlines of shrubs bordered the lawns, the fog floating in a ghostly-white layer above the grass.

"Aye, it really is odd," Sid repeated. "How that fog came down so bloody quick. There was nothing when we got here, did you notice? I mean, not even high up. I remember looking up at the stars. I'm into astronomy, did you know? Oh, yes. I know my Pisces from my Aquarius."

Toby laughed.

"I'm just kidding you, lad. Serious now. I saw the north star. It was a clear sky up there when we got out of the car."

"Even odder how fast this lot have fucked off. Like, how did they even know we got that woman? It was only a few hours ago. They've managed to clear out a house this size in hours making me look like a liar. Again. It was here, you do believe me, don't you?" He shook his head. "Times like this I wish I still smoked. I'd kill for one right now."

They sat in silence, both thinking.

And then it occurred to him. "Holy crap! Of course. The nasty little witch rang her solicitor, didn't she?"

"And?"

"Solicitors."

"Not with you, lad."

"Sid, think about it – police, lawyers, teachers, journalists, nurses, even bloody paediatricians. How many are bound into this? If Scutts was in it then why not the solicitor she rang?"

"So her solicitor tipped off Mullins, you reckon?"

"It's a fair guess."

After a while Sid said, "And there's serious money here – no doubt enough to pay a team of people to get everything sorted expediently. Okay." He heaved himself up. "If I get arthritis after tonight it's your bloody fault."

"Where are we going?" said Toby. "We've got nothing on them – nothing."

"No, but you're going to have to face the music some time. There's a whole cavalry after you, lad, and I can't fend them off forever."

***

In sombre mood they walked up the gravel driveway, through the side gate, and onto the unlit lane at the front.

Toby kept his head down, trying to hold himself together. At least Sid had believed him earlier tonight and taken his phone call - trusting him enough to pass on the information about

218

Sandi, so that within minutes of him detaining the woman the local police had arrived.

However, the officer who turned up had also been on the cusp of having him arrested too, which is where, thank God, his two closest allies had pulled rank. As Sandi was being led away, spitting and screeching like a harpy, Callum had finally burst in. After a few seconds of wild-eyed indecision, he had then instructed the officer to back off.

"We'll sort this out, officer. You can take that lowlife back to her cesspit and leave DC Harbour to us."

The officer looked from Toby to Callum, and back again. "There's a tape just come in you need to know about. I cannot—"

"Officer!"

"Alright. But I'm telling you his is a seriously high profile and I've had orders—"

"I know. And it's in hand."

Callum had a command of presence that few possessed; people didn't argue with him for long, and the officer had eventually, reluctantly acquiesced.

After the police had gone, Toby grabbed the nearest chair and stayed there, staring out of the window, waiting for the inevitable. Callum had bought him some time, that was all. Behind him, Becky was crying and several nurses, who had miraculously appeared when the police did, were now busy fussing around the new mother.

Misery hung over him like a wet rag in winter, as he sat, unaware of what had been about to happen to Molly, oblivious, at that point, of what would have happened to her had he not arrived when he did.

Even when Noel appeared, he could only turn and nod briefly, as the other man rushed over to Becky. She and Molly were safe and that was all that mattered; except he was probably going to be sent down for a very, very long time now. Amy had cited rape via one of the most aggressive solicitors in Leeds; and on top of that he had just been told there was footage of him physically murdering a local homeless man. A tape had been sent less than an hour ago, the remains of the man's body found dumped in a local graveyard. Everyone else wore masks except himself, the hand that had held his down airbrushed from existence. He was finished.

Hours passed, daylight fading from the rooftops. Streetlights reflected in amber blurs on the wet streets and shadow people hurried under umbrellas towards their cars. It took a long time for any awareness of his immediate surroundings to resurface, for the voices filtering in to make any sense.

"How's Ruby?" Becky was saying. "Please, please tell me she's going to be okay. Have you rung yet?"

Noel's voice, "She's in a coma but she's stable. All her vitals are good and it looks like she'll come round. God knows how she predicted what would happen to Molly, though. She knew. She's incredible."

Toby tuned in and glanced round. "Noel, what made you call me? I'm not even supposed to be on duty – I've been suspended. Set up, to be honest."

Becky's mouth fell open. "What?"

Noel looked from Toby to Becky and back again. "Well, after what happened on the ward, I called both Becky and Callum but got no reply. Honestly, I was calling them every other minute. But it wasn't until that dozy plonker, Ewan, finally told me Amanda had been wanting to speak to me for three days and she gave me Ruby's message, that it started to fit together. As it turned out, it really would all have been too late if it wasn't for you, Toby. You're a walking miracle."

Becky interrupted. "Hang on, I left countless messages for all of you, and I asked the staff to call as well – loads of times."

Everyone shook their heads. No one had had a message – either text or voicemail.

Becky frowned. "So how did you know where to look, Tobes?"

"I'm a detective, Becky."

She smiled. "Oh, yes."

His smile in response was weak. He looked down at the floor, blinking repeatedly. "Pregnant lady, attempted murder of her patient; she's not answering her phone and nor is her husband – tear-arse to hospital and hope to God she's there."

She reached over to him. "Come here and give me a hug because I bloody need it and so do you."

"We're all safe, that's what matters," said Callum. "It's just a damn good thing Noel got through to you, Toby, because if it wasn't for police radio I'm guessing I wouldn't have had your calls either and I'd be on me way to bloody Ipswich by now – that's where they were sending me next."

"How does that work, though?" Noel said. "Really? How does what they do block communications and send you all over the country like that? Some kind of dark arts to screw us up?"

"Well, they didn't get Molly, and we nabbed the old bitch who tried to kill Ruby so they're the ones who screwed up," said Toby. "God, I'm glad Ruby's okay."

"It was a sorry sight - her being lifted into the ambulance like that," said Noel. "You get attached to people, you know? Shouldn't, but we do. Oh, and I also spoke to Isobel. I had to tell her someone attempted to murder Ruby and to make sure Alice was safe. It wasn't difficult to persuade her of the gravity – she was in bits about Judy Harper. Do you know about that yet, Becky?"

Becky nodded. "I was the last person to see her. I'd only just had the call from her husband when the contractions started. Shock, I suppose."

"Oh, God. Alice's psychologist! Another bloody coincidence?"

Gripping Callum's hand, Becky said, "Isobel will guard that girl with her life, I'm sure of it. She knows what's been going on. I'm so upset about Judy, though, and Ruby – I really am." She turned to Callum. "Where they hell have you been, anyway?"

He looked as if he'd aged ten years, Toby thought, with dark shadows under red-rimmed eyes.

"Excuse my language but fuck knows. I've been sent on every wild goose chase imaginable. I get messages telling me to help with investigations only to turn up and find they've never heard of me. Other times it's cases I didn't really need to be involved in and I was like a spare prick at a party. Honestly, I was beginning to think I was jinxed – like someone didn't want me to be at home with my new wife. Thought it must be my ex."

They all laughed.

"We're laughing," said Noel. "But you probably were jinxed."

"And I definitely am," said Toby.

They all looked at him.

And then he told them. Everything. Blurting it out so they knew: Amy's weird behaviour in the cottage, the powerful persuasion to use the Ouija board, the S & M party at her parents' house; the rape allegations, and finally the gruesome snuff movie industry they seemed to be part of, and his own face on camera as he was forced to plunge a knife into the heart of a man who'd just had his throat cut in front of him.

"My God – so it's not just about perversions and black magic and helping each other up the greasy pole, it's big business too?"

Toby nodded. "Yes, and I'm up to my neck in it."

"You are a bit," said Callum. "This calls for Sid. I'll see how he's got on with reading the riot act to the old witch trying to hurt my child, and then we'll go looking for them, shall we?"

Noel shook his head. "Cal, they are absolutely bloody everywhere. Even in the church trying to disband it. It's like there's a curse on the entire area."

"No, honestly mate, you've got to stop all this witchcraft and curse stuff. I get that these people believe in it and it helps them get what they want, that they're okay with not having any kind of conscience; but what I won't buy into is all this dark arts mumbo-jumbo."

Noel looked into his eyes. "And I hope you never have to, mate, I really do. All I can tell you is when they come looking for you they are everywhere, even in your head. Isn't that right, Toby?"

Toby's shadow had spilled across the floor into the shape of an ogre. The four of them stared at it. "It's been like that for a while now," he said. "But there's only ever been one of them before – now look – one, two, three, four."

***

Chapter Thirty-One

Jasmine Cottage
Two weeks later

The knock on the door came at one in the morning. Callum answered to find Toby standing on the step holding a white cat. "Bloody hell mate, what are you doing here?"

The wind blew a swirl of leaves into the hall. "Is this yours?"

"Yeah." He took Louie from him. "It's whipping up a bit tonight. Come on in and get warm. Becky's going to be made up about this damn cat," he said, wandering into the kitchen. "He's been gone over two months. Where d'you find him?"

"Here on the mat waiting to come in."

"Well, I'll be buggered." With the cat under his arm he shook some biscuits into his dish. "Turns up just like that after all this time – makes you wonder where he's been." They stood watching the cat guzzle hungrily. "Fancy a brew, mate, or something stronger?"

"Stronger."

He poured them both a large glass of whisky. "Down the hatch."

Gasping at the burn they immediately chased it with another.

"How's Becky? Did she stay long at the hospital after I left?"

"Are you kidding? The minute she could stand up we got her out of there. She discharged herself. Probably the tender loving midwife she had put her off."

Toby laughed as they drew up chairs and sat next to the range.

"So how come they let you out? I thought you'd been sewn up like the proverbial kipper? I didn't think I'd see you again.

Not 'til we met up at a coppers' nursing home, dribbling soup and swearing at the telly, anyway."

"Neither did I. They put me on anti-depressants and suicide watch."

"The bloody lawyers wouldn't tell us anything and Becky rang every day."

"You're a lucky bastard having her, you know that don't you?"

"Yes, mate, I do. I'll tell you something else as well – I'm never leaving her alone as much as that ever again. I just didn't think anything of it at the time. It was like a slow dawning – every single request seemed so genuine, I just can't get my head round it."

"No, well, you'll not get your head round this one either. One minute I was sitting in my cell facing a life sentence, the next the door was opened and I was told I could go. Case dropped."

"How come?"

Toby shrugged. "Legals phoned to say the allegations had been withdrawn. I don't know what happened to the incriminating tapes either. Apparently the whole lot mysteriously vanished – every shred of evidence against me. Anyhow, it came from on high that I was free to go."

"By who, do you know? And why? 'Cos I just don't get it"

"No, I don't either. All I know is what I told you – case dropped, evidence gone, top brass tell me I'm good to go. To be honest, I don't think I'll ever find out who's up to what, who's in this bloody racket and why I'm out. The only thing I can say for sure is it's the best offer I've had in a while and I'm taking it."

"Bloody hell. I mean I'm chuffed to bits for you but it's very, very suspicious."

"All I can come up with is Mullins won't want his name in court… I honestly don't know."

"Beats me how you got tangled up with that Amy. I mean, how come you went into the woods with her and she managed to tape you at it, you daft git?"

"I know, I know…stop. The only thing I can say in my defence is that it felt like I was acting, going through the motions but with no control – like it was happening to someone else – a kind of waking dream."

"As in hypnosis? I can get my head round that one. Yeah, I could see how that might have happened."

"Yeah, suppose. But the violent rape I was accused of – well, I've seen the incriminating evidence and I just do not remember being that person or even being there. But it is me. No one could watch that tape and say that isn't me because it is."

"Were you drugged?"

"I think it was sex magic."

"Sex magic? What?"

"Yeah, honest…I think that's what it was."

"Bloody hell, you lucky bastard. How come you get sex magic and all I get is lousy motorway driving and Premier Inns?"

They both laughed, but Toby's smile clouded over quickly. "They'll keep the tapes though, won't they, Cal? All it takes is a threat to leak those onto social media and anytime they want to call in a favour or get someone in the force to do something for them… Anyway, the thing is, I don't know who I'm working with anymore. I know jack shit."

"You're theirs. They did actually recruit you, then? Fucking hell."

"Yes. And the only way out I can think of is to get the hell away from here. I couldn't ever have a family or even a relationship without putting them in danger. And if I want to keep my integrity I'll have to resign – become an invisible person on the backstreets or go on the run – and even then they'd catch up with me."

Callum narrowed his eyes, looking at him intensely. "Where is she now, our giggling Amy? In fact, where's the whole family?"

"Sid and I had a good look round their place, and it could only have been hours after they'd gone, but I'm telling you there wasn't a shred of evidence they'd ever even been there. And

Noel said Mullins cleared his desk that afternoon and vanished without a word."

"Like that Ida woman, then – just disappeared into thin air?"

"Seems so. Beats me how they can pack up so fast – how they see things coming and just move on."

"We'll not find them either. Not when it's underground and they've got serious money and connections."

"They must have one hell of a network at the ready, to transport them into another life at the click of their fingers like that – across continents even."

"Exactly. So think about it. What's the point of you flitting then? I mean if these bastards are everywhere you could up-sticks to anywhere from Brazil to Oklahoma and they'd still find you. At least here you've got us."

"You're right - they're bloody everywhere, aren't they? And they look normal, do normal jobs…I'd never know. I don't think I'll ever be able to trust anyone ever again. God help me if I ever need surgery."

A sharp wind gusted down the chimney flue, and his glance flicked automatically to the dark shapes scooting along the floor and up the walls. Would they ever leave him alone?

"Another scotch?"

"Thanks." He held out his glass. "Is Becky okay now?"

"She's shattered. I've taken all the annual leave owed to me so I can look after her for a bit. To be honest with you though, she's behaving a bit oddly, not quite her normal self. I suppose it's the hormones and stuff, but she'll not have the light switched off at night – goes ballistic. The place is lit up like a chuffing football stadium. I suppose it'll all calm down eventually. I hadn't realised she'd not been sleeping for weeks, either. Like I said, I'll not be leaving her on her own like that again – even if I have to take another job."

"Well, it all came on the back of what happened last year, didn't it? It gets to you, Cal, it really does. Oh, while I remember, I need to ask you something. Who's that bloke Noel was talking about – the one who helped him with bad dreams and stuff? Maybe Becky's suffering with that too, you know? Maybe she could do with some help?"

"Maybe Becky's suffering with what?"

Callum's glance flicked to over Toby's head. "Hello love, what are you doing up? Did we wake you?"

"I thought the slates were going to come off in the wind. The windows are rattling." She slid onto a chair next to Toby, then did a double take. "Oh my good God – if it isn't the ghost of Toby Harbour." Her eyes widened further when she saw the cat on his knee. "And Louie! I don't believe this, I must be dreaming. When did he show up?"

"Just now," said Callum. "He came in with Tobes."

Becky bent and kissed the cat's head; then looked up, a huge grin spreading across her face. "That means she's gone, then? She's gone...oh thank God and all his angels, she's gone...I'd do a little dance if I had the energy." Her eyes shone through all the tiredness.

"Who? Bloody hell woman, I wish you'd both stop talking in riddles."

About to say, 'Lilith', she changed her mind. "No one, Cal. Never mind, let's just say I'm deliriously happy about it."

Toby stroked the purring cat, nodding. "You're right though, Becks. This cat disappeared about the time you told us about her."

"I hope so. I honestly, truly bloody hope so. Anyway, what brings you to our door on this dark and rainy night, Toby Harbour? I've been ringing for weeks now and no one would tell me anything."

"You look done in, Becky - you really should be in bed. I'm ever so sorry if I woke you."

"That's fine. Just tell me – I need to know."

"Okay, well basically they dropped the charges."

"Cal, would you make me a cup of tea, love? Sorry, I'm just too knackered to walk as far as the kettle."

"Course I will."

As soon as he began to clatter around making tea, she inched closer to Toby and whispered, "What about the other business? Are you okay?"

"Ah, that. I was just asking Cal if he knew who the bloke was who helped Noel."

"Harry. Do you need him? To be honest, I could do with a chat with him too."

"Becky, can you see shadows following you around, or is it just me?"

She nodded, keeping her voice low. "Yes, out of the corner of my eye. At least I don't see *her* anymore - not since I got back, anyway. But yes, the man you need is Harry. Noel's got his number. Apparently he's run off his feet but I know he'll help us."

"Okay, I'll ring Noel. I'm worried on another level too, Becky - seriously worried. I was just telling Cal, they're everywhere. I've been freed for a reason and I think one of them is to call in favours whenever they want... the evidence disappeared, you know?"

She nodded. "Maybe we should move?"

Callum, swung round. "Move? Are you kidding?"

"Big ears. Well, they can't follow us to New Zealand, can they? I'm worried about Molly. I'm worried about all of us. The whole area is in some kind of stronghold."

"That's what I said," Toby agreed. "It's cursed, and until that's lifted this place is a magnet."

"Not you as well with these bloody curses. So the answer is to emigrate, then? Leave our country and run away?" Callum handed Becky a cup of hot tea. "What about Ruby? And Alice?"

Becky took a sip. "Yes, you're right. Sorry, it was just a panic reaction – I can't leave them, of course I can't."

"So we're not running away then?"

"No." She lifted her face to his. "No, we're damn well not. This is our home. We're staying and we're fighting."

"'Men get away with evil things when good men do nothing'," said Callum, pouring out more whisky.

"No, that's not right," Becky said. "It's, 'The only thing necessary for the triumph of evil is for good men to do nothing.'"

"I'll drink to that," said Toby.

"Can you pour me one, please?" said Becky. "I'd like to drink   to   that   as   well."

***

Chapter Thirty-Two

1583, Samhain

Nightfall came quickly, snuffing out the bright, crisp afternoon as Magda tore through the forest to the abbey. Skirting the perimeter, well away from the main track, she kept close to the shadows until finally the abbey walls came into view. From somewhere deep within the woods there came cries not of wolves but of men, and a bolt of fear riveted her to the spot.

The mob was out already – torches flickering with fire in the dark. They'd be looking for someone to hang for Lisbet's death - for their hunger, their disease and their fear. Who better than a lone woman who had lain with men twice her age and allowed her younger sister to be sacrificed instead of herself? How convenient it was to accuse her of witchcraft, something which would exact a humiliating trial and a public execution.

If they found her…

Before scaling the wall she checked over her shoulder. A crescent moon silhouetted an army of black trees. Motionless she stood listening, waiting…They were heading in this direction.

With moonlight shining on the wall she quickly located the same spot she and Cicely had discovered - a groove between the stones just big enough for foot leverage – then scrambled over the top and sprinted across the lawn to the abbey. On reaching the heavy wooden door, she hurled herself at it, hammering urgently with her fists.

No one came.

Precious seconds ticked by.

She paused and stepped back, scrutinising the darkened windows. There had to be someone here…There had to be…Next to the abbey, the little church sat in silent darkness. They were not at worship…So the sisters must surely be inside the abbey?

Smoke from the encroaching torch flames now reached her nostrils and her heart raced faster, hands trembling badly as she banged on the door.

Oh, please let someone answer…please…

Still with no response, she checked over her shoulder again, wondering if there was a back door or some other part of the abbey the nuns might be in. Perhaps they couldn't hear her? It would be far too dangerous to call out. What about hiding in the church? Surely they would not come looking for her there? Oh, what to do? What to do?

A sudden breath on her neck caused her to swing round. An elderly nun stood quietly behind her. "Make haste, Child," she whispered. "You must come with me."

There was no time for questions: shouts and barking dogs were getting louder by the second. Determined to track her down, it wouldn't be long before her scent was picked up and the abbey was searched.

Hurrying after the flowing robes of the nun, who was already disappearing round the corner of the building towards the church, she wondered how this woman had known immediately who she was and what she needed. On reaching the eastern porch, the old nun's face was in darkness as she stopped and turned, listening.

"Dear God, they're scaling the walls. They'll find you in here… No, follow me, I have a better idea."

"I don't understand," said Magda, scurrying after her. "Why would they come here? And how did you know they were coming?"

"My dear, you have no comprehension of what is going on in this village. We have to hide you. Hurry, quickly."

Magda looked behind them. Torch flames were leaping into the night air, and the heavy thud of men jumping over the walls was unmistakable.

They sped down the path to the rear of the abbey. "You're going to have to go down the well."

"What?"

"They'll be in the abbey in no time: the others are hiding down in the cellar – they'll hang us all for witches–" The elderly woman was out of breath as she used the winch to bring up a wooden pail inside the stone well. "They take the children to Tanners Dell and make them say things against us – in case we speak out, you see? We take in orphans from the streets – hurry get in. They have no birth certificates, no family. We can only watch as they're taken to the mill and never brought back. Sometimes, later, we're told to bury them. Come on, hurry, child. Now hold tight."

Magda gripped the sides of the pail as it swayed precariously.

"We found out the children were being used in most unspeakable ways, and we took the matter to the mill owner," she explained, lowering Magda down into the well. "Since then we've been threatened with the slur of witchcraft, using herbs to cast spells and talking to familiars in the forest. Some of the children have testified they're afraid of us, accusing us of talking in tongues, saying they've seen us using poison on people as they sleep."

Far below the water sloshed against the stones as progressively the descent became darker and colder, and the nun's voice became evermore faint.

Magda's voice resounded round the well. "But you're a religious order?"

"Yes."

From close by a window smashed and muffled screams echoed through the chambers of the abbey.

"Sit tight and keep quiet." The nun's voice was barely audible as she peeped over the rim. "I'll come back for you."

The rope had extended to its full length, the pail still oscillating, squeaking slightly as it knocked on the stones until finally it stilled; and she was left alone in the dripping, dark chill many feet below ground.

Desperate to cry out to the fleeing woman to remember to come back, please not to forget… she remained silent: the abbess would be running for her life. There was no choice but to sit this out, for however long it took.

After a while, her fear tempered and her sight adjusted to the slimy, dark walls. A steady drop, drop, drop of rain echoed in the well water as overhead the clouds grew heavier, and a brisk wind whipped up. Still she waited, hour after hour, straining to hear what was happening.

With time to think and gather her wits, she puzzled over what the abbess had said. Right back from being a child she'd been told the sisters looked after orphans until they were able to go back into town, acquire work and take care of themselves. Mostly they were young children, who were sick, or their families had been bankrupted or wiped out – grimy urchins found wandering round the back streets begging for food. The villagers held the sisters in reverence, believing the Church provided for them, contributing what little they could afford into the weekly collection box at church.

But why would William take those children to the mill? What for? What unspeakable deeds did she refer to, that meant the children did not return, or at least only to be buried in the little cemetery? Was it to work? Why would that be unspeakable? And why had her mother talked about depraved things and the nuns being paid for what they did? As if in answer to her questions, her head began to pound and a sudden vision appeared to her, of chains nailed into a wall, of a black altar and hooded men…

You know…Magda…you were there…Magda…

The whispers, they were coming from somewhere. She whirled around, staring into the dripping darkness of the well. Who was here?

"Are you here with me? Show yourself then. Help me!"

The sudden acrid pungency of fire and terrified screaming forced her back into the moment. They must have found the nuns. She covered her ears. What were they doing, hauling these religious women from a place of worship to try them for witchcraft? And why would the children they'd helped accuse them of such things? This was evil beyond all words and the men who did this should be punished in hell.

Daring a glance upwards, her heart lurched. A man was peering down the well staring directly at her. Instinctively she faced downwards, squeezing shut her eyes, thankful her hair and clothes were black. Surely he couldn't see, surely, surely…

"Found her?" said a man's voice.

"Nah, she's gone – probably off on her broomstick."

"They leave a pile of black soot. There'll be soot somewhere, you mark my words."

"I'll cut the rope anyway – if she's down there she'll drown then with her toads."

Magda clung onto the side of the wooden pail as the ropes were chopped, and the pail plunged deeply into the dark pool below, scraping her knuckles raw as it crashed sideways into the stones.

Even as her skull cracked and she sank under the freezing water, she made not a sound. And briefly the world eclipsed. Before a slam of pain thumped her hard in the chest, and she surfaced, fighting for air, gulping water. Desperately her fingers clutched at a jutting stone, and with her toes on a narrow ledge below water level, she held on, spewing out water from her lungs, gasping for air, teeth chattering uncontrollably. She would die down here. If the nuns had been taken she would die because no one was coming back.

Fleetingly, she wondered where the older lady had gone. Would she have gone to the church? Would they have dragged her from the altar?

She held on, gradually losing hope - her hands were too numb to grip on for much longer - until she began to lose consciousness. Resting her forehead against the slippery, lichen covered walls, she began to pray for forgiveness when a glint in the wall caught her eye. Something was there. Was it glass? Would it help her?

Inch by inch she edged a little further round. Overhead the clouds had now cleared to reveal a starry sky, and the facing wall had caught a shard of light. Curiosity drove her on. Reaching out, she strained as far as she could without falling back into the water, until finally she had it. A glass phial. She held it up to the silvery light and a stab of recognition twisted inside her. Inside the glass bottle were locks of hair, nail cuttings, a waxy substance and what looked like the bodies of insects.

Men's voices overhead made her start. Hadn't they gone? Frantically, she edged back to the dark side of the well, looking down, the phial clasped tightly in her hand.

"Is that all of 'em?"

A voice she recognised all too well replied, "Aye, we strung 'em all up. William said hang the lot in case they spoke out."

"Did they find Magda?"

"Nah, she's gone. We'll get her eventually, though, she won't be far off. He said keep going 'til we find her – those were his orders."

"At least we'll not go hungry this winter, eh? Not with this bloody, great feast. Mr Miller will just have to get his bairns another way now, won't he?"

"Be some money in it for us, I reckon then Mr Dean – you and your lads could go hunting for 'em? He'll pay handsome and no mistake."

"Could be, could be."

Magda's feet were as lead, the strength and the will to crawl out now having ebbed away. She closed her eyes. So he had deliberately had his own daughter and unborn granddaughter hunted down for slaughter...

Those were his orders...

The icy, black water closed over her head as she sank through its murky depths, clutching the phial she knew without doubt, had been placed there by her mother. It seemed so clear now – her mother had cursed the nuns who abandoned her in her hour of need. She had been raped. Of course...

And the whole of this village knew about it; knew about those children; and knew what happened at the mill. No wonder

Magda had been filled with rage. No wonder she had invited in the one who had not abandoned her: the one who had come to each of them in turn, bestowing the power to invoke a curse on the whole damn lot of them.

Icy black water filled her lungs with crushing pain as her eyes met with the white eyes she now knew were the same as her mother's; the same as her own. And her smile widened in the final moment.

Lucifer, take me for I am yours.

"May this whole village be cursed with misery and fear; and whoever looks into a mirror and sees me, be possessed by the spirit of Lilith for all eternity. This is my will. So mote it be."

***

Epilogue

Ruby
Doncaster Royal Infirmary
November

My window is different. No bars. And blobs of amber are fuzzy in the dark. Streetlights? Are they streetlights? A loud, rhythmic hissing and clunking fills my ears with every breath; my body weighted down...so heavy...

I wake again, blinking, to another change. To daylight radiating through cloud. To white uniforms. A stab of fear. Faces loom over me; something fizzing in my veins and once again the world spins away.

It feels like a limbo-land of time; an endless grey fog in here. We can talk and sometimes we see each other. And inside the fog there is a light – a lantern – we are being shown something...*Come with me, come and see...come and see...*

"Oh, God no....Celeste...no."

Her presence shines as a globe of brilliant light, her laugh tinkling. She is determined to show me this - reaching out to take my hand. Then suddenly we fall down a shute...a tunnel...plummeting into somewhere horrible, cold, dark and wet. There's a bad feeling in here...full of anguish, confusion and fear...and so much rage...

Below, the icy chill of stagnant water awaits, the drip-drip-drip of moss-coated stones all around us. Down and down... oh no, plunging into freezing water...it closes over my head, pressure swelling inside my lungs...bursting...silently screaming with fear and pain...something sharp cutting into the palm of my hand. I'm drowning...lungs heaving against my chest wall...exploding...

238

Suddenly a face swims into mine - eye whites bulging, long, black hair floating all around a bloated, mottled corpse...but there is light. All around, in these murky depths there is light. Celeste is here...she wants me to see...The girl's hand is unfurling. She is showing me something...a bottle...

Oh, it's gone black. No...I cannot breathe...I'm going to die...No...

"No, no, I want to live. Let me up, I want to live–"

"Ruby, you're okay. You're doing well. Spit the tube out, that's it. It's all over. Back in the land of the living, there we go–"

I blink. Unsure. "Where is Celeste?"

Remember to tell....

"Yes, yes..."

When I wake again it is into a room lit as starkly as an operating theatre. I have no idea where I am or what time of day it is.

"Hello, Ruby?"

A woman is standing over me with an armful of flowers. "We brought these for you."

She floats before me... She has a nice smile in a plump face, her hair tied back. My heart leaps. "Becky?"

She nods. "How are you doing?"

"I know where it is." These are my first words to her.

She shakes her head.

"I've seen it. I was there. There's a glass bottle in the well. Tell Harry to break it. That's what I have been shown. I'm told to tell Harry? Do you know a Harry?"

Her eyes glint and I see she understands whatever the hell it is I'm talking about.

"You're off the respirator, that's good. Do you want some water?"

"Yes. But the message...do you–?"

She nods and strokes my forehead. "Yes, I understand and yes there is a Harry, and yes I will tell him what we need to do. You are amazing." She has tears in her eyes even though she is smiling. "Don't worry, Ruby. Anyway, I have someone special here to see you."

I notice then, the small girl she has with her.

We lock eyes, this child and I. I've seen her before, many, many times... In my dreams, in my madness, in my despair and in my fears. She has gazed through her window at the same stars; and she has seen me too.

She doesn't hesitate. Alice puts her arms around my neck and cries.

My girl.

***

"The best thing about the future is that it comes one day at a time."
Abraham Lincoln

Acknowledgements and Glossary of Terms

The author of this book would like to add that a considerable amount of research was undertaken in order to broaden her knowledge of Dissociative Identity Disorder (DID), which affects many people, and in 90% of cases can be attributed to child abuse. Thank you very much to those who helped with this research.

RSA: Ritual Satanic Abuse

DID: Dissociative Identity Disorder (previously known as multiple personality disorder) is thought to be a complex psychological condition that is likely caused by many factors, including severe trauma during early childhood (usually extreme, repetitive physical, sexual, or emotional abuse).

PTSD: Post Traumatic Stress Disorder

bpm – beats per minute (heart rate/pulse)

Dystonia – A syndrome of abnormal muscle contraction that produces repetitive involuntary twisting movements and abnormal posturing of the neck, trunk, face, and extremities. (Farlex Partner Medical Dictionary © Farlex 2012)

Extrapyramidal syndrome: A condition characterized by a range of findings– rigidity, tremors, drooling, shuffling gait– parkinsonism, akathisia–restlessness, dystonia–odd involuntary postures, akinesia–motor inactivity, and other neurologic disturbances Etiology Extrapyramidal dysfunction, often a reversible side effect of certain psychotropics–eg, phenothiazines. (McGraw-Hill Concise Dictionary of Modern Medicine. © 2002)

IV – intra-venous

Haloperidol – an anti-psychotic agent.

Systolic and diastolic blood pressure – normally around 120/80.

Father of Lies – Book 1

A Darkly Disturbing Occult Horror Trilogy: Book 1

'Boy did this pack a punch and scare me witless..'
'Scary as hell...What I thought would be mainstream horror was anything but...'
'Not for the faint-hearted. Be warned - this is very, very dark subject matter.'
'A truly wonderful and scary start to a horror trilogy. One of the best and most well written books I've read in a long time.'
'A dark and compelling read. I devoured it in one afternoon. Even as the horrors unfolded I couldn't race through the pages quickly enough for more...'
'Delivers the spooky in spades!'
'Will go so far as to say Sarah is now my favourite author - sorry Mr King!'

***

Ruby is the most violently disturbed patient ever admitted to Drummersgate Asylum, high on the bleak moors of northern England. With no improvement after two years, Dr. Jack McGowan finally decides to take a risk and hypnotises her. With terrifying consequences.

A horrific dark force is now unleashed on the entire medical team, as each in turn attempts to unlock Ruby's shocking and sinister past. Who is this girl? And how did she manage to survive such unimaginable evil? Set in a desolate ex-mining village, where secrets are tightly kept and intruders hounded out, their questions soon lead to a haunted mill, the heart of darkness...and The Father of Lies.

http://www.amazon.co.uk/dp/B015NCZYKU
http://www.amazon.com/dp/B015NCZYKU

Tanners Dell – Book 2

Now only one of the original team remains – Ward Sister, Becky. However, despite her fiancé, Callum, being unconscious and many of her colleagues either dead or critically ill, she is determined to rescue Ruby's twelve year old daughter from a similar fate to her mother.

But no one asking questions in the desolate ex-mining village Ruby hails from ever comes to a good end. And as the diabolical history of the area is gradually revealed, it seems the evil invoked is both real and contagious.

Don't turn the lights out yet!

***

The Owlmen
Pure Occult Horror

If They See You They Will Come For You

Ellie Blake is recovering from a nervous breakdown. Deciding to move back to her northern roots, she and her psychiatrist husband buy Tanners Dell at auction - an old water mill in the moorland village of Bridesmoor.

However, there is disquiet in the village. Tanners Dell has a terrible secret, one so well guarded no one speaks its name. But in her search for meaning and very much alone, Ellie is drawn to traditional witchcraft and determined to pursue it. All her life she has been cowed. All her life she has apologised for her very existence. And witchcraft has opened a door she could never have imagined. Imbued with power and overawed with its magick, for the first time she feels she has come home, truly knows who she is.

Tanners Dell though, with its centuries old demonic history...well, it's a dangerous place for a novice...

http://www.amazon.co.uk/dp/B079W9FKV7
http://www.amazon.com/dp/B079W9FKV7

***

The Soprano:
A Haunting Supernatural Thriller

'It is 1951 and a remote mining village on the North Staffordshire Moors is hit by one of the worst snowstorms in living memory. Cut off for over three weeks, the old and the sick will die; the strongest bunker down; and those with evil intent will bring to its conclusion a family vendetta spanning three generations.

Inspired by a true event, 'The Soprano' tells the story of Grace Holland - a strikingly beautiful, much admired local celebrity who brings glamour and inspiration to the grimy moorland community. But why is Grace still here? Why doesn't she leave this staunchly Methodist, rain-sodden place and the isolated farmhouse she shares with her mother?

Riddled with witchcraft and tales of superstition, the story is mostly narrated by the Whistler family who own the local funeral parlour, in particular six year old Louise - now an elderly lady - who recalls one of the most shocking crimes imaginable.'

http://www.amazon.co.uk/dp/B0737GQ9Q7
http://www.amazon.com/dp/B0737GQ9Q7

***

Hidden Company

*An eerie, supernatural thriller set in a Victorian
asylum in the heart of wales.*

1893, and nineteen year old Flora George is admitted to a remote asylum with no idea why she is there, what happened to her child, or how her wealthy family could have abandoned her to such a fate. However, within a short space of time it becomes apparent she must save herself from something far worse than that of a harsh regime.

2018, and forty-one year old Isobel Lee moves into the gatehouse of what was once the old asylum. A reluctant medium, it is with dismay she realises there is a terrible secret here - one desperate to be heard. Angry and upset, Isobel baulks at what she must now face. But with the help of local dark arts practitioner, Branwen, face it she must.

This is a dark story of human cruelty, folklore and superstition. But the human spirit can and will prevail...unless of course, the wrath of the fae is incited...

http://www.amazon.co.uk/dp/B07JQYQ7R8
http://www.amazon.com/dp/B07JQYQ7R8

***

Monkspike

A Medieval Occult Horror

1149 was a violent year in the Forest of Dean.

Today, nearly 900 years later, the forest village of Monkspike sits brooding. There is a sickness here passed down through ancient lines, one noted and deeply felt by Sylvia Massey, the new psychologist. What is wrong with nurse, Belinda Sully's, son? Why did her husband take his own life? Why are the old people in Temple Lake Nursing Home so terrified? And what are the lawless inhabitants of nearby Wolfs Cross hiding?

It is a dark village indeed, but one which has kept its secrets well. That is until local girl, Kezia Elwyn, returns home as a practising Satanist, and resurrects a hellish wrath no longer containable. Burdo, the white monk, will infest your dreams....This is pure occult horror and definitely not for the faint of heart...

http://www.amazon.co.uk/dp/B07VJHPD63
http://www.amazon.com/dp/B07VJHPD63

***